A Passion
for Him

Also by Sylvia Day

A Passion for Him

SYLVIA DAY

KENSINGTON PUBLISHING CORP.
http://www.kensingtonbooks.com

KENSINGTON BOOKS are published by

Kensington Publishing Corp.
119 West 40th Street
New York, NY 10018

Copyright © 2007 Sylvia Day

All Kensington Titles, Imprints, and Distributed Lines are available at special quantity discounts for bulk purchases for sales promotions, premiums, fund-raising, and educational or institutional use. Special book excerpts or customized printings can also be created to fit specific needs. For details, write or phone the office of the Kensington special sales manager: Kensington Publishing Corp., 119 West 40th Street, New York, NY 10018, attn: Special Sales Department; phone 1-800-221-2647.

KENSINGTON and the k logo are Reg. U.S. Pat. & TM Off.

ISBN-13: 978-0-7582-1762-2
ISBN-10: 0-7582-1762-5
First Kensington Trade Edition: November 2007
First Kensington Mass Market Edition: July 2016

eISBN-13: 978-0-7582-9063-2
eISBN-10: 0-7582-9063-2

10 9 8 7 6 5 4 3 2

Printed in the United States of America

To my dear friends, Shelley Bradley and Annette Mc-Cleave. Thank you both for the friendship, support, and brainstorming you shared with me while I wrote this book. They were invaluable and deeply appreciated.

Acknowledgments

To Kate Duffy, for her forbearance and guidance. When I needed help, she was there for me. I couldn't have finished this book without her.

To Nadine Dupont, for her assistance with the French words used in this book. Any errors are mine alone.

To the fabulous gals on my wicked chat loop, for their aid and friendship.

To Patrice Michelle, Janet Miller, and Mardi Ballou, for their commiseration.

I'm grateful to you all. Thank you so much!

Chapter 1

London, 1780

The man in the white mask was following her. Amelia Benbridge was uncertain of how long he had been moving surreptitiously behind her, but he most definitely was.

She strolled carefully around the perimeter of the Langston ballroom, her senses attuned to his movements, her head turning with feigned interest in her surroundings so that she might study him further.

Every covert glance took her breath away.

In such a crush of people, another woman most likely would not have noted the avid interest. It was far too easy to be overwhelmed by the sights, sounds, and smells of a masquerade. The dazzling array of vibrant fabrics and frothy lace . . . the multitude of voices attempting to be heard over an industrious orchestra . . . the mingling scents of various perfumes and burnt wax from the massive chandeliers . . .

But Amelia was not like other women. She had lived the first sixteen years of her life under guard, her every movement watched with precision. It was a unique sensation to be examined so closely. She could not mistake the feeling for anything else.

However, she could say with some certainty that she had never been so closely scrutinized by a man quite so . . . compelling.

For he *was* compelling, despite the distance between them and the concealment of the upper half of his face. His form alone arrested her attention. He stood tall and well proportioned, his garments beautifully tailored to cling to muscular thighs and broad shoulders.

She reached a corner and turned, setting their respective positions at an angle. Amelia paused there, taking the opportunity to raise her mask to surround her eyes, the gaily colored ribbons that adorned the stick falling down her gloved arm. Pretending to watch the dancers, she was in truth watching him and cataloguing his person. It was only fair, in her opinion. If he could enjoy an unhindered view, so could she.

He was drenched in black, the only relief being his snowy white stockings, cravat, and shirt. And the mask. So plain. Unadorned by paint or feathers. Secured to his head with black satin ribbon. While the other gentlemen in attendance were dressed in an endless range of colors to attract attention, this man's stark severity seemed designed to blend into the shadows. To make him unremarkable, which he could never be. Beneath the light of hundreds of candles, his dark hair gleamed with vitality and begged a woman to run her fingers through it.

And then there was his mouth . . .

Amelia inhaled sharply at the sight of it. His mouth was sin incarnate. Sculpted by a master hand, the lips neither full nor thin, but firm. Shamelessly sensual. Framed by a strong chin, chiseled jaw, and swarthy skin. A foreigner, perhaps. She could only imagine how the face would look as a whole. Devastating to a woman's equanimity, she suspected.

But it was more than his physical attributes that intrigued her. It was the way he moved, like a predator, his gait purposeful and yet seductive, his attention sharply focused. He did not mince his steps or affect the veneer of boredom so esteemed by Society. This man knew what he wanted and lacked the patience to pretend otherwise.

At present it appeared that what he wanted was to follow her. He watched Amelia with a gaze so intensely hot, she felt it move across her body, felt it run through the unpowdered strands of her hair and dance across her bared nape. Felt it glide across her bared shoulders and down the length of her spine. *Coveting*.

She could not begin to guess how she had attracted his attention. While she knew she was pretty enough, she was not any more attractive than most of the other women here. Her gown, while lovely with its elaborate silver lace underskirts and delicate flowers made of pink and green ribbon, was not the most riveting on display. And she was usually disregarded by those seeking a romantic connection, because her long-standing friendship with the popular Earl of Ware was widely assumed to be leading to the altar. Albeit very slowly.

So what did this man want with her? Why didn't he approach her?

Amelia canted her body to face him and lowered her mask, staring at him directly so he would not have to wonder if she was looking at him. She left him no doubt, hoping his long legs would resume their deliberate stride and bring him to her. She wanted to experience all the details of him— the sound of his voice, the scent of his cologne, the impact of proximity to his powerful frame.

Then she wished to know what he wanted. Amelia had lived the entirety of her motherless childhood being secreted from place to place, her governesses changed often so that no emotional attachment could form, she was cut off from her sibling and anyone who might care for her. Because of this, she distrusted the unknown. This man's interest was an anomaly, and it needed to be explained.

Her silent challenge caused a sudden, visible tension to grip his body. He stared back, his eyes glittering from the shadows of the mask. Long moments passed, time she barely registered because she was so focused on his response to her. Guests walked past him, momentarily obstructing her view and then revealing him again. His fists clenched along with his jaw. She saw his chest expand with a deep breath—

—just as she was bumped roughly from behind. "Excuse me, Miss Benbridge."

Startled, her gaze turned to identify the offending individual and found a wigged man wearing puce satin. She muttered a quick dismissal of his concern, managed a brief smile, and swiftly returned her attention to the masked man.

Who was gone.

She blinked rapidly. *Gone.* Lifting to her tiptoes, Amelia frantically searched the sea of people. He was tall and blessed with an impressive breadth of shoulder. His lack of a wig provided an additional means of identification, but she could not find him.

Where did he go?

"Amelia."

The low, cultured drawl at her shoulder was dearly familiar, and she shot a quick, distracted glance at the handsome man who drew abreast of her. "Yes, my lord?"

"What are you looking for?" The Earl of Ware mimicked her pose, craning his neck in much the same fashion. Any other man would have looked ridiculous, but not Ware. It was impossible for him to appear anything less than perfect from the top of his wigged head down to his diamond-studded heels six feet below. "Would it be too much to hope that you were looking for me?"

Smiling sheepishly, Amelia abandoned her visual hunt and linked her arm with his. "I was seeking a phantom."

"A phantom?" Through the eyeholes of his painted mask, his blue eyes laughed at her. Ware had two expressions—one of dangerous boredom and one of warm amusement. She was the only person in his life capable of inspiring the latter. "Was this a frightening specter? Or something more interesting?"

"I am not certain. He was following me."

"All men follow you, love," he said with a faint curve to his lips. "At the very least with their gazes, if not with their legs."

Amelia squeezed his arm in gentle admonishment. "You tease me."

"Not at all." He arched one arrogant brow. "You often appear lost in a world of your own making. It is supremely appealing to men to see a woman content with herself. We long to slip inside her and join her."

The intimate timbre of Ware's voice was not lost on Amelia. She glanced up at him from beneath her lashes. "Naughty man."

He laughed, and the guests around them stared. So did she. Merriment transformed the earl from the epitome of an ennui afflicted aristocrat to a vibrantly attractive man.

Ware began to stroll, expertly carrying her along with him. She had known him for six years now, having met him when he was ten and eight. She'd watched him grow into the man he was today, watched him take his first steps into liaisons and the way relations with women had changed him, although none of his inamoratas held his attention long. They saw only his exterior and the marquessate he would rule upon his father's passing. Perhaps he could have lived with that depth of interest, if he had not met her first. But they *had* met, and become the closest of friends. Now lesser connections displeased him. He kept mistresses to relieve his physical needs, but he kept her close to see to his emotional ones.

They would marry, she knew. It was unspoken

between them, yet understood. Ware simply waited for the day when she would finally be ready to step beyond the boundaries of friendship and into his bed. She loved him for that patience, even though she was not *in* love with him. Amelia wished she could be; she wished it every day. But she loved another, and while death had stolen him from her, her heart stayed true.

"Where are your thoughts now?" Ware asked, his head tilting in acknowledgment of another guest's greeting.

"With you."

"Ah, lovely," he purred, his eyes lit with pleasure. "Tell me everything."

"I am thinking that I shall enjoy being married to you."

"Is that a proposal?"

"I'm not certain."

"Hmmm . . . well, we are getting closer. I take some comfort in that."

She studied him carefully. "Are you growing impatient?"

"I can wait."

The answer was vague, and Amelia frowned.

"No fretting," Ware admonished gently, leading her out a pair of open French doors to a crowded terrace. "I am content for now, so long as you are."

The cool evening breeze blew across her skin, and she inhaled deeply. "You are not being entirely truthful."

Amelia came to a halt at the wide marble railing and faced him. Several couples stood nearby, engaging in various conversations, but all were casting curious glances in their direction. Despite the shadows created by the cloud-covered moon, Ware's cream-colored jacket and breeches gleamed like ivory and enticed admiring perusals.

"This is not the place to discuss something as auspicious as our future," he said, reaching up to untie his mask. He removed it, revealing a profile so noble it should have graced a coin.

"You know that will not dissuade me."

"And you know that is why I like you so well." His slow smile teased her. "My life is regimented and compartmentalized. Everything is orderly and firmly in its place. I know my role and I fulfill the expectations of Society exactly."

"Except for courting me."

"Except for courting you," he agreed. His gloved hand found hers and held it. He adjusted his stance to hide the scandalous contact from the curious. "You are my fair princess, rescued from her turret tower by an infamous pirate. The daughter of a viscount hanged for treason and sister to a true femme fatale, a woman widely considered to have murdered two husbands before marrying one too dangerous to kill. You are my folly, my aberration, my peccadillo."

He brushed his thumb across her palm, making her shiver. "But I serve the opposite purpose in your life. I am your anchor. You cling to me because I am safe and comfortable." His gaze lifted to look over her head at the others who shared the terrace with them. He bent closer and murmured, "But on occasion, I remember the young girl who so boldly demanded a first kiss from me, and I wish I had responded differently."

"You do?"

Ware nodded.

"Have I changed so much since then?"

With his mask dangling from one hand and her hand captured in the other, he turned abruptly and led her down the nearby flight of stairs to the garden. A gravel pathway bordered low yew hedges, which in turn bordered a lush center lawn and impressive fountain.

"The passing of time changes all of us," he said. "But I think it was the passing of your dear Colin that changed you the most."

The sound of Colin's name affected Amelia deeply, provoking feelings of overwhelming sadness and regret. He had been her dearest friend, who later became the love of her heart. He was the nephew of her coachman and a Gypsy, but in her sheltered world they were equals. They had been playmates as children, then found their interest in each other changing. Deepening. Becoming less innocent.

Colin had matured into a young man whose exotic beauty and quiet strength of character had stirred her in ways she had not been prepared for. Thoughts of him had ruled her days, and dreams of stolen kisses had tormented her nights. He had been wiser than she, understanding that it was impossible for a peer's daughter and a stableboy to ever be together. He had pushed her away, pretended to feel nothing for her, and broken her adolescent heart.

But in the end he had died for her.

Her silent exhale was shaky. Sometimes, just before she drifted into sleep, she permitted herself to think of him. She opened her heart and let the memories out—stolen kisses in the woods, passionate longing and budding desire. She had never felt that depth of emotion again and knew she never would. Some childish infatuations faded away. Her love for Colin had been built with firmer stuff, and it stayed with her. No longer a raging fire, but a softer warmth. Adoration enhanced by gratefulness for his sacrifice. Trapped between her father's men and agents of the Crown, she could have been killed had Colin not spirited her away. A reckless, love-fueled rescue that had delivered her to safety at the cost of his precious life.

"You are thinking of him again," Ware murmured.

"Am I so transparent?"

"As clear as glass." He squeezed her hand, and she smiled fondly.

"Perhaps you think my reticence stems from my lingering affection for Colin, but it is my affection for you that restrains me."

"Oh?"

Amelia could see that she had surprised him. They turned back toward the manse, following the subtle urging of the path. Brilliant light and the glorious strains of stringed instruments spilled out in abundance from the many open doorways, enticing strolling guests to linger close to the festivities. Others wended their way through the rear garden as they did, but all resisted straying too far.

"Yes, my lord. I worry that perhaps I will steal you from your great love."

Ware laughed softly. "How fanciful you are." He grinned and looked so handsome, she gazed a moment longer to admire him. "I admit to curious musings when you wear that faraway look, but that is the extent of my interest in affairs of the heart."

"You have no notion of what you are missing."

"Forgive me for being callous, but if what I am missing is the melancholy that clings to you, I want none of it. It is attractive on you and lends you an air of mystery that I find irresistible. Sadly, I fear I would not fare so well. I suspect I would appear wretched, and we cannot have that."

"The Earl of Ware wretched?"

He gave a mock shudder. "Quite impossible, of course."

"Quite."

"So you see, you are perfect for me, Amelia. I enjoy your company. I enjoy your honesty and our ability to converse freely about nearly everything. There is no uncertainty or fear of reprisal for a careless act. You cannot hurt me, and I cannot hurt you, because we do not attribute actions to emotions that are not there. If I am thoughtless, it is not because I seek to injure you, and you know this. Our association is one I will appreciate and value until I take my last breath."

Ware paused when they reached the bottom step that would lead them back up to the terrace. Their brief spell of privacy was nearly at an end. Her desire to spend unhindered time with him was an added impetus to marriage. It was only the sexual congress that would end their evenings that she resisted.

The memory of feverishly exchanged kisses with Colin haunted her, and she could not bring herself to risk disappointment with Ware. She dreaded the possibility of awkwardness intruding on their closeness. The earl was comely and charming and perfect. How would he look when he was flushed and disheveled? What sounds would he make? How would he move? What would he expect of her?

It was apprehension that goaded these ponderings, not anticipation.

"And what of the sex?" she asked.

His head swiveled toward her, and he froze with his foot poised above the step. The depth of his blue eyes sparkled with merriment. Ware backed down from the stair and faced her directly. "What of it?"

"Do you not worry that it will be . . . ?" She struggled to find the correct word.

"No." There was a wealth of assurance in the negation.

"No?"

"When I think about sex with you there is no worry involved. Eagerness, yes. Anxiety, no." He closed the small gap between them and bent over her. His voice came as an intimate whisper. "Do not hesitate for that reason. We are young. We can wed and wait, or we can wait and then wed. Even with my ring on your finger, I will not ask you to do anything you do not wish to. Not yet." His mouth twitched. "In a few years, however, I may not be so accommodating. I must reproduce eventually, and I do find you supremely alluring."

Amelia tilted her head, considering. Then she nodded.

"Good," Ware said with obvious satisfaction. "Progress, however incremental, is always good."

"Perhaps it is time to post the banns."

"By God, that is more than an incremental move forward!" he cried with exaggerated verve. "We are actually getting somewhere."

She laughed and he winked mischievously.

"We will be happy together," he promised.

"I know."

Ware took a moment to once again secure his mask, and her gaze wandered as she waited. Following the line of the marble railing, she found a profusion of ivy climbing the brick exterior. That visual trail led to another terrace farther down, this one unlit in an obvious gambit to deter guests from lingering away from the ballroom. It appeared, however, that the lack of welcome was too subtle for two attendees, or perhaps they simply did not care to heed it. Regardless, the reason *why* they were there was not what caught Amelia's attention. She was more interested in *who* was there.

Despite the deep shadows that blanketed the second patio, she recognized her phantom follower by the pure white of his mask and the way his garments and hair blended into the night around him.

"My lord," she murmured, reaching out blindly to clutch Ware's arm. "Do you see those gentlemen over there?"

She felt his attention turn as she directed.

"Yes."

"The dark-clad gentleman is the one who held such interest in me earlier."

The earl looked at her in all seriousness. "You made light of the matter, but now I am concerned. Was this man an annoyance to you?"

"No." Her gaze narrowed as the two men parted and set off in opposite directions—the phantom away from her, the other man toward her.

"Yet something about him disturbs you." Ware rearranged her grasping hand to rest upon his forearm. "And his assignation over there is curious."

"Yes, I agree."

"Despite the years that have passed since you were freed from your father's care, I feel caution would be wise. When one has an infamous criminal for a relation, every unknown is suspect. We cannot have odd characters following you about." Ware led her quickly up the steps. "Perhaps you should stay close to me for the remainder of the evening."

"I have no cause to fear him," she argued without heat. "I think it is more my reaction to him that surprises me, as opposed to his interest in me."

"You had a reaction to him?" Ware paused just inside the door and drew her to the side, out of the way of those who entered and exited. "What sort of reaction?"

Amelia lifted her mask to her face. How could she explain that she had admired the man's powerful frame and presence without lending more weight to the sentiment than it deserved? "I was intrigued. I wished he would approach me and reveal himself."

"Should I be concerned that another man so quickly captured your imagination?" The earl's drawling voice was laced with amusement.

"No." She smiled. The comfort of their friendship was priceless to her. "Just as I do not worry when you take interest in other females."

"Lord Ware."

They both turned to face the gentleman who approached, a person whose distinctively short and portly frame made him recognizable despite his mask—Sir Harold Bingham, a Bow Street magistrate.

"Sir Harold," Ware greeted in return.

"Good evening, Miss Benbridge," the magistrate said, smiling in his kindly way. He was known for his tough rulings, but was widely considered to be fair and wise.

Amelia quite liked him, and the warmth of her returning pleasantries reflected this.

Ware leaned toward her, lowering his voice for her ears only. "Will you excuse me a moment? I should like to discuss your admirer with him. Perhaps we can learn an identity."

"Of course, my lord."

The two gentlemen moved a short distance away, and Amelia's gaze drifted over the ballroom, seeking out familiar faces. She spotted a small grouping of acquaintances nearby and set off in that direction.

After several steps she stopped, frowning.

She wanted to know who was behind the white mask. The curiosity was eating at her, niggling at the back of her mind and making her restless. There was such intensity in the way he had looked at her, and the moment when their eyes had met lingered in her thoughts.

Turning abruptly on her heel, she again walked outside and down the steps into the rear garden. There were many other guests about, all seeking relief from the crush. Rather than going straight along the path she had taken with Ware or to the right where the second terrace waited in the dark, she turned to the left. A few feet off to the side, a marble reproduction of Venus graced a semicircular space filled with a half-moon bench. It was bordered by the same low, perfectly shaped yew hedges that surrounded the lawn and fountain, and it was presently unoccupied.

Amelia paused near the statue and whistled a distinctive warble that would bring her brother-in-law's men out of hiding. She was guarded still, and suspected she would always be. It was an inevitable consequence of being the sister-in-law of a known pirate and smuggler such as Christopher St. John.

At times she resented the inherent lack of privacy that came with having one's every movement watched. She could not help but wish that her life was simple enough to make such precautions unnecessary. But at other times, such as tonight, she found relief in the unseen protection. She was never left exposed, which enabled her to view her phantom in a different light. Having St. John's men nearby also afforded her the opportunity to elicit help in relieving her curiosity.

Her foot tapped impatiently atop the gravel as she waited. That was why she did not hear the man's approach. She did, however, feel him. The hairs on her nape tingled with awareness, and she turned swiftly with a soft gasp of surprise.

He stood just barely within the entrance of the circle, a tall, dark form that vibrated with a potent energy that seemed barely restrained. Beneath the pale light of the moon, the man's inky locks gleamed like a raven's wing, and his eyes glittered with the very intensity that had goaded her to seek him out. He wore a full cape, the gray satin lining providing a striking backdrop to his black garments, enabling her to fully appreciate the size and power of his frame.

"I was looking for you," she said softly, her chin lifting.

"I know."

Chapter 2

Her phantom's voice was deep, low, and distinctly accented. Foreign, which complemented his swarthy complexion.

"Do not fear me," he said. "I wish only to apologize for my lack of manners."

"I am not frightened," she replied, her gaze darting past his shoulder to where other guests were clearly visible.

He stepped aside and bowed, gesturing her out with a grand sweep of his arm.

"That is all you have to say to me?" she asked, as she realized that he intended for them to part.

His beautiful mouth pursed slightly. "Should there be more?"

"I . . ." Amelia frowned and glanced away a moment, trying to gather her thoughts into coherent words. It was difficult to think clearly when he stood in such close proximity. What had been compelling at a distance was nearly overwhelming now. He was so somber. . . . She had not expected that.

"I do not mean to detain you," he murmured, his tone soothing.

"Lack of manners," she repeated.

"Yes. I was staring."

"I noticed," she said dryly.

"Forgive me."

"No need. I am not upset."

She waited for him to take some action. When he stepped out of the small circle and again gestured toward the main part of the rear garden, she shook her head in denial. Her mouth curved at his apparent haste to be rid of her.

"My name is Miss Amelia Benbridge."

The man stilled visibly, his only movement the lift and fall of his chest. After a moment's hesitation, he showed a leg in a courtly bow and said, "A pleasure, Miss Benbridge. I am Count Reynaldo Montoya."

"Montoya," she breathed, testing the name on her tongue. "Spanish, yet your accent is French."

His head lifted, and he studied her closely, his gaze caressing the length of her body from the top of her elaborate coiffure down to her kid slippers. "Your surname is English, yet your features are enhanced by a foreign touch," he pointed out in rebuttal.

"My mother was Spanish."

"And you are enchanting."

Amelia inhaled sharply, startled by how the simple compliment affected her. She heard such platitudes daily, and they held as much meaning as a comment on the weather. But Montoya's delivery altered the words, imbuing them with feeling and an underlying urgency.

"It appears I must apologize again," the count said, with a self-deprecating smile. "Allow me to escort you back before I make a further fool of myself."

She reached out to him, then caught herself and clutched the stick of her mask with both hands instead. "Your cloak . . . Are you departing?"

He nodded, and the tension in the air between them heightened. There was no reason for him to linger, and yet she sensed that they both wanted him to.

Something was holding him back.

"Why?" she asked softly. "You have not yet asked me to dance or flirted with me or made a casual remark about where you intend to be in the future so that we might find one another again."

Montoya reentered the small circle. "You are too bold, Miss Benbridge," he admonished gruffly.

"And you are a coward."

He drew up sharply just a few inches from her.

A cool evening breeze blew across the top of her shoulder, carrying with it one of the long, artful curls that hung down her back. The count's gaze focused on the glossy lock, then drifted over the swell of her breasts.

"You look at me as a man looks at his mistress."

"Do I?" His voice had lowered, grown softer, the accent more pronounced. It was a lover's tone, or a seducer's. She felt it move over her skin like a tactile caress, and she relished the experience. It was rather like exiting a warm house on a frosty day. The sudden impact of sensation was startling and stole one's breath.

"How would you know that look, Miss Benbridge?"

"I know a great many things. However, since you have decided not to acquaint yourself with me, you will never know what they are."

His arms crossed his chest. It was a challenging pose, yet it made her smile, because it signaled his intent to stay. At least for a short while longer. "And what of Lord Ware?" he asked.

"What of him?"

"You are, for all intents and purposes, betrothed."

"So I am." She noted how his jaw tensed. "Do you have a grievance with Lord Ware?"

The count did not reply.

She began tapping her foot again. "We are having visceral reactions to one another, Count Montoya. As attractive as you are, I would venture to say that you are accustomed to snaring women's interest. For my part, I can say with absolute certainty that a similar situation has never happened to me before. Stunning men do not follow me about—"

"You remind me of someone I used to know," he interrupted. "A woman I cared for deeply."

"Oh." Try as she might, Amelia could not hide her disappointment. He had thought she was someone else. His interest was not in *her*, but in a woman who looked like her.

Turning away, she sank onto the small bench, absently arranging her skirts for comfort. Her hands occupied themselves with twirling her mask between gloved fingertips.

"It is my turn to apologize to you." Her head

tilted back so that their gazes met. "I have put you in an awkward position, and goaded you to stay when you wanted to go."

The contemplative cant to his head made her wish she could see the features beneath the pearlescent mask. Despite the lack of a complete visual picture, she found him remarkably attractive—the purring rumble of his voice . . . the luscious shape of his lips . . . the unshakable confidence of his bearing . . .

But then he was not truly unshakable. She was affecting him in ways a stranger should not be able to. And he was affecting her equally.

"That was not what you wished to hear," he noted, stepping closer.

Her gaze strayed to his boots, watching as his cape fluttered around them. Dressed as he was, he was imposing, but she was unafraid.

Amelia waved one hand in a careless affectation of dismissal, unsure of what to say. He was correct; she was too bold. But she was not brazen enough to admit outright that she found the thought of his interest gratifying. "I hope you find the woman you are looking for," she said instead.

"I am afraid that isn't possible."

"Oh?"

"She was lost to me many years ago."

Recognizing the yearning in his words, she sympathized. "I am sorry for your loss. I, too, have lost someone dear to me and know how it feels."

Montoya took a seat beside her. The bench was small, and due to its curvature it forced them to sit near enough that her skirts touched his cape. It was improper for them to be seated so close to each other, yet she did not protest. Instead she breathed deeply and discovered he smelled like sandalwood and citrus. Crisp, earthy, and virile. Like the man himself.

"You are too young to suffer as I do," he murmured.

"You underestimate death. It has no scruples and disregards the age of those left behind."

The ribbons that graced the stick of her mask fluttered gently in the soft breeze and came to rest atop his gloved hand. The sight of the lavender, pink, and pale blue satin against his stark black riveted her attention.

How would they look to passersby? Her voluminous silver lace and gay multicolored flowers next to his complete lack of any color at all.

"You should not be out here alone," he said, rubbing her ribbons between his thumb and index finger. He could not feel them through his gloves, which made the action sensual, as if the lure of fondling something that belonged to her was irresistible.

"I am accustomed to solitude."

"Do you enjoy it?"

"It is familiar."

"That is not an answer."

Amelia looked at him, noting the many details one can see only in extreme proximity to another. Montoya had long, thick lashes surrounding almond-shaped eyes. They were beautiful. Exotic. Knowing. Accented by shadows that came from within as well as from without.

"What was she like?" she asked. "The woman you thought I was."

The barest hint of a smile betrayed the possibility of dimples. "I asked you a question first," he said.

She heaved a dramatic sigh just to see more of that teasing curve of his lips. He never set his smile completely free. She wondered why, and she wondered how she might see it. "Very well, Count Montoya. In answer to your query, yes, I enjoy being alone."

"Many people find being alone intolerable."

"They have no imagination. I, on the other hand, have too much imagination."

"Oh?" He canted his body toward her. The pose caused his doeskin breeches to stretch tautly across the powerful muscles of his thighs. With the gray satin spread out beneath him in contrast, she could see every nuance and plane, every hard length of sinew. "What do you imagine?"

Swallowing hard, Amelia found she could not look away from the view. It was a lascivious glance she was giving him, her interest completely carnal.

"Umm . . ." She tore her gaze upward, dazed by the direction of her own thoughts. "Stories. Faery tales and such."

With the half mask hiding his features she couldn't be certain, but she thought he might have arched a brow at her. "Do you write them down?"

"Occasionally."

"What do you do with them?"

"You have asked far too many questions without answering my one."

Montoya's dark eyes glittered with warm amusement. "Are we keeping score?"

"You were," she pointed out. "I am simply following the rules you set."

There! A dimple. She saw it.

"She was audacious," he murmured, "like you."

Amelia blushed and looked away, smitten with that tiny groove in his cheek. "Did you like that about her?"

"I loved that about her."

The intimate pitch to his voice made her shiver.

He stood and held his hand out to her. "You are cold, Miss Benbridge. You should go inside."

She looked up at him. "Will you go inside with me?"

The count shook his head.

Extending her arm, she set her fingers within his palm and allowed him to assist her to her feet. His hand was large and warm, his grasp strong and sure. She was reluctant to release him and was pleased when he seemed to feel similarly. They stood there for a long moment, touching, the only sound their gentle inhalations and subsequent exhales . . . until the gentle, haunting strains of the minuet drifted out on the night zephyr.

Montoya's grip tightened and his breathing faltered. She knew his thoughts traveled along the same path as hers. Lifting her mask to her face, Amelia lowered into a deep curtsy.

"One dance," she urged softly when he did not move. "Dance with me as if I were the woman you miss."

"No." There was a heartbeat's hesitation, and then he bowed over her hand. "I would rather dance with you."

Touched, her throat tightened, cutting off any reply she might have made. She could only rise and begin the steps, approaching him and then retreating. Spinning slowly and then circling him. The crunching of the gravel beneath her feet overpowered the music, but Amelia heard it in her mind and hummed the notes. He joined her, his deep voice creating a rich accompaniment, the combination of sound enchanting her.

The clouds drifted, allowing a brilliant shaft of moonlight to illuminate their small space. It turned the hedges silver and his mask into a brilliant pearl. The black satin ribbon that restrained his queue blended with the inky locks, the gloss and color so similar they were nearly one and the same. Her skirts brushed against his flowing cape, his cologne mingled with her perfume; together they were lost in a single moment. Amelia was arrested there, ensnared, and wished—briefly—never to be freed.

Then the unmistakable warble of a birdcall rent the cocoon.

A warning from St. John's men.

Amelia stumbled, and Montoya caught her close. Her arm lowered to her side, taking her mask with it. His breath, warm and scented of brandy, drifted across her lips. The difference in their statures put her breasts at level with his upper abdomen. He would have to bend to kiss her, and she found herself wishing he would, wanting to experience the feel of those beautifully sculpted lips pressed against her own.

"Lord Ware is looking for you," he whispered, without taking his eyes from her.

She nodded, but made no effort to free herself. Her gaze stayed locked to his. Watching. Waiting.

Just when she was certain he wouldn't, he accepted her silent invitation and brushed his mouth across hers. Their lips clung together and he groaned. The mask fell from her nerveless fingers to clatter atop the gravel.

"Good-bye, Amelia."

He steadied her, then fled in a billowing flare of black, leaping over a low hedge and blending into the shadows. He headed not toward the rear of the manse but to the front, and was gone in an instant. Dazed by his sudden departure, Amelia turned her head slowly toward the garden. She found Ware approaching with rapid strides, followed by several other gentlemen.

"What are you doing over here?" he asked gruffly, scanning her surroundings with an agitated glance. "I was going mad looking for you."

"I am sorry." She was unable to say more than that. Her thoughts were with Montoya, a man who had clearly recognized the whistle of warning.

He had been real for a moment, but no longer. Like the phantom she'd fancied him as, he was elusive.

And entirely suspect.

"Would you care to explain what happened last night?"

Amelia sighed inwardly, but on the exterior she offered a sunny smile. "Explain what?"

Christopher St. John—pirate, murderer, smuggler extraordinaire—returned her smile, but his sapphire eyes were sharp and assessing. "You know very well what I am referring to." He shook his head. "At times you are so like your sister, it is somewhat alarming."

What was alarming was how divinely handsome St. John was, considering how devilishly his brain worked. Despite the years she'd lived within his household, Amelia was still taken aback by his comeliness every time she saw him.

"Oh, what a lovely thing to say!" she cried, meaning every word. "Thank you."

"Minx. Fess up now."

Any other man would have difficulty prying information out of her that she didn't wish to share. But when the raspy-voiced pirate became cajoling, he was impossible to resist. With his golden hair and skin, thin yet carnal lips, and jeweled irises, he reminded her of an angel, for certainly only a celestial being could be formed so perfectly from head to toe.

The only outward sign of his mortality were the lines that rimmed his mouth and eyes, signs of a life that was fraught with stresses. They'd softened a great deal since his marriage to her sister, but they would never fully dissipate.

"I noted a man's uncommon interest. He noted that I'd noted, and approached me to explain."

Christopher leaned back in his black leather chair and pursed his lips. Behind him was a large window that overlooked the rear garden, or what would have been a rear garden if they'd had one. Instead, they had a flat, brutally trimmed lawn that made stealthy approach of the manse impossible.

When one had a great deal of enemies, as St. John did, one could never lower their guard, especially for frivolous aesthetic reasons. "What explanation did he offer?"

"I reminded him of a lost love."

He made a sound suspiciously like a snort. "A clever, sentimental ruse that almost embarrassed Ware and caused a terrible scandal. I cannot believe you fell prey to it."

Flushing with renewed guilt, she nevertheless protested. "He was sincere!" She did not believe anyone could pretend melancholy so well. That was not to say that she wasn't aware of something amiss, but she did believe his emotional response to her.

"My men followed him last evening."

Amelia nodded, expecting as much. "And?"

"And they lost him."

"How is that possible?"

St. John smiled at her astonishment. "It's possible if one is aware that he is being followed and is trained in how to evade shadows." His smile faded. "The man is no lovelorn innocent, Amelia."

She rose, frowning, which forced St. John to rise as well. Her floral skirts settled around her legs, and she turned to face the rest of the room, lost in thought. Appearances could be deceiving. This room and the criminal who owned it were prime examples. Decorated in shades of red, cream, and gold, the study could belong to a peer of the realm, as could the manse it was a part of. There was nothing here to betray its primary purpose— that of being the headquarters of a large and highly illegal smuggling ring.

"What would he want with me?" she asked, re-membering the previous night's events in crystal clarity. She could still smell the exotic scent of his skin and hear the slight accent to his words that made her insides quiver. Her lips tingled from the press of his, as did her breasts with the memory of the hardness of his abdomen.

"Anything from a simple warning to me, to something more sinister."

"Such as?" She faced him and found him watch-ing her with knowing eyes.

"Such as seducing you and ruining you for Ware. Or seducing you and luring you away to use as leverage against me."

The word "seducing" used in conjunction with the mysterious, masked Montoya did odd things to her. It should, perhaps, frighten her, but it didn't.

"You know as well as I how fortuitous it is that you met Ware while in your father's captivity and that he is willing to disregard your scandalous past and familial connections." His fingers drummed almost silently upon the desktop. "Your son will be a marquess and your children will have every ad-vantage. Anything that jeopardizes your future is cause for concern."

Amelia nodded and looked away again, hoping to hide how the reduction of her relationship with Ware to the material benefits made her feel. She was well aware that she stood to gain the most from their union. As Ware's friend, she wanted only the best for him. Marriage to her was anything but. "What do you want me to do?"

"Do not venture off by yourself. If the man ap-proaches you again, do not allow him within a few feet of you." The severity of his features softened. He wore cerulean blue today, a color that complemented both his tawny coloring and the beautifully embroidered waistcoat that hugged his lean waist. "I do not mean to chastise you. I want only to keep you safe."

"I know." But the entirety of her life had been spent in gilded cages. She found herself torn between loving the security of it and resenting the restrictions. She tried to behave, tried to follow the rules set for her, but at times it was difficult to conform. She suspected that was due to her father's blood in her veins. It was the one thing she most wished to change about herself. "May I be dismissed? Ware will be along shortly to take me for a ride in the park, and I must change."

"Of course. Enjoy yourself."

Christopher watched Amelia leave the room and then resumed his seat, only to stand a moment later when his wife entered in a profusion of pale pink skirts. As always, the sight of her made his heart race with a mixture of attraction and pure joy.

"You look a vision this afternoon," he said, rounding the desk to embrace her. As she had since the moment they had first met, Maria melted against him, a lush warm weight that he adored.

"You say that every day," she murmured, but her smile was filled with pleasure.

"Because it's true every day." He cupped her spine and molded her curves to his hardness. They fit together like two matching puzzle pieces, despite their disparity in height.

Maria shared the same glossy raven tresses as her

younger sibling, but that was the extent of their physical similarities. Amelia took after her father, the late Viscount Welton, with his emerald green eyes and tall, slender build. Maria, who gratefully claimed a different pater, took after their Spanish-blooded mother with her sloe eyes, short stature, and full figure.

St. John and his wife made a striking couple; their contrasting appearances complemented each other in ways oft commented on. But they drew the most attention for their reputations. The former Lady Winter was still known as the "Wintry Widow," a woman who was widely rumored to have murdered her first two husbands. Christopher was her third and last husband, the husband of her heart, and he was frequently celebrated for remaining alive.

You have survived another night in your wife's bed, they jested.

Christopher would smile and say nothing. It wasn't true, but he would not refute the misconception. Few would understand how he died in her arms every night and was reborn.

"I overheard the end of your conversation with Amelia," she said. "I think you are looking at the situation from the wrong perspective."

"Oh?" This was where their true similarities lay. As different as they were on the exterior, on the interior they were alarmingly alike, both criminally minded and quite wily. "What am I missing?"

"You are seeing only what interest the masked man had in Amelia. What of her interest in him? That is where my worry stems."

He frowned down at her, absently admiring the

artfully arranged curls that tumbled about her ears and shoulders, and her full bosom which swelled enticingly above her low, ribbon-edged bodice. "She has always been curious. That is how she met Ware to begin with."

"Yes, but she allowed this man to kiss her. A stranger. Why? She has been pining for her Gypsy sweetheart all these years and keeps Ware at bay. What was the fascination with this man that goaded such a response in her?"

"Hmm . . ." Lowering his head, he took her mouth in a long, luxurious kiss. "Would you mourn for me with such devotion, were I to pass on?" he queried, his lips moving against hers.

"No." Maria smiled with the hint of mystery that kept him endlessly enthralled with her.

"No?"

"Nothing or no one could ever take you from me, my darling." Her small hands brushed over his chest. "I will die alongside you. It is the only way I will allow you to go."

Christopher's heart swelled with love so fierce, it sometimes overwhelmed him. "So our young Amelia was drawn to this man in ways she has not been to anyone else. What do you suggest we do about that?"

"Watch her more closely, and find that man. I want to know him and his intentions."

"Done." He smiled. "Have you any plans for the rest of this afternoon?"

"Yes. I'm quite busy."

He hoped he hid his disappointment. While he had a great many items on his list of things to ac-complish, he would not have minded an hour or two of his wife's company. There was something delicious about making love in the middle of the day with the drapes thrown wide and the sun shining in. Especially when she took the top and writhed above him in the daylight.

Sighing dramatically, Christopher released her. "Enjoy yourself, love."

"That depends on you." Her dark eyes shined wickedly. "You see, my schedule says 'lovemaking' from two to four. I will need your help to accomplish that task."

Christopher was instantly aroused. "I am at your service, madam."

She stepped back and glanced down at the front of his breeches. "Yes, I see that you are. Shall we retire?"

"I should like that," he purred, his blood hot.

A knock intruded from the open doorway. They both looked over.

"Hello, Tim," Maria said, smiling at the giant whose great head was ducked to fit beneath the threshold.

He bowed in greeting, then rumbled, "Did you still wish to speak with me?"

"Yes." Tim was one of Christopher's most trusted lieutenants. He was also infinitely patient and had a way with women. His fondness for the fairer gender was obvious. They sensed it and were far more open with him than they were with other men. They listened to and trusted him, which would facilitate keeping Amelia in line.

Christopher looked down into Maria's uplifted face. "Don't undress," he whispered for her ears only. "I want to unwrap you myself."

"As if I'm a gift," she teased.

"You are. My most prized possession." Kissing the tip of her nose, he stepped back from her. "I must discuss Tim's new assignment to watch Amelia."

Her answering smile was a sight to behold. "You are so clever to anticipate my concerns. You never require my input in matters."

"But I do," he refuted, "and I value it." His voice lowered with promise. "Shortly, I shall show you how much."

Maria's fingertips brushed along his palm as she moved away and their hands separated. "See you at dinner, Tim," she said, sashaying past him as he entered the room.

"Yes, ma'am."

Tim looked at Christopher with a wry smile. "I know that look. This will be quick, eh?"

"Yes. Very. I want you to shadow Miss Ben-bridge."

"I 'eard about last night. No worries. She's in good 'ands with me."

"I would not ask you if I weren't confident in that." Christopher patted him on the shoulder as he headed out the door. "See you at dinner."

"Lucky bastard," Tim said after him.

Christopher grinned and sprinted up the stairs.

Chapter 3

France, a month earlier

"So," Simon Quinn said, setting his fork down. "The time has come."

"It has." And not a moment too soon in Colin Mitchell's estimation. He'd waited years for this day. Now that it had arrived, he found that sitting decorously at the table for dinner was nigh impossible. In mere hours he would set sail for England and the love of his life. He wished he were already there. With her.

All around them, revelry was the order of the day. Although raised in a boisterous Gypsy camp, Colin preferred quiet evenings. It was Quinn who sought out these loud venues. He claimed they made eavesdropping impossible and solidified their carefully affected mien of ennui and nonchalance, but Colin suspected the predilection was goaded by another reason entirely. Quinn was not a happy man, and it was easier to feign contentment when surrounded by gaiety.

Still, this establishment was one Colin tolerated better than most. It was clean, well lit, and the food was delicious. Three massive chandeliers hung from the wooden-beamed ceiling above them, and the air was redolent of various appetizing dishes and the perfumes of the many buxom serving wenches. Raucous laughter and a multitude of conversations fought to be heard over the frenetically playing orchestra in the far corner, which left them in relative privacy among the din, just two finely attired gentlemen enjoying an evening meal out.

"I had thought you might have grown beyond your feelings for the fair Amelia," Quinn said with a faint hint of his Irish brogue still evident. He lifted a glass of wine to his lips and studied Colin carefully above the rim. "You've changed a great deal from the young man who came to me searching for her so many years ago."

"True." Colin knew Quinn did not want him to go. He was too valuable a player in Quinn's games. He could become anyone, anywhere. Men trusted him and women found him irresistible. Perceptive creatures, they sensed that his heart was locked away, and it made them try harder to win him. "But that is one part of me that has not changed."

"Perhaps *she* has changed. She was a girl when you left her."

"She changed while I knew her." He shrugged. "It only deepened my feelings." How could he explain all of the many facets he had seen in her over the years?

"What allure does she possess that enslaves you so? The contessa adores you, and yet she is merely a diversion to you."

A vision of the lovely Francesca came to mind, and Colin smiled. "As I am a diversion to her. She enjoys the game, never knowing who will appear at her doorstep or which disguise I will be hidden beneath. I suit her reckless inclinations, but those extend only to the bedroom. She is too proud a woman to accept a man of my breeding in a capacity other than the one I fill presently."

Once, on assignment for Quinn, Colin had been chased into the first open door he'd come to during a ball. The room had been occupied by Francesca, who was adjusting her appearance and enjoying a small respite from the crush. He had bowed, smiled, and proceeded to divest himself of wig and clothing, turning his specially tailored garments inside out. The contessa had found the act of changing from a white-haired, black-clad gentleman to a dark-haired, ivory-clad rogue quite diverting. She'd eagerly assumed the ruse of his companion, exiting to the hallway with her hand firmly attached to his forearm, which effectively stumped the two scowling gentlemen who stumbled upon them in their search.

She'd taken him to her bed that night and kept him there the last two years, unconcerned when his employment forced him to leave her for weeks or months at a time. Theirs was an affair of convenience and mutual understanding.

I sometimes envy the woman who has such a tenacious hold on your heart, she once said to him.

Colin had swiftly turned the direction of her thoughts elsewhere. He could not bear to think of

Amelia while in the company of another woman. It felt like a betrayal, and he knew from experience that Amelia would be deeply wounded.

"Amelia holds the same allure for me as her sibling holds for you," Colin said, meeting Quinn's widening eyes. "Perhaps if you can explain to me why you still pine for Maria, it will help to answer your question regarding my feelings for Amelia."

A self-deprecating smile curved the Irishman's mouth. "Point taken. Will you return to her as Colin Mitchell or as one of your other aliases?"

Heaving out his breath, Colin glanced around the dining parlor at the many guests and overtly friendly serving staff. To Amelia, he was a part of her past . . . a deceased part of her past. A childhood friend who had grown into a young man who loved her with every breath in his body. She had loved him similarly, with the same wild, saturating, unrestrained adolescent passion. He had tried to stay away, tried to push her away, tried to convince himself that they would both grow beyond such impossible aspirations. As he was a Gypsy and a stableboy in her father's employ, there was no possibility of a future between them.

In the end, he had been unable to keep his distance. Her father, the late Viscount Welton, had been the worst sort of monster. Welton had used Amelia as leverage against her sister, selling the stunningly beautiful Maria to marriage-minded peers, whom he then killed for the widow's settlements. When Welton's machinations put Amelia in danger, Colin had attempted a daring rescue during which he'd been shot and left for dead.

How did one rise from the grave? And once he managed that task, would she accept him back into her life in the role he wished to fill—that of lover and husband?

"If she will have me, she will be the Countess Montoya," he said, referring to the title he had invented expressly for her. Over the years he'd built and strengthened the roots of that assumed nobility, purchasing properties and establishing wealth under that guise. He would not have her married to the common Colin Mitchell. She deserved better. "But perhaps it is her attachment to Colin that will win her heart."

"I will miss you," Quinn said, his blue-eyed gaze pensive. "In fact, I am not certain how I will manage without you."

Quinn had been enlisted by agents of the Crown of England to manage tasks more cautious agents wouldn't. He was not "officially" recognized, nor was Colin, which freed them both from the restrictions under which others labored. In return for their unacknowledged efforts, they kept most of the spoils, which made them exceptionally wealthy.

"You will find a way," Colin said, smiling. "You always do. You still have Cartland. In some respects, he is far more accomplished than I. He can track better than a canine. If something is lost, he is the best man to find it."

"I have my concerns about him." Quinn rested his elbows on the carved wooden arms of his chair and steepled his fingers together.

"Oh? You never said as much to me before."

"You were still in my employ then. Now I can speak to you as a friend who shares a joint past."

The logic to that was odd, but Colin played along. "What worries you?"

"Too many seem to die around Cartland."

"I thought that was by design."

"Occasionally," Quinn admitted. "He lacks the remorse that most would feel upon taking a life."

"You mean to say that *I* feel," Colin said wryly.

Quinn grinned and attracted the attention of a woman the next table over. His smile changed from one of amusement to one of sensual promise. Colin looked away to hide his chuckle. It amazed him that a man so widely lauded for his comeliness could hide such a covert livelihood.

"You never did enjoy that part of your employment," Quinn continued.

Colin lifted his glass in a mock salute and then swallowed the blood red contents in one uncouth swallow. "I always feared that every life I ended would cling to me in some way, taint me, and that eventually they would make me unsuitable for Amelia."

"How romantic," Quinn jeered softly. "One of the qualities I most loved in Maria was her ability to survive in the gutter. I could not live my life with a lily-white female. The weight of the façade would quickly fatigue me."

"You assume that the man you sit across from now is the real Colin and the one who longs for Amelia is the façade. Perhaps the opposite is true."

Quinn's gaze narrowed beneath boldly winged brows. "Then maintain the ruse a little longer."

Tensing, Colin set his empty glass down and listened alertly. "What do you want?"

He would do anything for Quinn, but the sudden portent of danger set him on edge. His bags were packed and loaded aboard the ship. In a few hours he would set sail and begin his true life, the one he had interrupted six years ago to become a man of means. A man of title, prestige, wealth. A man worthy of Amelia Benbridge.

"I have been told that Cartland is meeting often with confidants of Agent-General Talleyrand-Périgord."

Colin whistled. "Cartland is one of the most impious men I have ever met."

"Which is why his association with the equally impious agent-general is concerning. I want to search his lodgings tonight," Quinn said, "while you are still here to see to my safety. I simply need you to delay him if he attempts to retire early."

"Since he is aware that I depart at dawn, he will find it odd if I approach him."

"Be covert. Most likely he will cause you no grief. He is not known for being reclusive."

Nodding, Colin ran the posed scenario through his mind and could find nothing that would interfere with his removal from France. A few hours of his time and he would alleviate his feelings of guilt for abandoning Quinn. Cartland spent more time awake in the night hours than he did during the day. Chances were more than good that Colin would sit in a carriage watching the door of one establishment or another and go directly from there to the wharf.

"Of course I will help you," he agreed.

"Excellent." Quinn gestured to an attendant for more wine. "I am indebted to you."

"Nonsense," Colin dismissed. "I can never repay you for what you have done for me."

"I expect to be invited to the wedding."

"Never doubt it."

Quinn raised his refilled glass in a toast. "To the fair Miss Benbridge."

Filled with anticipation for the future, Colin drank eagerly to that.

"What are you about?" Colin muttered to himself just a few hours later as he clung to the shadows of an alleyway and followed Cartland at a discreet distance.

The man had left his mistress's home an hour past and had been strolling rather aimlessly ever since. Because he continued to move in the general direction of his lodgings, Colin followed. He could not have Cartland returning while Quinn might still be there.

The night was pleasant, the sky clear but for a few clouds. A full moon hung low, providing ample illumination when not blocked by a building. Still, Colin would much rather be in his cabin at the moment, sleeping away the hours until he could stand at the bow and breathe deeply of the crisp sea air.

Cartland turned a corner, and Colin fell behind, counting silently until the appropriate lapse had passed and he could round the building as well and continue his leisurely pursuit.

He made his move and paused, startled to find a private courtyard ahead. Cartland stood there, engrossed in discussion with someone who appeared to have been waiting. Two brick posts held lanterns marking the entrance to the outdoor retreat. A small fountain and a neatly trimmed, tiny lawn were the only other items in the space.

Colin hung back, drawing his cloak around him to better disguise his frame in the darkness. He was not an easy man to hide, not at a few inches over six feet in height and sixteen stone, but he had learned the art of concealment and practiced it well.

Oddly enough, while he could attribute his size to his laborer parents, Cartland was also quite large, and his breeding was more refined. He worked for a living only because his father had bankrupted them, and he made certain that everyone knew he was above certain tasks. Killing was not one of them. That was a duty he enjoyed far too much for Colin's taste, which was why they associated with each other only when forced to by necessity.

Creeping along the damp stone wall, Colin moved closer to the two men, hoping to hear something that would help to explain this assignation.

". . . *you may tell the agent-general* . . ."

". . . *forget your place! You are not* . . ."

". . . *I will see to it, Leroux, provided I am compensated* . . ."

The debate seemed to grow more heated with Cartland gesturing roughly with one hand, while the gentleman with whom he spoke began to pace. The sound of heels tapping restlessly along cobblestones helped to disguise Colin's stealthy approach. Cartland's evening garments were covered by a short cape secured with a jeweled brooch that gleamed in the lantern light. The other man was hatless, coatless, and much shorter. He was also highly agitated.

"You have not followed through with your end of our arrangement!" Leroux snapped. "How dare you approach me for more money when you have yet to accomplish the task you were previously paid for!"

"I was underpaid," Cartland scoffed, his features hidden beneath the rim of his tricorn.

"I will inform the agent-general of your ridiculous demands, and advise him to seek someone more trustworthy to work on his behalf."

"Oh?" There was a smugness to Cartland's tone that alarmed Colin, but before he could act, it was too late. The light of the moon caught the edge of a blade and then it was gone, embedded deeply within Leroux's gut.

There was a pained gasp and then a thick gurgle.

"You can pass along something else for me as well," Cartland bit out, as he withdrew the dagger and thrust it home again. "I am not a lackey to be set aside when I have outlived my usefulness."

Suddenly a dark form leaped from the shadows and tackled Cartland, knocking his hat aside. The blade slipped free and clattered to the cobblestone. Leroux sank to his knees, his hands clutching at the welling blood.

Rolling and writhing upon the ground, the would-be rescuer fought brutally, delivering blows that echoed off the buildings around them. Material ripped and venomous words were exchanged as Cartland gained the upper hand. Pinning his assailant to the ground, he reached for the knife lying just a few feet away.

"Cartland!" Colin abandoned his attempt at stealth and rushed toward the fray, tossing his cloak over his shoulder to bare the hilt of his small sword.

Startled, Cartland pulled back, revealing a face etched with bloodlust and cold, dark eyes. The man beneath him took the opening and swung his fist hard and fast, clipping Cartland in the temple and sending him reeling to the side.

Colin ran through the posts that marked the entrance and pulled his blade free. "You have much to answer for!"

"It won't be to you," Cartland cried, kicking out with his feet.

Sidestepping the assault, Colin lunged, piercing Cartland's shoulder. The man roared like a wounded animal and flailed in fury.

Circling, Colin turned his head to look at the unfortunate Leroux. His open, sightless eyes betrayed his demise.

It was too late. The man who had the ear of Talleyrand-Périgord was dead.

The dreaded feeling of portent once again hit Colin hard.

Distracted, he failed to anticipate the blow that came to the back of his knee, tumbling him to the ground. By instinct, he rolled to the side, avoiding another assault from Cartland, but coming up against the corpse and the pool of blood quickly spreading around it.

Cartland scrambled for his discarded knife, but the other man was there first, sending it skidding across the cobblestones with a well-placed kick. Colin was struggling to his feet when alarmed shouts sounded from the nearby street. All three of them turned their heads.

Discovery was near at hand.

"A trap!" Cartland hissed, leaping to his feet. He stumbled toward the low stone wall and threw himself over it.

Colin was already in motion, running.

"Halt!" came a cry from the alleyway.

"Faster!" urged Leroux's would-be rescuer, fleeing alongside him.

Together they took a different alley than the one Colin had arrived through . . . the one that was presently filling with authorities who pursued with lanterns raised high.

"Halt!"

When they reached the street, Colin ran to the left in the direction of his waiting coach; the other man fled to the right. After the explosion of activity in the small courtyard, the relative stillness of the night seemed unnatural, the rhythmic pounding of his footfalls sounding overly loud.

Colin weaved in and out among various buildings and streets, taking alleys whenever possible to lessen his chances of being apprehended.

Finally, he returned to Cartland's mistress's house

and caught the eye of his coachman, who straightened and prepared to release the brake.

"Quinn's," Colin ordered as he vaulted into the carriage. The equipage lurched into motion, and he hunched over, tearing off his blood-soaked cloak and tossing it to the floorboards. "Damn it!"

How the hell could such a simple task spin so far beyond his control?

Keep Cartland from returning home too early. A bloody simple task, that. One that should not have involved witnessing a murder and the drawing of his blade.

The moment his carriage drew to a halt before Quinn's door, Colin was leaping out. He pounded with his fist upon the portal, cursing at the lengthy delay before it opened.

A disheveled butler stood with taper in hand. "Sir?"

"Quinn. *Now.*"

The urgency in his tone was clear and undeniable. Stepping back, the servant allowed him entry and showed him into the lower parlor. He was left alone. Then a few moments later Quinn entered wearing a multicolored silk robe and bearing flushed skin. "I sent for you hours ago. When you did not reply, I assumed you had boarded your ship and gone to sleep."

"If you've a woman upstairs," Colin gritted out, "I think I might kill you."

Quinn took in his appearance from head to toe. "What happened?"

Colin paced back and forth before the banked fire in the grate and relayed the night's events.

"Bloody hell." Quinn ran a hand through his inky locks. "He will be desperate, running from both us and them."

"There is no 'us,'" Colin snapped. He pointed at the longcase clock in the corner. "My ship sets sail within a few hours. I've come only to wish you good riddance! Had I been caught tonight, I might have been delayed for weeks or months while this mess was sorted out."

More pounding came to the door. They both paused, hardly daring to breathe.

The butler rushed in. "A dozen armed men," he said. "They searched the carriage and took something from inside it."

"My cloak," Colin said grimly, "soaked with Leroux's blood."

"That they would come for you here would suggest that Cartland has offered you up as the sacrificial lamb." Quinn growled as commands were shouted from outside. "Answer that," he said to the waiting servant. "Delay them as long as possible."

"Yes, sir." The butler departed, closing the parlor door behind him.

"I am sorry, my friend," Quinn muttered, moving to the clock and shoving it aside, revealing a swinging panel behind it. "This will lead you to the stables. You may find trouble at the wharf, but if you can board your ship, do so. I will manage things for you here and clear your name."

"How?" Colin rushed over to the hidden portal. "Cartland was working with the French in some capacity. There must be some level of trust in him."

"I will find a way, never doubt it." Quinn set a

hand on his shoulder as voices were heard in the foyer. "Godspeed."

With that, Colin rushed through the door, and it was immediately shut behind him. Scraping sounds accompanied the moving of the clock back to its original position. He heard no more than that, because he was moving blindly through the dark tunnel, his hands held out to either side to feel his way.

His heart racing, his breathing labored, he fought against a rising panic. Not because capture was at hand, but because he had never been so close to reclaiming Amelia. He felt as if she were within his grasp and that if he were unable to board his ship, he would be losing her all over again. He'd barely survived the first time. He doubted his ability to survive another.

The tunnel became dank, the smell unpleasant. Colin reached what appeared to be a dead end and cursed viciously. Then the sounds of skittish horses caught his ear, and he glanced up, noting the faint outline of a trapdoor above him. He kicked around with his foot until he found the short stool; then he pulled it closer and stood upon it.

Quiet as a mouse, he lifted the door just enough to look through the strands of straw that covered it. The stable was still, though the perceptive beasts it housed shifted restlessly in response to his agitation. Throwing the hatch wide, he climbed out and sealed the door again. Colin grabbed the nearest bridle and horse, then opened the stable doors.

He walked his mount outside, eyes wide and ears open as he searched for those who might be hunting him.

"You, there! Halt!" cried a voice coming from the left.

Grabbing two fistfuls of silky mane, Colin pulled himself up and onto the horse's bare back.

"Go!" he urged with a kick of his heels, and they burst out to the mew.

The early morning wind whipped the queue from his hair. He was hunched low over his mount's neck, as they raced through the streets, breathing heavily in unison. Colin's gut knotted with anxiety. If he made it to the ship without incident, it would be a miracle. He was so close to leaving this life behind, damn it. So close.

Colin galloped as near to the wharf as he dared, then dismounted. He freed his horse, then traversed the remaining distance on foot, moving in and out among the various crates and barrels. Sweat coated his skin despite the chill of the ocean breeze and his lack of outerwear.

So close.

Later, he would not remember the climb up the gangplank or the journey from the deck to his cabin. He would, however, never forget what he found inside.

The door swung open, and he entered, gasping at the sight that greeted him.

"Ah, there you are," purred the unctuous voice of a stranger.

Pausing on the threshold, Colin stared at the tall, thin man who held a knife to his valet's throat. One of Cartland's lackeys or perhaps one working for the French.

Regardless, he was caught.

His valet stared at him with wide horrified eyes

above a cravat tied around his mouth as a gag. Bound to a chair, the servant was visibly trembling, and the acrid smell of urine betrayed just how frightened he was.

"What do you want?" Colin asked, holding both hands up to display his willingness to cooperate.

"You are to come with me."

His heart sank. *Amelia.* In his mind, she was retreating. Fading.

He nodded. "Of course."

"Excellent."

Before he could blink, the man moved, shoving his valet's head back and slitting his throat.

"No!" Colin lunged forward, but it was too late. "Dear God, why?" he cried, his eyes stung by frustrated, hopeless tears.

"Why not?" the man retorted, shrugging. His eyes were small and pale blue, like ice. Swarthy skin and late-night bristle on his jaw made him look dirty, although his simple garments appeared to be clean. "After you."

Colin stumbled back out the cabin door, inwardly certain that he would die this night. The deep sadness he felt was not due so much to the loss of his life, such as it was. It was mourning for the life he had dreamt of sharing with Amelia.

His hands were shaking as he gripped the railings that supported the stairs leading back up to the deck. A sickening thud and low groan behind him made him jump and turn too quickly. He tripped and landed on his arse on the second-to-bottom step.

There at his feet lay his captor, facedown with a

rapidly swelling lump protruding from the back of his head.

Colin's gaze lifted from the prone body and found the man who had fought with Cartland in the courtyard earlier. He was short of stature and stocky, his body heavily muscled and clothed in nondescript attire of various shades of gray. The man's features were blunt, his dark eyes wizened and jaded.

"You saved my life," the man said. "I owed you."

"Who are you?" Colin asked.

"Jacques."

Just the one name, no more than that.

"Thank you, Jacques. How did you find me?"

"I followed this man." He kicked at the fallen body with the tip of his boot. "It is not safe for you to remain in France, monsieur."

"I know."

The man bowed. "If you have something of value, I would suggest you offer it to the captain as enticement to set sail immediately. I will manage the bodies."

Colin heaved out a weary breath, fighting the flickering hope inside him. The chances of him actually making it to English soil were negligible.

"Go," Jacques urged.

"I will help you." He pushed heavily to his feet. "Then you should disembark before you are associated with me."

"Too late for that," the Frenchman said, his gaze direct. "I will remain with you until you are settled and this matter of my master's death is resolved."

"Why?" Colin asked simply, too weary to argue.

"Arrange our departure now," Jacques said. "We will have plenty of time to talk on the journey."

Unbelievably, within the hour they were out to sea. But the Colin Mitchell who stood at the mist-covered bow was not the same one who had shared a farewell dinner with Quinn.

This Colin had a price on his head, and the cost to pay it could be his life.

Chapter 4

*T*he fence was directly ahead. After making certain that the guard was still far enough away to miss seeing her, Amelia hurried toward it. She did not see the man hidden on the other side of a large tree. When a steely arm caught her and a large hand covered her mouth, she was terrified, her scream smothered by a warm palm.

"Hush," Colin whispered, his hard body pinning hers to the trunk.

Her heart racing in her chest, Amelia beat at him with her fists, furious that he had given her such a fright.

"Stop it," he ordered, pulling her away from the tree to shake her, his dark eyes boring into hers. "I'm sorry I scared you, but you left me no choice. You won't see me, won't talk to me—"

She ceased struggling when he pulled her into a tight embrace, the powerful length of his frame completely unfamiliar to her.

"I'm removing my hand. Hold your tongue or you'll bring the guards over here."

He released her, backing away from her quickly as if she were malodorous or something else similarly unpleas-

ant. As for her, she immediately missed the scent of horses
and the hard-working male that clung to Colin.

Dappled sunlight kissed his black hair and handsome
features. She hated that her stomach knotted at the sight
and her heart hurt anew until it throbbed in her chest.
Dressed in an oatmeal-colored sweater and brown breeches,
he was all male. Dangerously so.

"I want to tell you I'm sorry." His voice was hoarse
and gravelly.

She glared.

He exhaled harshly and ran both hands through his
hair. "She doesn't mean anything."

Amelia realized then that he was not apologizing for
scaring the wits from her. "How lovely," she said, unable
to hide her bitterness. "I am so relieved to hear that what
broke my heart meant nothing to you."

He winced and held out his work-roughened hands.
"Amelia. You don't understand. You're too young, too
sheltered."

"Yes, well, you found someone older and less sheltered
to understand you." She walked past him. "I found someone older who understands me. We are all happy, so—"

"What?"

His low, ominous tone startled her, and she cried out
when he caught her roughly. "Who?" His face was so
tight, she was frightened again. "That boy by the stream?
Benny?"

"Why do you care?" she threw at him. "You have
her."

"Is that why you're dressed this way?" His heated gaze
swept up and down her body. "Is that why you wear your
hair up now? For him?"

Considering the occasion worthy of it, she had worn
one of her prettiest dresses, a deep blue confection sprin-

kled with tiny embroidered red flowers. "Yes! He doesn't see me as a child."

"Because he is one! Have you kissed him? Has he touched you?"

"He is only a year younger than you." *Her chin lifted.* "And he is an earl. A gentleman. He would not be caught behind a store making love to a girl."

"It wasn't making love," *Colin said furiously, holding her by the upper arms.*

"It appeared that way to me."

"Because you don't know any better." *His fingers kneaded into her skin restlessly, as if he couldn't bear to touch her, but couldn't bear not to either.*

"And I suppose you do?"

His jaw clenched in answer to her scorn.

Oh, that hurt! To know there was someone out there whom he loved. Her Colin.

"Why are we talking about this?" *She attempted to wrench free, but to no avail. He held fast. She needed distance from him. She could not breathe when he touched her, could barely think. Only pain and deep sorrow penetrated her overwhelmed senses.* "I forgot about you, Colin. I stayed out of your way. Why must you bother me again?"

He thrust one hand into the hair at her nape, pulling her closer. His chest labored against hers, doing odd things to her breasts, making them swell and ache. She ceased struggling, worried about how her body would react if she continued.

"I saw your face," *he said gruffly.* "I hurt you. I never meant to hurt you."

Tears filled her eyes and she blinked rapidly, determined to keep them from falling.

"Amelia." *He pressed his cheek to hers, his voice carrying an aching note.* "Don't cry. I can't bear it."

"Release me, then. And keep your distance." She swallowed hard. "Better yet, perhaps you could find a more prestigious position elsewhere. You are a hard worker—"

His other arm banded her waist. "You would send me away?"

"Yes," she whispered, her hands fisted in his sweater. "Yes, I would." Anything to avoid seeing him with another girl.

He nuzzled hard against her. "An earl . . . It must be Lord Ware. Damn him."

"He is nice to me. He talks to me, smiles when he sees me. Today, he is going to give me my first kiss. And I'm—"

"No!" Colin pulled back, his irises swallowed by dilated pupils leaving deep black pools of torment. "He may have all the things that I never will, including you. But by God, he won't take that from me."

"What—?"

He took her mouth, stunning her so that she couldn't move. Amelia could not understand what was happening, why he was acting this way, why he would approach her now, on this day, and kiss her as if he were starved for the taste of her.

His head twisted, his lips fitting more fully over hers, his thumbs pressing gently into the hinges of her jaw and urging her mouth to open. She shivered violently, awash in heated longing, afraid she was dreaming or had otherwise lost her mind. Her mouth opened, and a whimper escaped as his tongue, soft like wet velvet, slipped inside.

Frightened, she stopped breathing. Then he murmured to her, her darling Colin, his fingertips brushing across her cheekbones in a soothing caress.

"Let me," he whispered. "Trust me."

Amelia lifted to her toes, surging into him, her hands

sliding into his silken locks. Unschooled, she could only follow his lead, allowing him to eat at her mouth gently, her tongue tentatively touching his.

He moaned, a sound filled with hunger and need, his hands cupping the back of her head and angling her better. The connection became deeper, her response more fervent. Tingles swept across her skin in a wave of goose bumps. In the pit of her stomach a sense of urgency grew, of recklessness and flaring hope.

One of his hands slipped, caressing the length of her back before cupping her buttock and urging her up and into his body. As she felt the hard ridge of his arousal, a deep ache blossomed low inside her.

"Amelia . . . sweet." His lips drifted across her damp face, kissing away her tears. "We shouldn't be doing this."

But he kept kissing her and kissing her and rolling his hips into her.

"I love you," she gasped. "I've loved you so long—"

He cut her off with his lips over hers, his passion escalating, his hands roaming all over her back and arms. When she couldn't breathe, she tore her lips away.

"Tell me you love me," she begged, her chest heaving. "You must. Oh, God, Colin . . ." She rubbed her tear-streaked face into his. "You've been so cruel, so mean."

"I can't have you. You shouldn't want me. We can't—"

Colin thrust away from her with a vicious curse. "You are too young for me to touch you like this. No. Don't say anything else, Amelia. I am a servant. I will always be a servant, and you will always be a viscount's daughter."

Her arms wrapped around her middle, her entire body quaking as if she were cold instead of blistering hot. Her skin felt too tight, her lips swollen and throbbing. "But you do love me, don't you?" *she asked, her small voice shaky despite her efforts to be strong.*

"Don't ask me that."

"Can you not grant me at least that much? If I cannot have you anyway, if you will never be mine, can't you at least tell me that your heart belongs to me?"

He groaned. "I thought it was best if you hated me." *His head tilted up to the sky with his eyes squeezed shut.* "I had hoped that if you did, I would stop dreaming."

"Dreaming of what?" *She tossed aside caution and approached him, her fingers slipping beneath his sweater to touch the hard ridges of his abdomen.*

He caught her wrist and glared down at her. "Don't touch me."

"Are they like my dreams?" *she queried softly.* "Where you kiss me as you did a moment ago and tell me you love me more than anything in the world?"

"No," *he growled.* "They are not sweet and romantic and girlish. They are a man's dreams, Amelia."

"Such as what you were doing to that girl?" *Her lower lip quivered, and she bit down on it to hide the betraying movement. Her mind flooded with the painful memories, adding to the turmoil wrought by the unfamiliar cravings of her body and the pleading demands of her heart.* "Do you dream about her, too?"

Colin caught her wrist again. "Never."

He kissed her, lighter in pressure and urgency than before, but no less passionately. Soft as a butterfly's wings, his lips brushed back and forth across hers, his tongue dipping inside, then retreating. It was a reverent kiss, and her lonely heart soaked it up like the desert floor soaked rain.

Cupping her face in his hands, he breathed, "This is making love, Amelia."

"Tell me you don't kiss her like this." She cried softly, her nails digging into his back through his sweater.

"I don't kiss anyone. I never have." His forehead pressed against hers. "Only you. It's only ever been you."

Amelia jerked awake with a violent start, her heart racing with the remnants of adolescent passion and yearning. Tossing back the covers, she sat up, allowing the chilly night air to seep through her thin night rail to her perspiration-damp skin. She lifted shaking fingertips to her lips, pressing hard against the swollen curves in an effort to stem their tingling.

The dream had been so vivid. She imagined that she could still taste Colin, a heady exotic flavor that she craved to this day. It had been years since she'd been plagued with such recollections. She'd thought they were fading, that perhaps she might be healing. Finally.

Why now? Was it because she had agreed to proceed with the wedding? Was Colin's memory rearing up and demanding that the love of her life not be set aside?

Amelia closed her eyes and saw a white mask above shamelessly sensual lips.

Montoya.

His kiss had made her tingle as well. From head to toe and everywhere in between.

She had to find him. She *would* find him.

* * *

"What does he say?"

Colin refolded the missive carefully and tucked it into a drawer of his desk. He looked at Jacques. "He believes Cartland is leading a group of men here in England."

"He will not want to bring you back alive." Jacques walked over to the window and brushed the sheer panel aside to look down at the front drive.

The town house they occupied was a rental in fine shape. It was a short distance from the city, near enough to be convenient, but far enough away to ensure that no one would find them noteworthy. The distance also allowed them to ascertain if they were being followed or not, which Colin had been just a few nights past. The night he had danced with and kissed Amelia.

"It is good that you stay indoors during the day," Jacques said, turning back to face him again. "You are being hunted on all sides."

Shaking his head, Colin closed his eyes and leaned into the back of his chair. "It was foolish of me to seek her out that way. Now I have attracted St. John's attention, and he will not rest until he knows why I displayed such interest in her."

"She is a beautiful woman," Jacques said, his voice laced with a Frenchman's innate appreciation of such delights.

"Yes, she is."

Beyond beautiful. Dear God, how was it possible for a woman to be so perfect? Stunning green eyes framed by sooty lashes. An imminently kissable mouth. Creamy skin, and the fully ripened curves of a woman grown. All carried with an air of latent sensuality that he had always found alluring.

He could admit now that his attendance at the ball had been goaded by his hope that he would see her and find his attraction unfounded. Perhaps absence had made his heart too fond. Perhaps he had embellished her memory in his mind.

"But that is not why you love her," Jacques murmured.

"No," Colin agreed, "it's not."

"I have rarely seen a woman with such yearning in her soul. Although I watched her as you did, she did not take note of my interest, only of yours."

That was his fault, he knew. Repeated glimpses of her profile had only whetted his appetite to see her directly. *Look at me,* he'd urged silently. *Look at me!*

And she had, unable to resist when followed with such ravenous attention.

The eye contact had cut him to the quick, piercing across the distance between them and stabbing deep into his heart. He'd felt it, the yearning Jacques spoke of. That longing elicited a primal response in him to deliver it, whatever *it* was that she wanted. Whatever she needed.

"You could take her from the other man," Jacques said.

He knew that, too. Had felt the wavering in her as they had danced and then again when they had kissed.

"I wish I'd never followed Cartland that night!" Colin growled, the frustration inside him a writhing, powerful thing. "Everything would be different."

She would be in his bed now, writhing and arching beneath him as he rode her hard and deep, awakening the wanton he sensed was waiting just beneath the surface. In his mind, he could hear her voice hoarse from crying out his name, her satin skin covered in a fine sheen of sweat.

He would push her beyond reason, take her body places she never knew it could go . . .

"The twists in our lives happen for a reason," Jacques said, returning to the desk and sitting across from him. "I could have lived the whole of my life without leaving France, yet I was destined to follow you here."

Colin pushed the lewd images from his thoughts and opened his eyes. "You are a good man, Jacques, to carry your debt beyond the grave."

"Monsieur Leroux saved the life of my sister and with her, the life of my niece," he said quietly. "I cannot proceed knowing his murderer has not paid for the crime."

"And how do we make him pay?"

The Frenchman smiled, bringing warmth to his hard features. "I would like to kill him, but that would put you at a marked disadvantage. With me as your only witness, you would find it extremely difficult to prove your innocence."

Colin said nothing to that. Jacques had already helped far beyond what he had any right to ask.

"So he must confess." Jacques shrugged. "I will take what pleasure I can from doing whatever is necessary to garner that confession."

Nodding, Colin looked toward the window. Night had fallen hours ago. Shortly, he could leave and make discreet inquiries in his efforts to find Cartland before the man found him. But first, he would need some rest. "I will retire for a few hours, then set out and see what I can discover. Someone will have a loose tongue, to be sure. I just have to find him."

"Perhaps you should contact the man you worked for here," Jacques said carefully. "The one who directs Quinn."

Colin had never met Lord Eddington, never exchanged a word or correspondence. All communications passed through Quinn, and as far as Colin knew, Eddington was unaware of the identities of the men working under Quinn. There would be no way to prove that he was a confidant. "No. That is not possible," he said grimly. "We do not know one another."

The Frenchman blinked, apparently so taken aback by the news that he lapsed into his native language. "*Vraiment?*"

"Truly."

"Well, then . . . that rules out that course of action."

"Yes. Unfortunately, it does." He pushed to his feet. "We will talk more when I awake."

Jacques inclined his head in agreement and waited until Colin had left the room. Then he moved to the desk, where he opened a drawer and pulled out the white half mask.

Colin would not be attending any balls or masquerades, so his continuing possession of the mask betrayed its sentimental value. Jacques had watched his new friend with Miss Benbridge and knew the woman meant a great deal.

So he would watch her when he could and keep her safe, if possible. If God was kind, Jacques would finish his task, Cartland would have his comeuppance, and Colin would have the woman he loved.

As a child, Amelia had learned how to socialize with giants.

Of course, at that time, they had been imaginary. The man standing before her was quite real, but she knew he was the same sort of giant as the one in her mind—gentle and kind beneath a gruff, formidable exterior.

"This is extortion!" Tim cried, looming over her.

Amelia set a hand at her neck to rub the ache caused by craning so far back. "No," she denied. "Not really. Extortion gives you only one choice. I am offering you options."

"I don't like yer options." He crossed his great arms over his barrel chest.

"I do not blame you. I don't care for them very much either."

She moved toward the nearby padded window seat. The upper family parlor was packed with people, all employees of St. John. Some played cards, others talked and laughed boisterously, and still others napped where they sat, exhausted from running errands all day long.

"It would have been much easier for everyone if the man had simply stated his intentions directly." Amelia shook out her skirts of yellow shot silk taffeta and settled as comfortably as possible in her evening attire. "But he did not, and so we must guess. I am not very good at guessing, Tim. I haven't the patience for it."

Looking up at him from beneath her lashes, she smiled prettily.

Tim snorted and scowled. "Don't you 'ave something else to worry your 'ead o'er? Wedding gowns and such?"

"No. Not really."

She should be consumed with the planning of her forthcoming nuptials. From waking to sleeping she should have no time for anything else. It was the most anticipated match of the Season and, if she maneuvered well, it could be a wonderful launch for her new position as a future marchioness.

Instead she was consumed by thoughts of her masked admirer. She was tenacious when intrigued and told herself that if she could only discern the man's motives, she would be free to concentrate on more pressing matters.

It was prewedding nervousness. The need for one last peccadillo. A farewell to childhood whimsy.

She shook her head. There were a hundred names she gave to why she was so distracted by the masked Montoya. But the reason's true identity eluded her.

"Well, *yer* not doing any searching," Tim grumbled. "Not on my watch."

"Fine," she said agreeably. "Just inform me when you find him."

"No." Tim's jaw took on that obstinate cant that was more bark than bite. He wore green wool trousers this evening and a black waistcoat trimmed with green thread. It was the most colorful ensemble she had ever seen him wear. His coarse gray hair was restrained in a braided queue, and his Vandyke was neatly trimmed.

Amelia adored him for the effort, knowing the care he displayed was due entirely to affection for her. He wanted to make her proud while he was following her about at the Rothschild ball this evening. He would not be attending, of course, merely watching from the outside perimeter, yet he'd taken pains with his appearance.

She was proud of him, regardless.

"Very well, then." She heaved a dramatic sigh. "I shall search for him myself and drag you along with me, since you are to be my nursemaid."

Tim growled and several heads turned in their direction. "All right," he snapped. "I'll tell you when, but not where or 'ow. But you should be forgetting about that man. 'E won't be troubling you again, I promise you that."

"Lovely." She patted the space next to her and held her tongue regarding any further discussion on the matter. She would see Montoya again, alone. Whether that was within St. John's captivity, or outside his reach. She had to. Something within her wouldn't allow the matter to rest. "Come and tell me about Sarah. Will you be making an honest woman out of her soon?"

The floor vibrated with Tim's heavy footsteps, and when he sat, the seat creaked in protest. Amelia smiled. "Was your mother a sturdy woman?"

His returning grin was infectious. "No. She was tiny, but then, so was I."

She laughed and he flushed, so she changed the subject. "About Sarah . . . ?"

Sarah was Maria's longtime abigail, a soul of discretion and loyalty. Tim had been soft on the maid for years, yet neither appeared to be hastening toward the altar.

"She won't 'ave me," he answered glumly.

Amelia blinked. "Whyever not?"

"She says my work is too dangerous. She won't be widowed with children. Too 'ard."

"Oh." She frowned. "I do not understand that, to be honest. Love is too precious to waste. Waiting for the right time, the right place . . . Sometimes that never comes and you will have missed out on what little happiness was yours to claim."

Tim stared at her.

"Do not discount me because I am young," she admonished.

"Ye've yet to 'ave life knock you down."

"I have had it hold me back, restrain me, keep me from the things I have wanted."

"'Tis different to see something through glass than it is to 'old it in your 'and and 'ave it taken from you." His eyes were kind. "Cease pining for yer stableboy. The earl is a good man to turn a blind eye to this." Tim waved his arm in a sweeping gesture that encompassed the whole room.

Amelia sighed. "I know. I do love him. But it is not the same."

"If the Gypsy 'ad lived, you would 'ave grown out of yer liking for 'im."

"I do not believe so," she refuted, seeing Colin clearly in her mind, laughing, his dark eyes bright with joy and affection. Then later, flushed and intent with passion. They'd done no more than kiss, but the ardor was there. The need. The sensation that the feeling would escalate into a blinding brilliance that might well be unbearable.

That sense of . . . anticipation . . . stayed with her. Unfulfilled. Untapped.

Until Montoya kissed her.

Then it had simmered inside her. Just for an instant, but long enough to reawaken what had long been dormant. *That* was what she could not explain. Not to anyone, not to herself. She had considered what, if anything, was similar about her two attractions. It was rather alarming to decide that she was attracted to the forbidden. To what she could not have. Should not have.

In the voluminous folds of her skirts, Amelia's hand clutched the secret bundle in her pocket that she carried with the mad hope that she might see Montoya again.

"The Earl of Ware has come to call," the butler intoned from the doorway.

Tim stood and held out his hand to her. "A good man," he said again.

Nodding, she released the note in her pocket and set her fingers within his palm.

The man in the white mask was following her.

The mask was the same, but the man wearing it was not. This man was shorter, stockier. His garments, though of the same austerity as Montoya's, were of lesser quality.

Who was he? And why did he hold such interest in her?

Amelia was crestfallen, but prayed she hid it well. Although she had known it was a possibility that Montoya had approached her for a reason beyond attraction to her, she had chosen to believe that it was personal, in the best possible way. His mourning for his lost sweetheart had been so like her own. She had felt a connection to him that she had previously felt only with Ware and Colin.

Had it all been a lie?

She suddenly felt alone and very naïve. The ballroom was a crush, the earl whose arm she held was charming and devoted, and someone was speaking to her, but she felt as if she were an island in a vast sea.

"Are you unwell?" Ware whispered.

Shaking her head, she tried to look away from the man in the white mask and was unable to. She damned herself for looking for Montoya. If she had not, she could have kept the fantasy of his interest alive within her. Now that it was gone, she felt its loss keenly.

"Should we stroll?" Ware suggested. He bent over her in a highly intimate pose made acceptable by his smile and a wink at the gentleman speaking to them. "Lord Reginald's discourse is coaxing me to sleep, as well."

Amelia fought a smile, but felt it tugging at the corner of her lips. She turned her gaze from the masked man who watched her so closely and met Ware's concerned blue eyes. "I should like that, my lord."

He made their excuses and began to lead her away. As often happened when he sheltered her, her heart swelled with gratitude. She prayed that the feeling would grow into love and thought perhaps after they consummated their marriage it might turn into that. He would have a care for her in that regard, too, she knew.

She glanced at him, and he caught her gaze and held it. "Everything I do for you, sweet Amelia, is for the occasional moments when you look at me as you are doing now."

Blushing, she looked away and watched the man in the mask moving, circling the room at the same pace she was, keeping himself directly opposite her.

"Would you excuse me for a moment?" she asked Ware, smiling.

"Only a moment."

A female guest walked past them, her appreciative gaze roving the length of Ware's tall frame.

"You provocative devil, you," Amelia teased.

He winked, stepped back, and kissed her gloved hand. "Only for you."

She rolled her eyes at the blatant lie, then made her egress, heading toward the hallway that led to the retiring rooms. She took her time, making certain it would be easy to follow her, then slipped down the hall. There were plenty of guests mingling about. Music swelled from the open ballroom doors. Candlelight flickered in sconces along the wall. She felt safe.

Taking a deep breath, she pivoted on her heel and faced him.

He stood several feet back. Amelia arched a brow and gestured him closer. He smiled and approached, but stopped a discreet distance away.

"Y-your mask . . ." she began.

"*His* mask," he corrected with a definite French accent.

"Why? Does he want me, or St. John?"

"I do not know who St. John is."

Amelia hesitated a moment, inwardly debating the wisdom of her actions; then she reached into her pocket. She withdrew what she hid there and held it out to him.

The Frenchman's head tilted to the side as he considered her. He took what she offered and sketched a gallant bow. "Mademoiselle."

"Give him that," she said. Then, lifting her chin, she walked past him and returned to Ware's side.

Chapter 5

"For God's sake! Why did you go?"
Colin paced back and forth before the fire in his study and growled low in his throat.

"Because," Jacques said easily.

"Because? *Because!*" Colin glanced down at the object in his hand, a miniature of Amelia as only a lover should see her. *En dishabille,* one shoulder provocatively bare almost to the nipple, her hair loose and flowing, her lips red and slightly parted. As if she'd been fucked long and well.

Who was this made for? Not for him certainly. It would have been commissioned many months ago.

"She looked beautiful, monsieur."

Pausing before the fire, Colin leaned heavily against it, wishing he could have seen her. "What color was she wearing?"

"Yellow."

"She approached you?"

"In a fashion." Jacques sat on the settee and tossed one arm over the back, at ease. Which was completely opposite of Colin's own turmoil. "I admire her."

Colin released his breath in a rush. "Damn it. I wanted to keep my distance."

"Why? To keep her safe? She is heavily guarded." The Frenchman's fingertips drummed silently against the wooden lip which framed the back of the settee. "Why is that?"

"Her sister and her sister's husband are both notorious criminals. They fear she will be used against them, just as I do." Leaving the grate, Colin sank heavily into his seat behind his desk.

"I thought her father was a man of some consequence."

"A viscount, yes." At Jacques's raised brows, he continued. "His avarice was exceeded only by his cruelty. He could see nothing beyond his own wants and desires. He married a lovely widow to gain access to her daughter, Amelia's sister. He sent Maria to the finest schools, then sold her into marriage to men he eventually killed to obtain their widow's settlements."

"*Mon Dieu!*" Jacques's fingers stilled. "Why did she not flee?"

"Lord Welton had Amelia and was using her to gain Maria's cooperation."

The Frenchman's face hardened. "I hope he has met his reward. There are very few things in this life that I find more detestable than crimes against one's family."

"His lordship was tried and hanged. In the course of her efforts to free her sister, Maria met Christopher St. John, a known pirate and smuggler. Together, they were able to manage a rescue and implicate Welton in the murders of Maria's two husbands."

Colin ran a hand through his hair. "The tale is far more complicated than that, but suffice it to say that St. John and his wife are two people with a multitude of enemies."

"Considering Miss Benbridge's past and present circumstances, it is even more curious that she would approach me as she did."

"Amelia was never one to do what was expected." His gaze returned to the miniature in his hand. It was an irresistible enticement that he must find a way to ignore.

"What did she give you?"

"An invitation." A private request to meet with her at the Fairchilds' musicale. Another chance to see her and speak with her.

"Will you go?"

"I think it would be best if I leave Town," he said, considering alternative locations. He could travel to Bristol, where Cartland's brood originated, and see what might be of interest there. A man like Cartland would not have a sterling past. There could be something Colin could use to lure the man into the open. "We cannot risk remaining in one location too long."

"And I was just beginning not to thoroughly detest London," Jacques said wryly.

Colin knew that although the Frenchman tried valiantly to hide it, he found England distasteful and obviously longed to go home.

"You do not have to come with me." Colin smiled

to soften his words. "Frankly, I do not know why you are here."

Jacques shrugged his sturdy shoulders. "Some men are born to lead. I was born to serve." He stood. "I will begin packing our belongings."

"Thank you." Colin closed his fist around the precious image of Amelia, then put it away in his drawer next to the mask. "I will join you."

Rising to his feet, he told himself distance from Amelia was the best thing he could do for her.

But the image of her portrait refused to leave his mind, gnawing at his soul in a way he wondered if he would survive.

Amelia had always been known for her wanderings. Her unusual childhood led her to detest solitude as much as she craved it. She was never one to sit still for long, and she often made excuses to be alone, even at the most intimate of dinner parties. Ware understood her restless wanderlust, which was why he was always quick to suggest a stroll and a breath of fresh air.

So when she begged a few moments' absence to use the retiring room, Ware paid her no mind, nor did Lady Montrose, who acted as her chaperone. They both smiled and nodded, freeing her to attend her assignation.

If Montoya came.

She moved through the downstairs as silently as possible, slipping once into a conveniently located alcove when the sound of approaching voices made discovery a very real hazard. With a racing heart, she waited for the guests to pass.

Would he appear? Would he have found a way? His attendance at the masquerade led her to believe that he was a man of some consequence. A casual introduction to Lady Fairchild would have sufficed to be extended an invitation to tonight's event. However, she had inquired about him and was answered with a blank stare.

He had not been invited.

That did not mean he would not be here.

If his interest in her was related to St. John, she imagined he would have the knowledge required to gain entry to the house and find the private sitting room. She could not decide if that meant it would be best for him not to come. With the household she lived in and the man she was promised to marry, she could not afford any more trouble. But her heart recklessly ignored the situation as a whole and concentrated solely on what it wanted. She wasn't certain what she would do if he responded to her invitation; she knew only that she wished he would.

Anticipation and heady expectation filled her at the thought. She had dressed with purpose this evening, choosing a gown made of dark, thick sapphire damask accented with delicate silver lace at the bodice, elbows, and underskirts. With sapphires in her hair, at her throat, and adorning her fingers, she looked older and worldlier.

If only she felt that way inside. Instead she felt as she had as a young girl—breathless with the desire to see Colin and eager to feel the emotions that only he roused in her. She had thought she would never feel similarly again. It was both thrilling and frightening to feel that way about a masked stranger.

Finally, she reached the small sitting room she had specified in the note. Sarah had learned of the room from her cousin who worked in the Fairchild household. The abigail passed the information on to Amelia, wanting her to have a quiet place to retreat if necessary.

Pausing a moment with her hand on the knob, Amelia took a deep breath and attempted to calm her riotous nerves. It was hopeless, so she abandoned the effort. Opening the door, she slipped inside. The drapes were open, allowing a sliver of silver moonlight to slant in through the sash.

She waited just inside the door, giving her eyes the time necessary to adjust to the reduced lighting. She held her breath expectantly, her ears straining to listen above the rushing of blood, hoping that he would be there and call out to her.

But there was nothing more than the ticking of the clock on the mantel.

Amelia moved to the window and turned, taking in the contents of the room. Two settees, one chaise, two chairs, tables of various sizes scattered about . . . There was more, but no Montoya.

She sighed, and her hands moved restlessly over her voluminous skirts. Perhaps she had arrived too early, or he was having some difficulty gaining entry. She looked out the window, half frightened by the thought that he might be standing outside. But there was no Montoya there either.

A few minutes. She could spare that much.

As she began to pace, the clock ticked relentlessly. Her heart rate slowed and her breathing settled into a natural rhythm. Disappointment weighed on her shoulders and the corners of her mouth. After ten minutes passed, Amelia knew it was impossible to linger, though she thought she might wait all night if not for those who would seek her out in worry.

She walked toward the door. "Well . . . Now there is nothing to distract from the wedding plans," she muttered.

"Who was the miniature created for?"

Amelia paused with her hand on the knob, shivering as that dark, deep voice wrapped around her like a warm embrace. Gooseflesh covered her bared skin, and her lips parted on a silent gasp. Wide-eyed, she pivoted slowly to face the room. It was then that she saw the faint glow of the white half mask and cravat in the far corner. Montoya wore black again, enabling him to hide in the shadows of the unlit room.

"Lord Ware," she answered, slightly dazed by her phantom's sudden appearance and the realization that he had been there the whole time. Watching her. Why the mask? What was he hiding?

"Why was it created?" he asked gruffly. "It is not a gift commonly given from a virginal bride to her fiancé."

She took a step toward him.

"Stay there and answer the question."

Amelia frowned at his curtness. "I wanted him to see me in a different way."

"He will see you in all ways, in the flesh." There was bitterness in his tone, and the sound of it softened her apprehension, which enabled her to say what she might not have said otherwise.

"I wanted him to see that I was willing to share that side of myself with him," she admitted.

The sharp alertness that tensed his frame was palpable. "Why would he doubt it?"

"Must we talk about him?" Her foot tapped impatiently. "We have so little time since you spent all of it hiding in that corner."

"We are not talking about him," Montoya said silkily. "We are discussing why an intimate gift meant for your fiancé found its way into my possession. Did you intend for me to see you in a different way as well?"

Amelia caught herself fidgeting nervously and hid her hands behind her back. "I think you see me differently," she murmured, "regardless."

His smile flashed white in the darkness. "So if I, a stranger, can see you as a sexual creature, why would your future husband have difficulty doing the same?"

She held her breath, considering his perceptive probing. "What is it that you want me to say? It is inappropriate for me to discuss private matters."

"Sending me a provocative image of you is appropriate?"

"If it troubles you so, return it." She held out her hand.

"Never," he growled. "I will never give it back."

"Why not?" She raised one brow in challenge. "Do you seek to use it against me?"

"As if I would ever allow anyone else to see it."

Possessiveness. Clear as day. He was possessive over *her*. Amelia was both startled and pleased.

"Why does Lord Ware not see you as you wish to be seen?" he asked, finally approaching.

His tall form stepped out of the shadows and into

the moonlight, setting her heart racing. There was something so predatory, yet elegant in the way he moved, his tails swaying gently with his determined stride. Power leashed and clad in a civilized veneer. It made his allure even more seductive, made her want to see him unrestrained and free. His features were austere, his beautifully etched lips enticing her to kiss him.

That is what I want, she realized suddenly. *That is why I needed to see him again.*

She was willing to be honest with him in order to achieve that aim. "We are longtime companions."

"Is it not a love match?" he asked, stopping a few feet away.

"I should not answer that."

"And I should not be here. You should not have lured me."

"You had me followed."

He shook his head. "No. Jacques took it upon himself. I am leaving Town. I need distance from you, before this matter progresses any further."

"How can you leave? Are you not haunted by our dance in the garden?" Her hand lifted to the sapphires at her throat. "Don't you think about the kiss we shared?"

"I cannot cease thinking of it." He pounced and caught her hard against him, as if something in him had broken free of its bonds. "Waking. Sleeping."

She felt his gaze heating her mouth. She licked the lower curve and breathed in the scent of his skin. He smelled exotic, spicy, purely male animal.

Something instinctive inside her stirred in response.

"Do it," she goaded, her chest moving against his with rapid pants.

Montoya whispered a low curse. "You do not love him."

"I wish I did." Tentatively, her hands slipped beneath his coat and settled at his waist. His skin was hot, so feverish, she could feel the heat through his garments.

"Is your heart already taken?"

Her exhale was shaky. "In a fashion."

"Why me?"

"Why the mask?" she retorted, hating the feeling of being stripped bare by his questions.

He stared down into her upturned face. "My visage is not one you would wish to see."

She was deeply disquieted by the finality in his tone. The feeling of incertitude disturbed her to the point that she released him and attempted to step back. He held fast.

"Let us settle this now," he said, reaching up to brush callused fingertips along her cheekbones. "What do you want from me?"

"Did you approach me because of St. John?"

Montoya shook his head. "My motives were simple. I saw a beautiful woman. I lost all sense of manners and stared, which made her ill at ease. I attempted to apologize. That is all." His hands cupped her spine and stroked downward, arching her into him.

He was so hard, so solid, Amelia wanted to cling to him and touch him without impediments. Only one man had ever held her this closely. Only a short time ago, she would have said her ability to enjoy such an embrace with every fiber of her being had passed with Colin. Now, she knew that wasn't true.

How extraordinary to have found Montoya.

Or more aptly, how extraordinary that he had found her.

"That night . . . You recognized that others were coming," she pointed out.

"I did." The line of his lips hardened. "I am a man encumbered by a tainted past. It is why you should not send for me."

"You did not have to come." A tainted past, one that allowed him to recognize covert signals that most aristocrats would fail to notice. *Who was he?*

The corner of his mouth twitched with amusement, and she touched it with her fingertip. She could not see any deformity through the eyeholes of the mask or around his mouth. What she could see were dark eyes of a slightly exotic slant and a mouth made for sin. The curvature, shape, and firmness were perfection. She could imagine hours of kissing him and never growing bored. Whatever else may be wrong with him, she thought she might be able to bear it.

She touched the edge of the mask. "Let me see you."

"No!" He pushed her hand away roughly, then caught it again and kissed the back. The press of his lips left tingles, even through her glove. "Trust me. It would be difficult to bear the truth of it."

"Is that why you will not court me?"

Montoya stilled. "Would you wish me to?"

"Do you feel this way about many women?" Her gaze dropped to his throat where she watched him swallow hard. "I have felt this way about only one other man, and he is lost to me, as your love is to you."

Suddenly his embrace tightened, and he pressed his lips to her forehead. "You have mentioned a lost loved one before," he rasped.

"Sometimes it feels as if a piece of me is missing. It is unbearable. I do not understand why I feel so vividly about him after all these years, as if he might return, as if some part of me expects him to." Her hands fisted in his coat. "But when I am with you, I think only of you."

"Do I remind you of him?"

She shook her head. "He was vital and unrestrained; you are more subdued, but in a . . . primitive way." Her smile was sheepish. "That sounds silly."

"The primitiveness comes in response to you," he said, nuzzling his jaw against her temple. He was so close, the smell of him inundated her senses and made her giddy. Joy, hot and sweet, filled her. The sensation of being alive after years of numbness. She felt guilty for that, burdened by a sense of betraying Ware, but she could not fight the attraction to Montoya. It was too strong, too heady and intoxicating.

"I would be willing to explore it . . ." she offered shyly.

"Are you propositioning me, Miss Benbridge?" he asked with a low laugh that she adored from the moment she heard it. It was the kind of laugh one worked to hear again. Already her mind was sifting through anecdotes she could share that might make him merry.

"I want to see you again."

"No." He cupped her nape and held her cheek to his chest, wrapping his big body around her. It was safe in his embrace. Warm. Delightful. Could two people spend hours hugging? A derisive snort escaped her. Hours of kissing and hugging. She was deranged.

"Was that a snort?" he teased.

She flushed. "Do not attempt to change the subject."

"We should part," he said, sighing with what sounded like regret. "You have already been absent from the festivities too long."

"Why did you not say something when I first arrived?"

Montoya tried to retreat, but she held him to her. There was power in her proximity, she thought. The two halves warring within him—the part that wanted to hold her and the part that wanted to push her away—seemed stalemated when she was near.

Amelia smiled a woman's smile. "You could not allow me to walk away, could you?"

"Is that vanity I hear?"

"Is that evasion?"

The flash of a rakish dimple made her stomach flutter. "If my circumstances were different, nothing could keep me from making you mine."

"Oh?" She looked up at him from beneath her lashes. "Would you come bearing honorable intentions, or would you seduce me as you are doing now?"

"Sweet . . ." He laughed again. "The only seduction at work here is yours."

"Truly?" Her breasts were full and heavy, pressing uncomfortably against her corset. Her mouth was dry, her palms damp. She *felt* seduced. Could it be that his body was responding to her as well? "What am I doing to you?"

"Why?" His smile was charming. "So you can do more of it?"

"I might. Would you like that?"

"When did you become so flirtatious?"

"Perhaps I have always been so," she rejoined, batting her lashes coyly.

Montoya turned pensive. "Can Ware manage you?" He caught her wrists and pulled her hands away from his waist.

"I beg your pardon?" Amelia frowned as he evaded her and moved toward the door.

"You are mischievous baggage." His gaze narrowed as his hand wrapped around the knob.

"I am not baggage." She set her hands atop her pannier.

"You will forever land into trouble if not watched carefully."

She arched a haughty brow. "I have been watched my entire life."

"And yet here you are, luring strangers with tantalizing miniatures and holding a highly inappropriate assignation."

"You did not have to come!" She stomped one slippered foot, irritated by his condescending tone.

"True. And I shan't come again."

His tone was too familiar. He had asked her if he reminded her of Colin. Up until this moment, he had not. They were built differently, their voices were inflected with dissimilar accents, and their strides boasted different kinds of confidence. Colin had a bit of a stomp, as if to forcibly establish his presence. Montoya had sultriness to his gait, a more understated way of defining his dominance.

But in their mulish determination to set her aside, they were the same. As a young girl, she'd no choice but to tolerate it. That was not the case now.

"As you wish," she said, moving toward him with a deliberate swaying of her hips. "If it is so easy for you to walk away and leave me behind, it would be best if you go."

"I did not say it would be easy," he bit out.

Amelia set her hand atop his where it gripped the knob. "Good-bye, Count Montoya."

He turned his head, and she lunged, pressing her lips to his. He froze, and she took the advantage, tilting her head to deepen the contact. His breathing grew labored, his skin hot. Still, he did not move. She was unsure of how to proceed, and without his participation the kiss became awkward. Then she thought perhaps she was overthinking the thing.

Closing her eyes, Amelia allowed instinct to take over. Her hands settled lightly upon his tense shoulders, and he shuddered. She licked his lower lip, and he groaned. Her stomach churned madly with delight and fear. What if they were caught? How would she explain?

Then she did not care because it was too delicious taking him as she wanted. He did nothing to help her, but he did nothing to stop her either. Stretching her arms up, she reached behind him and tugged off her glove; then she curled her fingers around his nape. The moment their bare skin touched she was lost to him. His mouth opened on a gasp, and she pushed her tongue inside, licking the taste of him as she would a favorite treat. She tugged on his queue, and he growled.

His tongue stroked along hers, a practiced, smooth glide that made her moan into his mouth. The tiny sound broke him. He moved so quickly, she barely registered it. The next she knew, she was pinned to the door by over six feet of aroused male, and he was kissing her back, ardently and possessively.

"Damn you," he cursed in a harsh whisper. "I can't have you."

"You will not even try!"

"I have done nothing but try. *Nothing*. That does not change the fact that my circumstances make me unsuitable and dangerous for you."

Montoya cupped her nape and slanted his mouth hungrily over hers. It was a dark kiss, rife with sensual intent. Delicious. She sagged into the door and took it, all of it. Every thrust of his tongue, every nibble of his teeth, every caress of his beautiful lips. She took it and begged for more with pleading whimpers that drove his fervency to greater heights.

There was a mask between them and endless secrets. There was the wall that existed between strangers who shared nothing of each other beyond a single moment in time, yet the connection she felt with him was there, threading through all of that.

Was it mere lust? How could it be when she could not see all of him? But this thrumming in her veins, the ache in her breasts, the dampness between her thighs . . . Lust was there, part of the greater whole.

"Amelia," he breathed roughly, his warm breath gusting across her damp skin. His parted lips drifted across her face, from jaw to cheekbone. Then higher. "I want to strip you bare, lay you on my bed, and kiss you all over."

She shivered, both at the serrated way he said her name and the images his words invoked in her mind. "Reynaldo."

"I must leave Town or that will happen, and I cannot lay claim to you if we progress that far. Not now."

"When?" Tormented by yearning and a body that was wracked with unappeased desire, she would promise anything in this moment to see him again.

"You have Ware, a friend of long acquaintance who can give you things that I cannot."

"Perhaps you and I can be friends."

"You do not know me well enough to say that."

"I want to know you." Her voice was a throaty purr. Never in her life had she sounded like that, and it affected him. She could tell by the way he wrapped himself around her in an even tighter embrace. "I would like you to know me."

He pulled back, and she realized she found the mask attractive. Arousing. How odd, but true, nevertheless. She did not find it alarming, but rather comforting. She felt too open, and the sight of the mask shielded her as well as him.

"The only thing you need to know about me," he said in a rasp, "is that there are those who want me dead."

"Such a statement might frighten other women away," she retorted, tugging his mouth back down to hers, "but I live with people who have similar problems. Some would say I live a similar circumstance simply by association."

"You won't change my mind," he grumbled, licking at her parted lips, his body acting in opposition to his words.

"*I* was attempting to leave the room; *you* detained me."

"You kissed me!" he accused.

Amelia shrugged. "Your mouth was in the way. I could not avoid it."

"You *are* trouble." Bending his head, he kissed her one last time. Softer. Lingering. Her toes curled in her slippers. "*Now*, we must part, before we are discovered."

She nodded, knowing it was true, understanding that she had been absent far too long. "When will I see you again?"

"I cannot say. After your wedding, perhaps. Maybe never."

"Why?" She'd asked that question endlessly tonight and still couldn't collect the answer. Did he not understand how precious it was to feel this alive around another being? She had not realized that she was dormant until she'd met him.

"Because Ware can give you things that I cannot."

She was about to retort, when the doorknob jiggled. Her breath caught and held. She froze. Montoya did not.

He moved quickly, pulling back from her and fading again into the shadowy corner. She stumbled away from the door when it pushed open behind her. Turning, Amelia faced the intruding party.

"My lord," she breathed, curtsying.

Ware entered with a frown. "What are you doing in here? I have been searching the house for you." He studied her carefully; then his jaw tautened. "You have something to tell me, don't you?"

She nodded and held a shaking hand out to him. He took it and drew her out of the room, pausing a moment to sweep the contents with his gaze. Finding nothing amiss, he led her away from Montoya and into a future that was far less orderly than it had been mere days ago.

Chapter 6

"**S**o that is the whole of it," Amelia said, her fingers fidgeting with her teaspoon.

The Earl of Ware reached over and stilled his fiancée's restless movement by covering her hand with his own. "No need to be nervous," he murmured, his mind sifting through everything she had related.

"You are not angry?" Her green eyes were wide with a mixture of surprise and apprehension.

"I am not pleased, but I am not angry." He smiled ruefully and settled back more firmly in his chair.

They were seated on the terrace of the St. John house, enjoying tea before their customary ride through the park. It was with some trepidation that he had passed the hours waiting to speak with her. He knew what a woman looked like after a heated assignation, so while Amelia's revelation was in keeping with his own suspicions, he was sorry to have them confirmed.

"I do not know what to do," she said, sounding forlorn. "I fear I am out of my depth."

"And I fear I am not going to be much help," he admitted. "We are friends, love, but I am a man first and foremost. It does not sit well with me to hear that you feel things for this stranger that you do not feel for me."

As her hand twisted and gripped his tightly, a becoming blush spread across her cheeks. "I do not like myself very much at this moment. You are dear to me, Ware. You always have been, and I have not acted as you deserve. I pray you can find it in your heart to forgive me."

He stared pensively over the rear "garden." The word barely applied to the outdoor space that surrounded the St. John manse. Only low-lying flowerbeds alleviated the stark severity of the spacious lawn.

"I forgive you," he said. "And I admire your honesty. I doubt I would have the fortitude to reveal so much were I in your stead. However, I cannot have a fiancée who is engaging in such behavior, especially in public venues."

She nodded, looking like a chastened schoolgirl. While the scolding was required, he took no pleasure in it.

"You will have to decide, once and for all, whether you wish to wed me or not, Amelia. If you choose to proceed with our arrangement, you must act in good faith and deport yourself properly." Ware pushed to his feet and rolled his shoulders back to alleviate the tension there. "Damnation, I do not like feeling as if you are being coerced to marry me!"

Amelia stood as well, her floral muslin skirts falling to a graceful drape. "You are angry." She held up a delicate hand to stem his reply. "No. I understand. You have the right to be. Had you acted similarly, I would have been equally furious with you."

Blowing out her breath, she walked to the marble terrace railing and leaned her weight upon her hands. He joined her, the lawn to his back, she to his side.

She was lovely this afternoon, as she was every afternoon. Her dark hair was arranged in artless, powdered curls that swayed around her shoulders. Her skin was pale as cream, her eyes as green as jade, her lips red like dark wine. He had once jested that she was the only woman he thought of in poetic prose, and she'd laughed with him, delighted at what she called his "fancifulness." He was only fanciful with her.

"If we wed," she murmured, "do you intend to be faithful to me?"

"That depends on you." He considered her carefully. "If you lie there and pray for a swift finale, I probably will not be. I enjoy sex, Amelia. I crave it. I would not give up the pleasure of sexual congress for anything, even a wife."

"Oh." She looked away with a sigh.

A stray breeze blew by, rolling a tight curl along the tender, bared skin where her neck met her shoulder. She shivered, not with cold, but from the sensation. Ware noted that reaction, as he noted everything about her. Cataloguing the finer details for future use. Amelia was a tactile, sensual creature. Something he appreciated and had been gentle not to exploit, biding his time for the day when she would be his and he could teach her how to embrace that side of herself. With him alone.

Now, he had much to consider.

"I believe we could enjoy each other," he offered, teasing her fingers on the ledge with his own. "I think sex between us could be much more than a chore, but only if you open yourself to me completely in that way. No shyness, no reserve. If our marital bed is welcoming, I will not go elsewhere. I am not a man given to the pursuit of conquests. I simply want to fuck and have a splendid time doing it. If I can do that with one woman, more the better in my estimation. Less work."

The coarse word shocked her, he could tell, but it was the right word for how he liked his bedsport, and it was best she know that now. There would be no brief groping and grunting in the darkness. There would be illumination, flushed and sweaty skin, and many hours.

"Is that what passion in the bedroom is?" she asked, with what appeared to be genuine curiosity. "Animal urges given free rein? Is there nothing more involved in the process?"

It took him a moment to comprehend the question. "Are you referring to the glances your sister shares with St. John? Or how the Westfields look at one another?"

"Yes. They are . . . indecent, yet romantic."

"You are not the only one to see such affection and covet it." The inquisitiveness in her gaze made him smile.

"Do you?"

Ware shrugged and crossed his arms over his chest, leaning his hip into the railing. "On occasion. But I do not pine for it or suffer from its lack. I think, however, that you do."

As honest as ever, she nodded.

"I begin to see that my straightforward approach to wooing you was not the best," he mused aloud. "I assumed that the miserable end to your first love affair would make you inclined to appreciate a more . . . *grounded* relationship. But you want the opposite, do you not?"

She pushed away and began to pace, which was her wont when agitated. At times like this, she reminded him of a caged cat prowling in its boredom. "I do not know what I want, that is the problem." The look she gave him pinned him in his place.

"I am content. There is nothing more that I need."

"Are you truly content?" she challenged. "Or do you simply accept that friendship is all that one can hope for in your position?"

"You know the answer to that."

"Who would you wed, if not for me?"

"I've no notion, nor do I care to think about it until absolutely necessary. Are you suggesting I consider alternatives to you?"

Coming to a halt, Amelia released a sound that reminded him endearingly of a kitten's growl. "I want to be mad for *you!* Why is the choice not mine to make?"

"Perhaps you suffer from bad taste?" He laughed when she stuck her tongue out at him. Then he lowered his voice and stared at her with heavy-lidded eyes. "If it's the mask that arouses you, I can wear one to bed. Such games can be fun."

When her eyes went big as saucers, he winked.

Her hands went to her hips as she bristled; then her head tilted to the side. "Perhaps it is the mystery that intrigues me so? Is that what you are suggesting, my lord?"

"It is a possibility." Ware's smile faded. "I intend to make inquiries about your admirer. Let us see if we can unmask him."

"Why?"

"Because he is not for you, Amelia. A foreign count? You have always longed for a family. You would not move away from your sister now that you are reunited, so what future do you have with this man? And let us not discount the fact that he may seek to wound me through you."

She began pacing again, and he watched, admiring the inherent grace in her movements and the way her skirts swirled enchantingly around her long legs. "Everyone appears to believe that Montoya has no interest in me as an individual, only in the people connected to me. I admit I find it rather insulting to learn that those who claim to love me find it impossible to imagine a man desiring me for myself."

"I can more than imagine it, Amelia. I feel it. Do not take my courtesy as a lack of desire for you. You would be wrong."

Heaving out her breath, she said, "St. John is also attempting to find him."

He expected as much. "If the man is hiding in

the rookeries, St. John might succeed. But you said the count was finely dressed and cultured. He sounds as if he is a denizen of my social circles, rather than the pirate's. My search may prove more fruitful."

Amelia paused again. "What will you do if you find him?" There was more than a small measure of suspicion in her voice.

"Are you asking me if I will hurt him?" The question was not frivolous, as he was a swordsman of some renown. "I might."

Her beautiful features crumbled. "I should not have said anything to you."

Straightening, Ware moved toward her. "I am pleased you spoke the truth. Our relationship would have been irreparably damaged if you had presented a lie to hide your guilt." As he reached her, he breathed deeply, inhaling the innocent scent of honeysuckle. He had long suspected that her body resembled the flower she favored, fragrant and sweet as honey upon the lips.

He cupped her face in both hands and tilted her gaze upward to lock with his. Something new swirled in the emerald depths and he found himself falling into them. "But that does not change the fact that the man knew you were mine and took liberties regardless. A grave insult to me, love. I can forgive you, but I cannot forgive him."

"Ware . . ." Her lips parted, the seam glistening in the soft afternoon light.

Leaning over her, he bent to take her mouth. Her breath caught as she recognized his intent.

"Good afternoon, my lord."

They sprung apart as Amelia's sister and her husband joined them on the terrace, followed shortly by a maid bearing a new tea service.

"It is a lovely day," the pirate said in his distinctive raspy voice. "We thought we would join you in the sunshine."

Ware understood the warning. With a slight bow of his head, he stepped back farther. The former Lady Winter smiled at his perceptiveness. It was a bedroom smile, the one a woman shared with her lover after a bout of great sex. For Mrs. St. John, it was her only smile, and it was a lauded part of her appeal.

"We would enjoy the company," Ware said, leading Amelia back to their table.

He spent the rest of the afternoon trading inanities with the St. Johns and, later, with those he and Amelia passed during their drive through the park. But part of his mind was actively occupied with the logistics of his hunts—the one for Amelia's favor and the other for the masked man who sought to steal it from him.

"Are you certain the man's name is Simon Quinn?"

"Aye," the tavern keep said, setting another pint on the bar.

"Thank you." Colin accepted the ale and moved to a table in the corner. The report of a man searching for him was disturbing, even more so because the one making the inquiries was using Quinn's name. It could be Cartland, or one of the men with him, though the owner of the tavern was fairly certain the man did not have a French accent.

There was nothing Colin could do aside from settling in to wait, using techniques of concealment in which he was well versed. A man of his size could never hide completely, but he could make himself less noticeable by sprawling low to disguise his height and breadth of shoulder. He also left his hair unrestrained, which roughened his overall appearance.

The establishment itself made it easy to lose oneself among the crowd. The lighting was kept low to hide a multitude of faults and dirt. The dark-stained walnut furnishings—round tables and spindle-backed chairs—only added to the dimness of the interior. The air was filled with the smells of old and new ale and crackling grease from the kitchen. Patrons wandered in and out. Several were regulars whom Colin had spoken to previously.

Long ago, in his past life, he had frequented such places with his uncle, Pietro. Those lazy afternoons off had been spent listening to the imparted wisdom of a good and decent man. Colin missed him, thought of him often, and wondered how he was faring. Pietro had instilled strength of character in him and a belief in honor that had stood him in good stead these many years.

Colin's hand fisted on the table.

One day, they would be reunited, and he would show his uncle how he had heeded those early teachings. He would free Pietro from his life of servitude and establish him in comfort. Life was too short, and he wanted his beloved uncle to enjoy as much of it as possible.

"Evenin'," greeted a voice to his side, drawing Colin from his introspection.

Beside him stood an elderly gentleman who spent most of his life in the taverns on this street, offering companionship to those who would buy him a drink or something to eat. Occasionally, the man overheard something worth selling, and Colin was willing to pay for it, as he was well aware.

"Have a seat," Colin replied, gesturing to the chair opposite his own.

Hours passed. He used the time to question those who found him familiar from his previous sojourns there. Many hoped to earn a coin or two by passing along information of note. Sadly, there was nothing of interest about Cartland, but Colin bought a pint for anyone who talked with him and used their company to deepen his disguise.

Then, quite miraculously, the man he most hoped to see appeared in a swirl of heavy black cape. Simon Quinn paused at the bar and exchanged words with the keep, then turned with wide eyes to find Colin waving from the corner.

"By God," Quinn said as he approached, unclasping the jeweled frog that secured his cloak to his neck. "I have been searching all over London for you, half-starved, and you have been here in my lodgings the entire time?"

"Well"—Colin grinned—"the last few hours, at least."

Quinn muttered a curse under his breath and sank wearily into the seat across from him. A pint was brought over, then a plate of food. Once he was fully settled, he said, "I come bearing both good and bad news."

"Why am I not surprised?" Colin said dryly.

"I have been betrayed in France."

Colin winced. "Did Cartland forfeit the names of everyone?"

"It would appear so. I believe that is how he was able to prove his loyalty."

"The man has loyalty to no one but himself."

"Very true." Quinn stabbed a piece of meat, brought it to his mouth, and chewed angrily.

"So that is the bad news, then. What is the good?"

"I have been able to secure a promise of a pardon for all of us, including you."

"How is that possible if they hunt you as well?"

Quinn's smile was grim. "Leroux was valuable to the agent-general, enough so that the capture of his killer is of greater concern than the routing of English spies. I was allowed to leave on the promise that I would return with the murderer—whoever that may be. To guarantee my return, they hold the others Cartland betrayed."

Colin straightened. "By God . . . we must work swiftly, then."

"Yes." Quinn finished off his pint. "And there are conditions to complicate matters. First, I must persuade Lord Eddington to release a French spy whom he has in captivity. Then, we must convince a member of Cartland's group—a man named Depardue—to vouch that Cartland has confessed to the crime."

The first seemed unlikely, and the second seemed highly difficult, but Colin would take what opportunities were given to him and gladly.

I want to know you, Amelia had said. If only he had the chance to make that happen.

"You seem unduly pleased by this," Quinn said around a bite. "It is not much."

"I saw Amelia," Colin confessed. Held her, touched her, tasted her.

Quinn stilled with a forkful of food lifted halfway to his mouth. "And?"

"It is complicated, but hopeful."

Setting his utensils down, Quinn gestured for more ale. "How did she take your emergence from the grave?"

Colin smiled ruefully and explained.

"A mask?" Quinn asked when he finished. "Out of all the guises you are capable of donning, you chose a *mask?*"

"Originally, it suited the masquerade. Later, she saw it on Jacques and it drew her to him. It seemed appropriate to wear it a third time under those circumstances."

"She is more like her sister than I thought." Quinn's lips curved into the slight smile he always wore when referring to Maria. "However, I fail to see how the situation is hopeful. Amelia has no idea who you are."

"That is a bit of a problem," Colin agreed.

"A bit? My friend, you are the master of understatement. Trust me, she will not take the news well. She will take it as lack of affection. When she discovers that you were not chaste and pining for her the entire time, she will have her proof that you do not love her."

Colin heaved out a sigh and sank back into his chair. "This was *your* plan! *You* said that I should become a man of means in order to make her happy."

"Also to make you happy. You would always doubt your worth if you came to her as an underling." Quinn smiled at the serving girl who brought over the fresh pint, then sat back and studied Colin for a long moment. "I hear she is betrothed to the Earl of Ware."

"Not yet."

"She could be a marchioness, despite her father's scandal and her sibling's reputation. Quite an accomplishment."

Glancing around the room, Colin's gaze paused a moment on every patron, taking stock of each one. "Yes, but she does not love him. She still loves me. Or rather, the boy I used to be."

A lovely blonde entered the room from the staircase that led to the bedchambers above. Dressed in deep purple and wearing a black ribbon and cameo at her throat, she reminded Colin of a doll. Her delicate features and slender build roused protective instincts, her heavy-lidded eyes and full, red lips inspired carnal musings.

His brows lifted as she turned her head and locked eyes with him. Her smile made him frown in confusion, and he watched her approach with much curiosity, pushing to his feet when she came to a halt behind Quinn.

She set her hands on the Irishman's broad shoulders. "You should have told me you were back, *mon amour,*" she said, her voice inflected with an unmistakable French accent.

The look Quinn shot Colin was intriguing, bearing more than a trace of irritation. He did not stand, merely caught the blonde's hand and tugged her around, directing her to a chair he pulled closer with his foot. Considering Quinn's love of females, his apparent disinterest in such a beautiful woman was beyond surprising. In close proximity, she was a delight. Pale blue eyes were framed by long, thick chocolate lashes and accented by finely arched brows.

"Is this him?" she asked, studying Colin with an appreciative eye.

Quinn growled.

She smiled wide, revealing straight white teeth. She offered her hand and said, "I am Lysette Rousseau. You are Monsieur Mitchell, *oui?*"

Colin glanced at Quinn, who cursed under his breath and resumed his meal. "Perhaps," he replied with caution.

"Excellent. Should it become necessary to kill you, it will be much easier now that I have catalogued your appearance."

Blinking, he asked, "What the devil did you just say?"

"Provoking wench," Quinn muttered. "He is innocent."

"They all say that," she replied sweetly.

"It is true in this case," Quinn argued.

"They all say that, too."

"Pardon me." Colin glanced between them. "What are you talking about?"

Quinn gestured toward Lysette with an off-hand jerking of his fork. "She is an additional part of my guarantee. She is to return to France with either Cartland, you or me."

"Or a confession," she purred. "A confession from any of you would suffice. See? I am not so difficult to please."

"Christ." Resuming his seat, Colin examined the Frenchwoman. It was then that he noted a hardness to her eyes and mouth that he had missed before. "How do you find these femmes fatales, Quinn?"

"They find me," Quinn grumbled, biting into a potato with gusto born of frustration.

"You see only the negatives," Lysette said, gesturing for service. "There are three of us at this table, all searching for the same thing. I am here to assist you."

Quinn glared. "If you think holding a sword over my head is endearing, you are sadly mistaken."

Colin was not so quick to dismiss her. "How can you help?"

"In many ways." The blonde took a brief moment to order wine from the attending serving girl. "Think of the places I can go where you cannot. All the people who might speak to me but not to you. All the wiles I employ as a woman that you cannot employ as a man. Why, the possibilities are endless!" She lifted a delicate hand to the cameo at her throat, and he found it nearly impossible to imagine her killing anyone.

"How does your participation relate to Depardue?" Colin asked.

Something dark passed over her features. "If he resolves this, it will save me the trouble."

"The agent-general is determined to leave nothing

to chance," Quinn explained. "Depardue watches Cartland. Lysette watches me. They perform the same service. She is an added . . . warranty."

Colin winced. "I cannot imagine Depardue appreciates the intimation that he might not be successful." He looked at Lysette, wondering what the lure of such a position would be. "Why are you doing this?"

"My reasons are my own. A word of advice"—she stared at him intently—"you can trust nothing about me except this: I want Leroux's killer brought to justice."

Exhaling harshly, Colin drummed his fingertips atop the table. "I do not like this. While Cartland hunts me, we have a serpent in our midst."

Quinn nodded his agreement.

Lysette pouted as she accepted the goblet she had ordered previously. "I would rather be Eve than the snake."

"Eve was alluring," Quinn retorted.

Colin choked, never having heard the Irishman say an unkind word to a female before.

"What have you accomplished up to this point?" she asked, dismissing Quinn's rudeness and directing her attention to Colin.

"My days are spent evading Cartland and anyone who sounds French, and my nights are spent searching for him."

"That is the most ridiculous plan I have ever heard," she scoffed.

"What do you suggest I do, then?" he challenged. "I know nothing."

"So you must learn." Lysette took a dainty sip of

the blood red wine and licked her lips. She sat with a ramrod straight spine and uplifted chin, the hallmarks of good breeding and proper schooling. "You cannot do that while hiding, which is exactly what Cartland will expect you to be doing. Why do you not contact the man you both work for? Surely, he has the resources to help you bring this to a swift end."

"That is not his purpose," Quinn argued. "We are responsible for the managing of our assignments. If we are caught, the cost is ours to pay. I expect your arrangement is similar."

For a moment, it seemed frustration marred the Frenchwoman's lovely features, and then it was gone, replaced by a honeyed, careless smile.

Colin could not help but wonder at her, and contemplate how much of a risk she presented. She was so slender and feminine, yet he knew from tales of Amelia's sister that appearances could be very deceiving. "Do you have other suggestions, mademoiselle? Perhaps you think I should search in the bright light of day?"

"Will you wear a mask?" Quinn asked, finally pushing his plate aside.

"Why would he?" She raked Colin with an assessing glance from the top of his head, down the length of his outstretched legs, to his booted feet. "It would be a shame to conceal such comeliness." Her mouth curved seductively. "I should like to view all of it."

Quinn snorted. "Now, you see, love. That is why you are not Eve. You lack the sense required to see the man is taken."

"You may wear a blindfold," she offered Colin with a wink, "and call me by whatever name you prefer."

Colin laughed for the first time in days.

"Watch out for her," Quinn warned.

"I will leave that task to you. I leave for Bristol in the morning. Cartland's past may be affecting his present. I hope that something can be discovered that might give me some advantage."

"Good thinking." Quinn's lips pursed with thought. "Lysette and I will stay behind and make inquiries here."

"I am not comfortable allowing him to go off alone," she said, with an underlying note of steel to her voice.

"You will grow accustomed." Quinn lounged in his chair with his usual insolent grace—his body canted to the side, his arm slung across the spindle back, his legs spread wide.

"As handsome as you are," she sniffed, "I sometimes find it difficult to like you."

Quinn grinned. "So we are in accord. Mitchell will search elsewhere. You and I will work together in Town."

"Perhaps I wish to go with him instead." Lysette's smile did not reach her lovely eyes.

"Oh, would you?!" Quinn's exaggerated pleasure made Colin laugh again. "How delightful. At least for me, if not for Mitchell. Sorry, chap." He shrugged one shoulder and set his hand on the table.

Before either of them could anticipate the action, Lysette was on her feet and Quinn's discarded knife was piercing the table with precision . . . directly between his casually splayed fingers.

He froze and stared at how close he had come to losing a finger or two. "Damnation."

She leaned over him. "Do not mock or underestimate me, *mon amour*. It is not wise to prick my temper."

Colin stood. "Thank you for the kind offer of your companion's company," he said hastily, "but I must respectfully decline."

Lysette looked at him with a narrowed glance.

"You trust me not at all," he said, "but I promise you this: I have every reason to clear my name and no reason to flee."

For a moment, she did not move. Then her mouth lifted slightly at the corner. "Your woman is here."

He said nothing, but an acknowledgment wasn't necessary.

She waved him off with a graceful toss of her wrist. "You will not stray far. Good luck to you."

After a quick bow, Colin reached into his pocket and tossed coins on the table. "I will pray for you," he said to Quinn, squeezing his friend's shoulder as he passed.

Quinn's reply was a blistering curse.

Chapter 7

It was a small but fine house in a respectable neighborhood. The Earl of Ware had owned it for three years now, and during that time, it had rarely been unoccupied.

Tonight the lower windows were dark, but candle-light flickered from one upper sash. He pushed his key into the front door lock and allowed himself entry. The home was maintained by two servants, a husband and wife pair who were trustworthy and discreet. They were abed now, and since he did not require their services, Ware did not disturb them.

He set his hat on the hook, followed by his cloak. Beneath that he wore the evening garments he had donned for another night in an endless string of nights spent at balls and routs. Except this evening had been slightly different. Amelia was different. *He* was different. The awareness between them had changed. She saw him in a new light, as he saw her in altered fashion as well.

Climbing the steps to the upper floor, he paused

a moment outside the one door where light peeked out from the gap at the bottom. Ware exhaled, taking a moment to relish the thrumming of blood in his veins and the quickening of his arousal. Then he turned the knob and entered, finding his dark-haired, sloe-eyed mistress reading quietly in bed.

Her gaze lifted to meet his. He watched her breathing quicken and her lips part. The book was shut with a decisive snap, and he kicked the portal closed behind him.

"My lord," Jane breathed, tossing back the covers, revealing a shapely figure. "I was hoping you would come tonight."

Ware's mouth curved. She was hot for it, which meant the first fuck could be hard and swift. Later, they would take their time, but now such dalliance would not be necessary. A circumstance that suited his mood.

From the moment he had first seen the stunning widow, he'd wanted her. When her last arrangement with Lord Riley ended, Ware approached her with haste before anyone else could lure her away. She was flattered and, later, enthusiastic. They suited each other well, and the sex was pleasurable for both.

He shrugged out of his coat; she untied the belt of her robe. Within moments he was deep inside her—her hips on the edge of the mattress, his feet on the floor as he drove powerfully into her writhing body. His frustration and unease were forgotten in the maelstrom of carnal sensation, much to his relief.

But the surcease did not last long.

An hour later he rested on his back with his hand tucked behind his head, his sweat-drenched skin cooling in the evening air.

"That was delicious," Jane murmured, her voice throaty from passionate cries. "You are always so primitive when aggravated."

"Aggravated?" He laughed and tucked her closer to his side.

"Yes. I can tell when something is troubling you." Her hand stroked down the center of his chest.

Ware stared up at the ornate ceiling moldings and thought again of how well the room suited her, with its rose and cream colors and gilded furnishings. He had encouraged her to spare no expense and to think only of her own comfort, having found over the course of several mistresses that a woman's taste in décor spoke a great deal about her. "Must we talk of things unpleasant?"

"We could work your frustrations into exhaustion," she teased, lifting her head to reveal laughing dark eyes. "You know I will not complain."

He brushed back the damp strands of hair that clung to her temple. "I prefer that solution."

"But it would be only a temporary measure. As a woman, I might be able to assist you with your problem, which I suspect is feminine in nature."

"You *are* helping me," he purred.

Her raised brows spoke of her skepticism, but she did not press him.

Exhaling harshly, he shared his thoughts aloud, trusting Jane as a friend and confidante. She was a sweet woman, one of the sweetest he knew. She was not the kind of soul who sought to hurt others or advance herself at another's detriment.

"Do you realize that a man of my station is rarely seen as a man?" he asked. "I am lands, money, and prestige, but rarely more than that."

She listened quietly but alert.

"I spent my youth in Lincolnshire, raised to think of myself only as Ware and never as an individual. I had no interests outside of my duties, no goals beyond that of my title. I was trained so well that it never occurred to me to want something of my own, something that had nothing to do with the marquessate and everything to do with me."

"That sounds like a very lonely way to live."

He shrugged and shoved another pillow under his head. "I had no notion of any other way."

When he held his silence, she prompted, "Until?"

"Until one day I traversed the perimeter of our property and chanced upon an urchin preparing to fish in my stream."

Jane smiled and slid from his arms and the bed, donning her discarded robe before moving to the console and pouring a libation. "Who was this urchin?"

"A servant from the neighboring property. He was waiting for the young lady whose father he worked for. They had struck up a friendship of sorts, which intrigued me."

"As did the young lady." She warmed the brandy expertly by rolling the glass over the flame of a taper.

"Yes," he agreed. "She was young, wild, and free. Miss Benbridge showed me how different the world looked through the eyes of one who suffered under no one's expectations. She also completely disregarded my title and treated me just as she treated the urchin, with playful affection."

Jane sat on the edge of the bed and drank lightly, then passed the goblet over to him. "I think I would like her."

"Yes." He smiled. "I believe she would like you, as well."

They would never meet, of course, but that was not the point.

"I admire you for marrying her," she said, "despite the sins of her father."

"How could I not marry her? She is the person who taught me that I had value in and of myself. My aristocratic arrogance is now tempered with personal arrogance."

Laughing, Jane curled over his legs. "How fortunate for the rest of us."

Ware ran a hand through his unbound hair. "I will never forget the afternoon when she said, quite innocently, that I was devilishly handsome, which was why she sometimes halted her speech midsentence. No one had ever said such a thing to me. I doubt anyone had ever felt it. When they stuttered it was because of intimidation, not admiration."

"I tell you that you are comely, my lord," she said, the sparkle in her eyes giving proof to her words. "There are few men as handsome as you are."

"That may be true. I do not compare myself to other men, so I would not know." He drank in large swallows. "But I suspect my attractiveness has more weight when I believe in it myself."

"Confidence is a potent lure," she agreed.

"Because she had no expectations of me, I was able to be myself with her. It was the first time in my life that I spoke without considering the confines of my station. I practiced wooing with her and said things aloud that I had never allowed myself to even consider." He looked down the foot of the bed and into the fire in the grate. "I suppose I grew into my own by knowing her."

Running her fingertips down his bare thigh, she asked, "Do you feel as if you owe a debt to her?"

"Partly, but our relationship has never been one-sided. We practiced deportment together and conversation. I had experience with such things; she was so sheltered."

"You gave her polish."

"Yes. We both gained."

"And now she belongs to you," Jane pronounced, "because you helped to create her."

"I—" Ware frowned. Was that where this disgruntlement came from? Did he simply feel proprietary? "I am not sure that is it. She was in love once—or so she says—and she still pines for him. I do not resent that. I accept it."

"Perhaps 'appreciate' would be a more apt word?" Her lips lifted in a kind smile. "After all, she cannot burden you with elevated feelings if they are engaged elsewhere."

He tossed back the rest of his brandy, filling his belly with fire, then thrust the goblet at her in a silent demand for more. "If that were true, why am I so annoyed by her fascination with another man?"

As she accepted the glass, her brows rose. "Annoyed? Or jealous?"

Ware laughed. "A little of both?" He waved one hand carelessly. "Perhaps my masculine sensibilities are piqued because she never felt such interest in me? I cannot say for certain. I only know that I doubt myself again. I am wondering if my decision to give her the space and time to heal was an error in judgment."

Jane paused halfway to the console. "Who is this other man?"

He explained.

"I see." She refilled his glass and warmed the liquor, then returned to him. "You know I cared deeply for my late husband."

Nodding, Ware patted the spot next to him. She crawled up beside him, baring her lithe legs to his view. "But I was tempted to marry another, whom I did not love."

"You jest," he scoffed. "Women want nothing so much as they want devotion and pronouncements of undying affection."

"But we are also pragmatic. If you offer Miss Benbridge all the practical things she covets that this other man cannot provide, she will be more tempted to select you."

"I pointed out that his foreign title would require her to leave her sister behind."

"Verbally, you did, yes. Now make it even more difficult by proving it in fact. Take her to see your properties, purchase a home near her sibling . . . things of that nature. Then, consider her love of romance and mystery. Put that into play, as well. You can seduce her easily. You have the skill and she is susceptible. Flowers, gifts, stolen kisses. Your competition is working in the shadows. You have no such limitations."

"Hmm . . ."

"It could be fun for you both. A chance to learn more about each other than you now know."

He reached over and linked his fingers with hers. "You are so clever."

Jane's mouth curved in her winsome smile. "I am a woman."

"Yes, I am ever aware of that fact." Reaching to the side, Ware set his goblet atop the bedside table and pulled her beneath him. He kissed her, then moved lower, nudging the edge of the robe aside to take a nipple in his mouth.

"Oh, that's nice," she sighed.

Lifting his head, he grinned. "Thank you for your help."

"My motives are not entirely altruistic, you know. Perhaps you will become aggravated during your attempts to woo Miss Benbridge. I do so love it when you are less than controlled."

"Minx." He gave a mock growl and she shivered.

Which prompted Ware to spend the rest of the hours until morning playing the primitive lover to both their delights.

Amelia peeked around the corner of the house, her lower lip worried between her teeth. She searched for Colin in the stable yard, then heaved a sigh of relief when she found the area empty. Male voices drifted on the wind, laughter and singing spilling out from the stables. From this she knew Colin was hard at work with his uncle, which meant that she could safely leave the manse and head into the woods.

She was becoming quite good at subterfuge, she thought as she moved deftly through the trees, hiding from the oc-

*casional guard in her journey toward the fence. A fort-
night had passed since that fateful afternoon when she
had caught Colin behind the shop with that girl. Amelia
had avoided him since, refusing to speak with him when
he asked the cook to fetch her.*

*Perhaps it was foolish to hope that she would never see
him again, given how closely their lives were entwined. If
so, she was a fool. There was not an hour of the day that
passed without her thinking of him, but she managed the
pain of her grief as long as he stayed away from her. She
saw no reason for them to meet, to talk, to acknowledge
each other. She traveled by carriage only when moving to
a new home, and even then, she could deal exclusively
with Pietro, the coachman.*

*Espying the waited-for opening, Amelia hopped deftly
over the fence and ran to the stream, where she found
Ware coatless and wigless, with his shirtsleeves pushed
up. The young earl had caught some color to his skin
these last weeks, setting aside his life of book work in
favor of hard outdoor play. With his dark brown locks
tied in a queue and his cornflower-colored eyes smiling,
he was quite handsome, his aquiline features boasting
centuries of pure blue blood.*

*He did not set her heart to racing or make her ache in
unfamiliar places as Colin did, but Ware was charming
and polite and attractive. She supposed that was a sufficient enough combination of qualities to make him the recipient of her first kiss. Miss Pool told her to wait until
the right young man came along, but Colin already had,
and had turned to another instead.*

*"Good afternoon, Miss Benbridge," the earl greeted
with a perfect bow.*

*"My lord," she replied, lifting the sides of her rose-
hued gown before curtsying.*

"I have a treat for you today."

"Oh?" Her eyes widened in anticipation. She loved gifts and surprises because she rarely received them. Her father simply could not be bothered to consider such things as birthdays or other gift-giving occasions.

Ware's smile was indulgent. *"Yes, princess."* He offered his arm to her. *"Come with me."*

Amelia set her fingers lightly atop his forearm, enjoying the opportunity to practice her social graces with someone. The earl was kind and patient, pointing out any errors and correcting her. It gave her a higher polish and a deeper confidence. She no longer felt like a girl pretending to be a lady. Instead she felt like a lady who chose to enjoy her youth.

Together they left their meeting place by the stream and wended their way along the shore until they reached a larger clearing. There Amelia was delighted to find a blanket stretched out on the ground, the corner of which was held down by a basket filled with delicious smelling tarts and various cuts of meat and cheeses.

"How did you manage this?" she breathed, filled with pleasure by his thoughtfulness.

"Dear Amelia," he drawled, his eyes twinkling. *"You know who I am now, and who I will be. I can manage anything."*

She knew the rudiments of the peerage, and saw the power wielded by her father, a viscount. How many more times the magnitude was the power wielded by Ware, whose future held a marquessate?

Her eyes widened at the thought.

"Come now," he urged. *"Have a seat, enjoy a peach tart, and tell me about your day."*

"My life is dreadfully boring," she said, dropping to the ground with a sigh.

"*Then tell me a tale. Surely you daydream about something.*"

She dreamt about kisses given passionately by a dark-eyed Gypsy lover, but she would never say such a thing aloud. She rose to her knees and dug into the basket to hide her blush. "I lack imagination," she muttered.

"Very well, then." Ware situated himself on his back with his hands clasped at his neck and stared up at the sky. He looked as at ease as she had ever seen him. Despite the rather formal attire he wore—including pristine white stockings and polished heels—he was still a far more relaxed person than the one she met weeks ago. Amelia found that she rather liked the new earl and felt a touch of pleasure that she had wrought what she considered to be a positive change in him.

"It appears I must regale you with a story," he said.

"Lovely." She settled back to a seated position and took a bite of her treat.

"Once upon a time . . ."

Amelia watched Ware's lips move as he spoke, and imagined kissing them. A now-familiar sense of sadness shivered through her, an effect of leaving her beloved romantic notions behind and embracing unfamiliar new ones, but the sensation lessened as she thought of Colin and what he had done. He certainly did not feel any sadness about leaving her behind.

"Would you kiss me?" she blurted out, her fingertips brushing tart crumbs from the corners of her lips.

The earl paused midsentence and turned his head to look at her. His eyes were wide with surprise, but he appeared more intrigued than dismayed. "Beg your pardon. Did I hear you correctly?"

"Have you kissed a girl before?" she asked, curious. He

was two years older than she was, only one year younger than Colin. It was quite possible that he had experience.

Colin had an edgy, dark restlessness about him that was seductive even to her naïve senses. Ware, on the other hand, was far more leisurely, his attractiveness stemming from innate command and the comfort of knowing the world was his for the taking. Still, despite her high regard for Colin, she could see how Ware's lazy charm appealed.

His eyebrows rose. "A gentleman does not speak of such things."

"How wonderful! Somehow, I knew you would be discreet." She smiled.

"Repeat the request again," he murmured, watching her carefully.

"Would you kiss me?"

"Is this a hypothetical question, or a call to action?"

Suddenly shy and unsure, Amelia looked away.

"Amelia," he said softly, bringing her gaze back to his. There was deep kindness there on his handsome patrician features, and she was grateful for it. He rolled to his side and then pushed up to a seated position.

"Not hypothetical," she whispered.

"Why do you wish to be kissed?"

She shrugged. "Because."

"I see." His lips pursed a moment. "Would Benny suffice? Or a footman?"

"No!"

His mouth curved in a slow smile that made something flutter in her belly. It was not an outright flip, as was caused by Colin's dimples, but it was certainly a herald of her new awareness of her friend.

"I will not kiss you today," he said. "I want you to think upon it further. If you feel the same when next we meet, I will kiss you then."

*Amelia wrinkled her nose. "If you have no taste for
me, simply say so."*

*"Ah, my hotheaded princess," he soothed, his hand
catching hers, his thumb stroking the back. "You jump to
conclusions just as you jump into trouble—with both
feet. I will catch you, fair Amelia. I look forward to catching you."*

*"Oh," she breathed, blinking at the suggestive under-
tone to his words.*

"Oh," he agreed.

Amelia was awakened by the knock that came to
her bedchamber door. She lay curled in a ball, her
eyes closed, her sleep-foggy mind praying that she
could drift back into sleep and rejoin her vivid
dreams. Dreams that reminded her of the rare
connection she had with Ware and how precious
that bond was to her.

But the knocking came again, more insistent.
Harsh reality intruded, and she mourned the loss
of her nocturnal reminiscences.

"Amelia?"

Maria. The one person in the household that
she could not ignore.

Calling out in a sleep-husky voice, Amelia struggled to a seated position and watched as the portal
swung open and her sister stepped into view.

"Hello, poppet," Maria said, gliding toward her
with an elegance she had long envied. "Sorry to
wake you. It is late morning, however, so I did wait.
Sadly, the length of my patience is probably not as
long as you would like."

"I do so love that gown on you," Amelia replied,

admiring the cream-colored muslin and its appeal next to Maria's olive skin.

"Thank you." Maria took a seat on the slipper chair near the window. "Did you have a good evening?"

Visions of Ware, dashing in evening attire, filled Amelia's mind. Last night had been one in an endless string of nights spent at balls and routs. Except last evening had been marginally different. She was different. *Ware* was different. The awareness between them had changed, and she knew instinctively that it would never be the same.

He was pressing forward, maneuvering expertly, forcing her to see their situation in cold, hard facts. After an entire childhood filled with falsehoods and evasions, she was normally grateful for his candor. In this instance, however, it served only to increase her feelings of guilt and confusion.

"It was a lovely evening," she replied.

"Hmm . . ." The sound was clearly skeptical. "You have been melancholy of late."

"And you are here to talk about it."

"Lord Ware almost kissed you on the terrace yesterday afternoon, and yet last night you did not appear any more eager to see him than usual. How could I not ask you about it?"

Closing her eyes, Amelia's head dropped back onto the pillow.

"If you would share your burdens with me," Maria coaxed, "perhaps I could help. I should like to."

Opening her eyes, Amelia looked up at the satin lining of her canopy and remembered an earlier time. Her room was decorated in various shades of blue, from pale to dark, just as her childhood bedchamber had been. She'd made the choice consciously, an external declaration of her decision to pick up where her relationship with her sister had been cruelly severed. Her father had stolen years from them, but in this room she felt as if she reclaimed them.

"There is nothing to help me with, Maria. There is nothing to mend or alter."

"What of your masked admirer?"

"I will not be seeing him again."

There was a pregnant pause, then, "The last you spoke of him was not with such finality in your tone. You saw him a second time, did you not? He sought you out."

Amelia turned her head to meet her sister's gaze. "*I* lured him to me, and he was angry at me for doing so. He intends to leave Town now, to keep his distance and to prevent me from reaching out to him again."

"He shows a care for your reputation by this action, but you are upset by it." Confusion filled Maria's dark eyes. "Why?"

Tossing up her hands, Amelia said, "Because I do not want him to go! I want to know him, and it pains me greatly that I will not be given that chance. I am distressing Ware and you, yet I cannot seem to set aside my fascination nor can I ignore how weary I am of being left behind. I had enough of such treatment with my father."

"Amelia . . ." Maria held out a hand to her. "What is it about this man that has captured you so? Is he comely? No . . . don't become angry. I simply wish to understand."

Amelia sighed. Lack of sleep and inability to eat

were taking their toll. She could not fight the feeling that Montoya was slipping away, that every moment when she did nothing took him farther from her. It frustrated her and made her snappish.

"He wore the mask again," she said finally. "I've no notion of what he looks like beneath it, but I do not care. I am moved by the way he talks to me, the way he touches me, the way he kisses me. There is reverence in his handling of me, Maria. Longing. Desire. I do not believe such depth of affection can be feigned. Not the way he expresses it."

Frowning, Maria looked away, lost in thought. Dark ringlets swung around her bared shoulders and betrayed how unsettled she felt. "How can he feel such things for you after only a few moments' acquaintance?"

"He says I remind him of a lover lost to him, but in truth I sense he wants me for myself in addition to that." Amelia's fingertips plucked at the edge of her bed linens. "He originally approached me because of her, but when he came again it was for me."

"How can you be certain?"

"I am certain of nothing, and now I suppose I never will be." She looked toward the open door to her boudoir, afraid her features would reveal too much.

"Because he is departing." Maria's voice softened. "Did he say why or where he intends to travel?"

"He says he is in danger of some sort. Deadly danger."

"From St. John? Or someone else?"

Amelia's hands fisted into the counterpane. "He has nothing to do with your husband. He said as much and I believe him."

"Shh," Maria soothed, standing again. "I know you are distraught, but do not vent your frustration on me. I want to help you."

"How?" Amelia challenged. "Will you help me find him?"

"Yes."

Frozen with disbelief, Amelia stared at her sibling. "Truly?"

"Of course." Maria's shoulders went back, a sure sign of her determination. "St. John's men look for him, but we have an advantage. You are the only person to manage close proximity to this man."

Amelia was speechless for a moment. She had not expected anyone to champion her desire to pursue Montoya, and she could not have selected a better person to help her than Maria, who was afraid of nothing and well versed in finding things that did not wish to be found. "Ware searches for him, too."

"Poor Count Montoya," Maria said, sitting on the edge of the bed beside her and collecting her hands. "I pity him. He espies a pretty woman and because of it, becomes hunted from all sides. St. John will seek him in a criminal's fashion. Ware will seek him in a peer's fashion. So you and I must seek Montoya in a woman's fashion."

"And how would that be?" Amelia asked, frowning.

"By shopping, of course." Maria smiled, and the entire room brightened. "We will visit all the purveyors of masks that we can find and see if any recall the count. If he always covers his face, he must procure a great many of the things. If not, perhaps it was a recent purchase and he left an indelible impression. It is not much, but it's a start. We will have to take care, of course. If he is in danger, finding him will bring that danger to us. You must trust me and listen to me implicitly. Agreed?"

"Yes." Amelia's lower lip quivered, and she bit it to hide the betraying movement. Her hands tightened on her sister's. "Thank you, Maria. Thank you so much."

Maria caught her close and kissed her forehead. "I will always be here to help you, poppet. Always."

The quiet declaration gave Amelia strength, and she clung to it as she slipped from the bed and began to prepare for the day ahead.

Chapter 8

There was a leisurely pace to the pedestrians, carts, and carriages that traveled down the street. The day was sunny and comfortably warm, the air cleansed from a brief spate of early morning rain. Colin, however, was far from relaxed. Something about the day did not sit well with him.

"You should not worry so much," Jacques said. "She will be fine. No one has connected you to your past or to Miss Benbridge."

Colin smiled ruefully. "Am I so transparent?"

"*Oui.* In your unguarded moments."

Staring out the carriage window, Colin noted the many people going about their daily business. For his part, his business this afternoon was leaving Town. His carriage was presently wending its way toward the road that would lead them to Bristol. Their trunks were loaded and their account with the rental property was settled.

He remained *un*settled.

The feeling that he was leaving his heart behind

was worse than before. His mortality was some-thing he began to feel more keenly each day. Life was finite, and the thought that the entirety of his would be spent without Amelia in it was too painful to bear.

"I have never shared a carriage with her," he said, his gloved fingers wrapping around the win-dow ledge. "I have never sat at a table with her and shared a meal. Everything I have done these last years was in pursuit of a higher station, one that would afford me the privilege to enjoy all the facets of her life."

Jacques's dark eyes watched him from beneath the rim of his hat. He sat on the opposite squab, his compact body as relaxed as Colin had ever seen it, but still thrumming with energy.

"Soon after my parents died," Colin murmured, staring out at the view of the street, "my uncle ac-cepted the position of coachman to Lord Welton. The wages were dismal and we were forced to leave the Romany camp, but my uncle felt it was more stable than the Gypsy life. He had been a dedicated bachelor prior to my arrival, but he took the burden of my care very seriously."

"So that is where your honor comes from," the Frenchman said.

Colin smiled slightly. "I was wretched at the change. At ten years of age, I felt the loss of my friends keenly, especially following so soon after the loss of my father and mother. I was certain my life was over and I would be miserable forever. And then, I saw her."

In his mind's eye, he remembered the day as if

it were yesterday. "She was only seven years old, but I was awed. With her dark curls, porcelain skin, and green eyes, she looked like a beautiful doll. Then she held out a dirty hand to me, smiled a smile that was missing teeth, and asked me to play."

"*Enchanté,*" Jacques murmured.

"Yes, she was. Amelia was a dozen playmates in one—adventurous, challenging, and resourceful. I rushed through my chores just so I could be with her." Sighing, Colin leaned his head back against the squab and closed his eyes. "I remember the day I first rode as rear footman on the carriage. I felt so mature and proud of my accomplishment. She was happy for me, too, her eyes bright and filled with joy. Then, I realized that while she sat inside, I stood outside, and I would never be allowed to sit with her."

"You have changed a great deal since then, *mon ami*. There is no such divide between you now."

"Oh, there is a divide," Colin argued. "It just is not a monetary one any longer."

"When did you know that you loved her?"

"I loved her from the first." His hand fisted where it rested atop his thigh. "The feeling just grew and changed, as we both did."

He would never forget the afternoon when they had played in the stream, as they often did. He in his breeches, she stripped to her chemise. She had just reached fifteen years, he ten and eight. He had stumbled across the pebbled shore, attempting to catch a fleeing frog, when he'd fallen. Her delighted laughter turned his head, and the sight of her had changed his life forever. Bathed in sunlight, drenched in water, her beautiful features transformed by merriment, she had seemed a water nymph to him. Alluring. Innocently seductive.

His breath had caught in his throat; his body had hardened. Heated cravings burned in his blood and dried his mouth. His cock—which had become an aching, demanding torment as he'd matured—throbbed with painful pressure. He was no innocent, but the physical urgings he'd appeased before were merely annoying when compared to the need wrought by the sight of Amelia's semi-nude body.

Somehow . . . sometime, when he hadn't been looking, Amelia had grown into a young woman. And he wanted her. Wanted her as he'd never wanted anything before. His heart clenched with his sudden longing; his arms ached to hold her. Deep inside him, he felt an emptiness and knew she would fill it. Make him whole. Complete him. She'd been everything to him as a child. He knew she would be everything to him as a man.

"Colin?" Her smile had faded as tension filled the air between them.

Later that evening, Pietro noted his somberness and questioned him. When he'd spilled out his discovery, his uncle reacted with novel ferocity.

"Stay away from her," Pietro growled, his dark eyes burning in their intensity. "I should have ended your friendship long ago."

"No!" Colin had been horrified at the thought. He couldn't imagine his life without her.

Pietro slammed his fist on the table and loomed over him. "She is far above you. Beyond your reach. You will cost us our livelihood!"

"I love her!" As soon as the words left his mouth, he knew they were true.

Grim-faced, his uncle had dragged him out of their quarters in the stables and taken him into the village. There, he'd thrusted Colin into the arms of a pretty whore who delighted in exhausting him and wringing him dry. A mature woman, she was unlike the marginally experienced girls he'd dallied with before. She made certain he was spent. He left her bed with muscles turned to jelly and a need for a long nap.

When he'd staggered into the nearby tavern hours later, his uncle had met him with a jovial smile and fatherly pride. "Now you have another woman to love," he'd pronounced, slapping him affectionately on the back.

To which Colin had corrected, "I'm grateful to her, yes. But I love only Amelia."

Pietro's face had fallen. The next day, when Colin saw Amelia and felt the same lustful longing as he'd experienced at the stream, he'd known instinctively that the sexual act would be different with her. Just as she'd made the days brighter and his heart lighter, he knew she would make sex deeper and richer, too. The hunger he felt for that connection was inescapable. It gnawed at him and gave him no rest.

Over the next few months, Pietro told him daily to leave her be. If he loved her, his uncle said, he would want the best for her, and a Gypsy stableboy could never be that.

And so he eventually found the fortitude to push her away out of love for her. It had killed him then.

It was killing him anew now.

The carriage dipped, swayed, and rumbled over the streets beneath it, every movement a signal that he was moving farther and farther away from the only thing he'd ever wanted in this world.

"You will return to her," Jacques said quietly. "It is not the end."

"Until we finish this matter with Cartland, I cannot even consider having her. There is a reason Quinn continued to use Cartland even though he was troublesome—he is an excellent tracker. As long as he is searching for me, I have no future."

"I believe in destiny, *mon ami*. And yours is not to die at that man's hands. I can promise you that."

Colin nodded, but in truth, he was not so optimistic.

The white-gloved fingers that were curled around the carriage windowsill belonged to Montoya. Amelia knew it with bone-deep surety.

As the nondescript equipage passed her, she chanced a stray glance through the open window and spotted Jacques. Frozen in surprise, a shiver of discovery moved through her and filled her with hope. Then she noted the many trunks strapped to the back of the coach.

Montoya was leaving Town, just as he'd said he would.

Fortuitously for her but unfortunate for him, his driver had chosen to travel along the very street she and Maria traversed in their search for him.

"Maria," she said urgently, afraid to tear her gaze away for fear she would lose sight of him.

"Hmm?" her sister hummed distractedly. "I see masks in the display here."

Before Amelia could protest, Maria slipped into the nearest store, the merry chiming of bells heralding her departure.

A multitude of pedestrians milled around them, though many steered clear due to Tim, who towered over everyone and guarded his charges with an eagle eye.

"Tim." Amelia lifted her hand and pointed at the carriage, which continued to move farther away. "Montoya is in that black travel coach. We must move swiftly or we shall lose him."

The sensation of something precious sifting through her fingers caused a sort of anxiety she had never felt before. She grabbed her skirts and followed at a near run.

A hackney discharged its passengers a few yards up the street. Amelia hurried toward it with one hand lifted in a frantic wave.

Realizing her intent, Tim cursed under his breath, grabbed her elbow, and dragged her along. "Halt!" he roared as the driver raised his whip.

The man turned his head and froze at the sight of Tim. Swallowing hard, he nodded. When they reached the coach, Tim yanked the door open and thrust her up into it. He looked at the two lackeys who followed them. "Go back with the others and find Mrs. St. John. Tell her what happened."

Sam, a red-haired man who had been in St.

John's employ for years, gave a jerky nod. "Aye. Be careful."

Tim lunged into the coach, forcing Amelia back into the interior. "I don't like this," he said gruffly.

"Hurry!" she urged. "You can chastise me on the way."

He glowered and cursed again, then yelled instructions to the driver.

The hackney lurched into motion, pulling away from the milling pedestrians and into the traffic of the street.

The doorbells were still chiming when Maria came to an abrupt halt just inside the door of the shop.

A tall, elegantly attired gentleman blocked her way to the deeper interior. At his side, a lovely blonde was wearing the very latest in French fashion. Maria's gaze moved from one to the other, noting what a handsome couple they made.

"Simon!" Maria gaped in startled recognition.

"*Mhuirnín.*" As he captured her hand and lifted it to his lips, the tender affection in the beloved voice was palpable. "You look ravishing, as always."

Simon Quinn stood before her looking more sinfully delicious than any man had a right to. Dressed in buff-colored breeches and a dark green coat, his powerful frame drew the eye of every woman within viewing distance. He bore the form of a laborer, while clad in superbly tailored garments fit for the king himself.

"I was not aware that you had returned to London," she chastised gently. "And I admit I am more than slightly piqued that you did not seek me out immediately."

The Frenchwoman smiled a smile that never reached her cold, blue eyes. "Quinn . . ." She shook her head, setting the festive ribbons that adorned it to swaying. "It appears your poor treatment of women is an unfortunate recurring trait in you."

"Hush," he snapped.

Maria frowned, unaccustomed to Simon being curt to lovely females.

The bells chimed again, and she attempted to step out of the way when her arm was caught by a grasping hand. Taken aback, she pivoted in a swirl of deep rose-colored skirts and found Sam looking far too anxious beside her.

"Miss Amelia saw 'is coach," the lackey blurted out, "and ran after 'im. Tim's with 'er, but—"

"Amelia?" It was then that Maria realized her sister was not beside her. She rushed back out the door and onto the crowded street.

"There," Sam said, pointing at a hackney moving down the street.

"She saw Montoya?" Maria asked, her gut knotting with apprehension. Lifting her skirts, she pushed her way through the milling pedestrians. Simon and the blonde came fast on her heels, and more of St. John's men barreled through directly after them. They were causing somewhat of a melee, but she did not care. Reaching Amelia was her only concern.

When it became apparent that there was no hope of catching up to them on foot, she stopped. "I need my carriage."

"I sent for it," Sam assured from his position at her side.

"Seek out St. John and explain." Her mind rushed ahead, planning out the possibilities of the next few hours. "I will take the rest of the men with me. Once we find Amelia, someone will be sent back with our direction."

Sam nodded his agreement and departed to collect his mount.

"What the devil is going on?" Simon asked, a frown marring the space between his brilliant blue eyes. The blonde, for her part, looked only vaguely interested.

Maria sighed. "My sister has become enamored of a masked stranger she met at a ball several nights ago, and she is chasing him."

The sudden tension that gripped Simon's frame increased her anxiety. If he sensed some danger from the situation, she knew it must be more than worry for a sibling that drove her.

"I have been fretting over it ever since," she continued, "but she cannot be swayed. I attempted to reason with her, but she is determined to find him. As is St. John. I offered to assist Amelia in her search as a way to control at least a part of the whole affair, but apparently she spotted him on the street a few moments ago and is now giving chase."

"Good God!" Simon cried, eyes wide.

"Oh, this is delightful!" Miss Rousseau said, her eyes finally showing some signs of life.

"I will come with you," Simon said briskly, gesturing to his footman who waited nearby. The boy rushed off to fetch Simon's carriage.

"You do not have to become involved," Maria said, heaving out her breath. "You are presently engaged. Enjoy your day."

"You are upset, *mhuirnín*. And perhaps I can help. We were on our way out of Town for holiday, as it was. Miss Rousseau does not mind the alteration of our destination."

"No, no indeed," the Frenchwoman said, smiling. "In fact, I should like to come along. Foolish young lovers are always so diverting."

Simon growled, the sound so edgy that Maria reconsidered her continuing protests and held her silence instead. Simon had been her lieutenant for many years, and his assistance would be tremendously valuable. Whatever the situation was between him and Miss Rousseau, it was for them alone to work out. She had enough trouble of her own to manage.

It was a few moments longer before the gleam of highly polished black lacquer heralded the approach of the St. John town coach. Maria hoped that the distance to be traveled was not one that would need the sturdier travel carriage.

Simon's equipage drew up behind hers, and with laudable haste they were all in hot pursuit.

Colin vaulted down from his travel coach with relief, his long legs cramped from the many hours spent traveling from London to the small posting inn just past Reading. He stood in the courtyard a moment and surveyed his moonlit surroundings. Jacques alighted behind him, and together they entered the inn to secure their lodging for the night.

The dim interior was quiet. Only a few patrons remained in the main room; the rest had retired. The necessary arrangements were quickly dealt with, and shortly, Colin found himself in a small, sparsely furnished room that was clean and comfortable.

As soon as he was alone, melancholy descended in a cold, weighty mantle. He was a day's ride away from Amelia, with the morrow bringing even more distance between them. Frustrated by the progression of events, he prayed sleep would offer him a brief respite, but after years of dreaming of Amelia, he did not hold out much hope.

He was reaching to close the curtains when the door opened behind him. Gripping the hilt of the dagger hidden in his coat, he canted his torso to make himself a smaller target.

"Montoya."

Amelia's sweetly feminine voice caused him to freeze in midturn. He had hoped to be followed, but not by her. Now the danger that stalked him shadowed her as well.

"I had to see you," she murmured. "Your carriage passed me in the street, and I could not allow you to go."

Only years of training and living by his wits leashed his surprise, preventing him from ruining everything by facing her. Instead he closed the drapes, dimming the gentle light of the moon before turning toward her. If he was fortunate, the banked fire in the grate would keep his face mostly in shadow, lessening the possibility of recognition.

Mentally prepared only for her reaction to him, Colin was completely vulnerable to his own reaction to her. The sight of her by the door—and near a bed—hit him like a blow, freeing a possessive, primitive growl from his tightened throat. She shivered at the sound, her lips parting with quickened breaths.

His hands clenched into fists at his sides. Did she know what she did to him?

She stood proud and undaunted before the door, a beribboned hat tied at a jaunty angle, her slender body encased in a gown of shimmering satin and delicate white lace. The innocent cut of the dress made the years fall away, made him hard as a rock and hot to claim her. He loved her deeply and completely with lingering traces of his boyish adoration, but he also lusted for her with every drop of the wild Gypsy blood in his veins.

"Tell me you did not travel alone," he bit out, hating to think of such beauty unattended. She was a treasure to be secured and valued. The thought of her on the journey without a guard, unwittingly in jeopardy, tied him in knots.

"I am protected." Her eyes glittered in the muted light, and she queried in a whisper, "Are you angry with me?"

"No," he said hoarsely, his heart thudding with rhythmic violence in his chest.

"The mask . . ." She inhaled audibly. "Most men look especially dashing in evening attire. You—"

"Amelia—"

"—move me always. Whatever you wear, wherever we are."

His eyes closed as her praise rippled through him. He took an involuntary step toward her, then jerked to a halt. The room was suddenly too small and airless; the need to divest them both of every stitch of cloth was nearly overwhelming. His craving for her grew more ferocious, clawing and biting in its desire to be appeased.

"Are you happy to see me?" she asked in a small voice.

Colin shook his head, his eyes opening because he couldn't bear not to see her. "It kills me."

Tenderness swept over her finely wrought features and called to something deep inside him.

"It is the yearning I sense in you that lures me." She stepped closer, and he lifted a hand to halt her progress before she came too near. "As long as you want me, I will want you in return."

"I would have ceased wanting you long ago," he rasped, "if such a thing were possible."

Her head tilted to the side as she considered him. "You lie."

Unable to resist, he smiled at that. She was audacious still.

"You enjoy wanting me," she said, with purely female satisfaction.

"I would enjoy having you more," he purred.

When her gaze shot to the bed, his cock swelled to full arousal. Her tongue darted out to lick her lower lip, and a rough, edgy sound rumbled from his chest.

"Come with me," she entreated, her gaze returning to his. "Meet my family. My sister and her husband can assist you. Whatever plagues you, they can help to resolve."

Colin's gut tightened. He should say no . . . He should avoid bringing any danger into her life . . .

But the possibility of having her *now* . . . No more waiting, no more hiding . . .

It was night, a bed was near, and they were alone. His deepest fantasy made reality.

He stepped toward her. "There is something I must tell you. Something you will find difficult to understand. Do you have time to hear me out?"

She lifted her gloved hand and extended it to him. "As much as you need."

"What of those who came with you?"

"He is drinking below." She smiled. "I lied, you see. I pointed out a different patron and said I suspected he was you. So Tim is occupied with watching him, while I inquired discreetly and found you. You have a unique form—so tall and broad. The maids noticed you when you came in."

"What of your reputation, then? A young woman of obviously fine breeding making inquiries about a bachelor."

"Once I learned where you were, I described my relief at finding my brother who is wearing dark green."

Colin glanced down at his blue garments. *Dear God, was it true? Could he have her?*

She beamed with obvious pride in her cleverness.

"You have gone to a great deal of trouble to find me, Miss Benbridge."

"Amelia," she corrected. "And yes I have."

He smiled. "Turn around, then, and face the door."

Amelia frowned. "Why?"

"Because I need to approach you, and I am not certain how much of my face can be seen in this light." When she hesitated, he said, "*You* pursue *me*. You want me. I will be yours, in every sense, but in return you must listen to me without question. Does that frighten you?"

She swallowed hard, her irises overtaken by dilated pupils. Then she shook her head.

"It excites you," he murmured. Hot, potent lust intoxicated him, easing the relentless drive that set him on edge. He had always led the way with her. It was highly arousing to lead the way in their bedsport, as well. "Turn."

Complying, she faced away from him, and Colin approached with a rapid stride, freed from the fear of untimely recognition. He pressed up against her, breathing in the scent of honeysuckle, placing his palms flat to the panels on either side of her head.

The vein in her throat fluttered with her increasing heartbeat, arresting his attention.

The sound of the bolt sliding home stiffened his frame and drew his gaze away.

How simple the action was, that of locking the door, but it aroused him as nothing ever had. She *wanted* him to take her, to strip her bare, to fuck her sweet little body until he was spent and conquered.

Though he knew it, he still wanted her to say the words aloud.

"There is no chance that you will depart this room as virginal as you entered it," he murmured, his tongue stroking over her racing pulse.

In answer, she reached for the chair by the door and pushed back hard against him, creating a gap that allowed her to wedge the spindle back beneath the knob.

"Do you anticipate interruptions?" he asked, with laughter in his voice and heart. "Or do you simply wish to keep the world at bay?"

The thought of Amelia forsaking the world at large to be with him made his chest tight. She had promised to do so as a young girl. Would she recommit to that promise as a woman?

"You assume I wish to lock others out." Her mouth curved in a woman's smile. "Perhaps I wish to lock you in."

Colin threw back his head and laughed at that, his arms banding her torso and squeezing her tightly. "Ah, love. How glad I am that you remain so spirited."

"The threat of lovemaking is not sufficient to repress me," she retorted.

No, but his identity might be. The thought was sobering. He inhaled sharply. "Amelia, I must share my face and past with you before we can proceed."

The tension that gripped her was palpable. "Will it change how I feel about you?"

"Most definitely, yes."

"Do not reveal anything."

He blinked. "I beg your pardon?"

"Right now, in this moment, I feel as if I could not breathe without you near." Her voice was low and earnest. "I've no desire to be disillusioned. Not after these last years when nothing was vital to me. It seems almost as if I walked through life wearing a veil. Only when I am with you do I see the world in all its many colors."

Pressing his cheek to hers, he whispered, "You should place greater worth upon your virginity. I cannot take you—"

She turned her head and pressed her lips to his. The sudden rush of sensation was dizzying. Then unbearably arousing. He felt her moving, but was unable to break the contact to discover why. His tongue stroked across her lips, licking the innocently sweet flavor that was innate to her. The taste was addicting, destroying him. He was helpless to resist it. When her bare fingertips wrapped around his wrist and lifted his hand to her breast, he knew there was no fighting her. He could not simply blurt out who he was. The revelation required more tact than that.

"I can see you with my heart," she said breathlessly, her lips moving against his. "I want to have you while I feel for you as I do at this moment— wild and hot and free. Does that make me reckless and naïve? Do you find me foolish and fast?"

With every word that left her mouth he grew harder and less controlled. *Wild. Hot. Free.* The combination was a potent allure for a Gypsy male. Amelia had lived outside the boundaries of Society for so long, she found it easier than most to ignore its constrictions. He suspected that contributed to their affinity. At heart, they were both desperate to run laughing through the fields without any restraints.

Colin reached around her and unfastened the jeweled brooch that secured her lace fichu. "Can I cover your eyes?" he asked in a dark voice. "Would that dampen your ardor?"

She tried to turn her head to meet his gaze, and

he stopped her with a kiss. "I would not have the revelation occur during the act. I want nothing to mar our first time together. I have waited too long for it and desired it too deeply to see it ruined."

Nodding, she held still as he twisted the expensive lace loosely, then tied it around her head in a makeshift blindfold.

"How does that feel?"

"Strange."

"Do not move." Colin backed up and shed his coat. He unwound his cravat, then began to work on the carved ivory buttons of his waistcoat.

"Are you undressing?" she asked.

"Yes."

He watched a shiver move through her and smiled. How erotically beautiful she looked with her kiss-swollen lips and covered eyes. His to savor and enjoy. Pietro had attempted to dissuade him away from Amelia by insisting that Englishwomen lacked the fire a Gypsy man needed. Colin hadn't believed it then; he certainly did not believe it now.

Her lovely breasts lifted and fell with her rapid breathing; her hands clenched rhythmically at her sides. She was ripe and ready, an oasis in the desert of his barren life.

Shrugging out of his waistcoat, Colin tossed it over the back of a chair and returned to her. "I want you to speak your thoughts to me. Tell me what feels good, what doesn't. I will know if you lie. Your body will betray you."

"Then why should I speak?"

"For your benefit." He caressed her shoulders, then reached for the tiny row of cloth buttons that followed the line of her spine. "Speaking aloud will force you to think in minute detail about what I am doing to you. It will anchor you to the pleasure and this moment."

"Anchor me to you."

"Yes, that, too." He kissed her throat. "It will empower you, be the telling of your desires. You may hesitate to touch me or wonder what is allowed or what is not allowed. But if you sense how the sounds of your pleasure in turn please me, you will know that this is a joining of two lovers playing equal parts."

"It sounds so intimate," she breathed.

"For us, my love, it will be."

Chapter 9

Ware entered Christopher St. John's study shortly after ten in the evening. The infamous pirate was pacing between the back of his desk and the window beyond that with a sort of restlessness the earl had never seen in him before. Sans coat and bearing a skewed cravat, St. John looked rumpled and anxious, which set the hairs on Ware's nape to rising. After seeing the travel coach hitched in the front circular drive, it was apparent that a journey of some distance was planned.

"My lord," St. John greeted absently.

"St. John." He cut straight to the heart of the matter. "What has happened?"

Rounding the desk, the pirate moved to the nearby console and held up a decanter in silent query. Ware shook his head in the negative and sank onto one of the matching settees that sat perpendicular to the grate. He was here to collect Amelia for the evening's social rounds. It was unlike her to leave him waiting. Her punctuality was one of the many traits he enjoyed in her.

"There is no way for me to relate the day's events without awkwardness," St. John began, pouring a hefty ration.

"Never mind that. I prefer bluntness to anything else."

Nodding, St. John took the seat opposite and said, "Mrs. St. John and Miss Benbridge went into Town today. I was told they meant to spend the day shopping. I have since learned that they were hunting the masked man who has so captured Amelia's interest."

Ware's brows rose. "I see."

"By some stray chance, Count Montoya—if that truly is his name—was seen departing London. Miss Benbridge hailed a hackney and set off in pursuit. My wife followed shortly after."

"Bloody hell."

"Would you care for that drink now, my lord?"

The earl seriously considered it, then shook his head. "I have made some inquiries of my own regarding this matter. I had hoped Lady Langston would shed some light on the man's identity; however, no invitation was ever issued to a Count Montoya."

St. John's lips pursed grimly. "I am at a loss for how to view this situation. If the man meant to hurt her in some fashion or seduce her, why leave London?"

There was jealousy and possessiveness laced with all the other emotions Ware was presently experiencing, but there was also resignation. Some part of him had known that Amelia held off on marriage to him because of a need for . . . *more.* He had no idea what she felt was missing, but in truth their relationship could not progress any further and still end happily without first resolving that lack.

"I am surprised to find you still at home," the earl said. "Amelia is not my wife, yet I feel a pressing need to go after her."

The glare the pirate shot at him was cutting. "I am near maddened with the need to follow, but I have no notion of their direction. I am awaiting word."

"Forgive me, I meant no offense. I was merely making an observation." He considered his options, then said, "I should like to go with you, if you have no objection."

St. John seemed ready to argue; then his scowl cleared and he nodded. "If you wish to come along, do. But your formal attire will be a burden."

Ware stood, as did the pirate. "I will change and pack lightly. If you depart before I return, please leave a note so that I may follow."

"Of course, my lord." St. John offered a commiserating smile. "I must apologize to you, as well. Your courting of Amelia has done much for her. Mrs. St. John and I are both exceedingly grateful, as is Amelia."

"St. John." Ware laughed ruefully. "At this moment, the matter of my pride is secondary to Amelia's safety."

They clasped hands in a gesture of mutual respect. Then the earl hastened to depart before he was left behind. As his carriage rolled away from the St. John residence, Ware began a mental list of what to bring with him.

His small sword and pistol were among the items

he catalogued. If Amelia's honor was to be impugned, he considered it his right and duty to correct the slight.

As Colin spread open the back of Amelia's gown, his thoughts were already rushing ahead, considering how this one night would change their lives forever. "Do you have an abigail with you?"

The blindfold might make some women more timid and hesitant. Not so with Amelia. Her voice came sure and strong. "No. I saw your carriage and gave chase."

Warring with the primitive need to mark her as his, his heart still wanted to protect her even at great cost to himself. "There will be no way to hide that you have been ravished. In the heat of passion, our better sense deserts us. What you want now, you may regret in the morning."

"I know my own mind," she said stubbornly.

"You will give up Ware." He gently withdrew one of her arms from a sleeve, then repeated the movement on the other side. "And you will belong to me."

"I think it more likely that you will belong to me."

Smiling, he bent at the knees and pulled her gown down with him. Amelia stepped out of the garment without urging, balancing her weight by leaning against the door. He deliberately delayed the joy of seeing her stripped from her outer garments. He took his time laying the dress over the back of a wing chair in an effort to spare it the most wrinkling.

"You are so calm," she murmured. "So controlled. You must have many affairs."

"This is not an affair." He turned his head, raking her lithe body with a heated glance. Still too many garments, but he knew that he was seeing her as no other man ever had.

She set her hand on her hip, and a finely arched brow lifted above the fichu. "Perhaps I want an affair."

"Well, you are not having one with me," he growled, reaching her in two strides and lifting her feet from the floor. "You will not be having one ever, because no other man will come after me in your bed."

Amelia laughed and wrapped her arms around his neck. "My . . . how delightful you are when you become possessive."

He pressed his lips to her ear. "Wait until my cock is inside you. See how delightful my possession is then."

"Tease," she said breathlessly, with a slight note of anxiety. "At this rate, the sun will be rising before I am naked."

"You do not have to be naked to be fucked," he whispered, deliberately challenging her to revive her spirits. "I could toss up your underskirts, undo my breeches, and pin you to the door."

"If your intent is to frighten me, you should know that I am difficult to scare." The anxiousness was gone from her voice, banished by her impressive inner fortitude. "I have lived in the most rustic of places. I have seen all sorts of animals doing all sorts of things to each other."

He buried his grin in her tender throat.

"Do not find amusement at my expense," she said. "Your threat is groundless. You would not take my virginity in so callous a manner. You worship me too much."

"So I do, Your Highness." Setting her back on her feet, Colin dropped to his knees and kissed her feet.

As she laughed, he moved upward, sliding beneath the masses of skirts, pressing open-mouthed kisses up the length of her stocking-clad legs. Her laughter turned into a gasp, then a soft whimper.

The intimate smell of her drove him insane, and with a tentative finger, Colin tested her, gritting his teeth at finding her slick and hot. Startled by his bold caress, Amelia stumbled and fell into the door with a soft thud.

"Not while I am standing!" she protested.

Pressing a final kiss to the back of her knee, Colin crawled free and stood before her. He gently turned her, then set to work on her tapes and stays, taking the brief respite to regain his control. He focused on his breathing and hers instead of the animal need that clawed inside him.

Finally, she was left with only her chemise, a garment made of material so fine he could almost see clear through it. It was enough to drive him to madness, the far-too-vague hints of her body beneath.

"I want you to remove the rest," he said, stepping back.

"Why?"

"Because it will please me."

"It is not as easy as you intimate. I have never been naked before a man."

"Do it, Amelia," he ordered, near desperate to see all of her.

With no further hesitation, she reached down and removed her shoes. The hem of her chemise lifted as she reached for the ribbons that secured her stockings. His mouth watered at the sight, every movement she made erasing similar memories from his past. No other woman could compete with the innocent, unaffected fashion in which Amelia undressed. Her movements were not practiced or planned with an eye for seduction, but they aroused him unbearably, nevertheless.

Aching with lust for her, he freed the placket of his breeches and took his cock in hand. He was thick and hard, slick at the tip with wanting her. Stroking leisurely down the length, he groaned in need.

Amelia froze at the sound, unsure of what she had done to distress him. "What is it? What's wrong?"

"Nothing is wrong," Montoya assured in a gruff voice that belied his words. "Everything is perfect."

She listened carefully, regulating her breathing in order to take in every nuance of sound. "What are you doing? I hear you moving."

"I am fondling my cock."

Images filled her mind, incomplete due to her inexperience, but arousing regardless. The flesh between her legs throbbed in response, making her squeeze her thighs together in a vain effort to ease the ache. "Why?"

"Because it pains me, love. I am hard and ready for you. Harder and thicker than I have ever been."

"Can I touch it?"

He made a choked noise, and the sounds of his

movements became more pronounced. "Bare yourself first."

Amelia finished undressing with haste, forcibly shoving aside thoughts of her imperfections. Unlike Maria, she was not lushly curved and built for a man's pleasure. She was taller, thinner, and smaller-breasted. She was too active, enjoying riding and fencing more than card games and teas.

"Dear God," he gasped when she dropped her chemise to the floor.

Her hands moved to cover herself, but he moved swiftly, catching her wrists. "Never hide from me."

"I am nervous," she retorted.

"My love . . ." He wrapped her against him, and she felt his erection between them. Smooth as silk, but hard as a rock and hot to the touch. Despite the shock of it, her body delighted in the feel and grew slicker.

"You are so beautiful, Amelia. Every inch of you. I dreamed of seeing you like this, naked and willing. How sorry those fantasies were compared to the reality."

She pressed her forehead to his chest and said, "You are being kind."

Montoya brought her hand to his cock and wrapped her fingers around it. "This is not how a man feels when he finds his lover inadequate."

Amelia moved, squeezing and caressing, exploring. His breath hissed out between his teeth. "You will make me spend," he gritted out.

"If it would please you to do so, go ahead," she replied, wanting to give him pleasure. Wanting to satisfy him in a way that would brand him as hers.

"Minx."

She stilled as a big, warm hand cupped her breast. Immediately, her nipple, already tight and hard from the chill of the open air, pebbled further.

"See how you fit so perfectly within my palm," he murmured, his hips beginning to thrust into her movements. "You were built for me, Amelia." She whimpered as his thumb and forefinger surrounded her nipple and tugged on it, sending pangs of intense pleasure straight to her womb. Everything tightened and coiled, making her move restlessly.

"And how quickly you respond to me." He leaned back, and a moment later she cried out as hot, wet suction surrounded the tender peak of her breast. Her hands gripped his cock convulsively, and he growled against her skin, the vibration driving her wild.

His powerful arms banded her waist, supporting her as he pushed her backward and worshipped her breast, his tongue curling around her nipple as his cheeks hollowed with drawing pulls.

Just as he had said, every thought left her mind, leaving her a creature of lust and desire. The lack of reason bound her tighter to him. There was only one other man she had ever considered sharing herself with in this way. That Montoya was scarred and haunted had no bearing on the emotions he aroused in her.

"Tell me you love this," he said, as he moved to her other breast. "Let it out, Amelia. Do not be silent."

His teeth nipped the hard peak and she cried out. He began licking her, his tongue stroking with maddening leisure. It was not enough, not nearly. She began to writhe, whimpering, arching her back in an attempt to push deeper into his mouth.

"What do you need?" he asked in a dark whisper. "What do you want? Tell me, and I will give it to you."

Desperate, she begged, "Suck it . . . please . . . I need—"

She gasped as he obliged, his lips closing around her. In her hands his cock throbbed, and a hot trickle of moisture tickled the backs of her fingers. She touched it, found its source at the tiny hole at the head. The pad of her thumb smoothed it around, and he shuddered and suckled her harder.

With her sight stolen from her, every other sense was heightened. As his skin heated, her nostrils filled with his unique scent, increasing her desire. Her sense of touch was painfully acute; even the slight rustle of the air prickled across her flesh.

"Please," she cried, wanting more.

With one last lingering suck, Montoya straightened and pulled her up with him. Then he lifted her into his arms and moved toward the waiting bed.

Simon was in a foul mood by the time Maria's coach pulled off the main road and into the courtyard of an inn just shy of Reading. Two of St. John's outriders traveled on ahead, freed of the burden of the slow-moving carriages. If they were fortunate, they would return with a more solid direction or perhaps even a sighting.

The entire day had been a study in frustration.

The hackney carrying Amelia had discharged her and her guard shortly after collecting them, unwilling to travel beyond the city. They had then secured another carriage and continued on. That progression of events was to be expected. What most concerned Simon were the reports of an inordinate number of French-speaking riders moving in the same direction ahead of them.

It could be nothing, or it could be Cartland.

Simon had longed to disclose the whole of the matter to Maria over dinner, but he felt a similar level of loyalty to Colin, who had risked his life for Simon on more than a few occasions. So he said nothing, holding his tongue when they parted ways to retire for the night.

In the meantime, neither he nor Lysette had any of the items required for comfortable travel. They had no change of clothes and no servants. They did not even have the proper equipage, which led him to having an aching arse and a sore back.

At least Colin had mentioned traveling to Bristol, which gave Simon an advantage. He subtly urged Maria in that general direction, while quietly sending a lone footman back to his lodgings to inform his valet of their change of plans. The servant would manage the settling of the accounts, the packing of their things, and the rounding up of Lysette's maid and belongings.

Thinking of the Frenchwoman, his gaze moved to where she sat before the fire. By necessity, they shared a bedchamber, the size of their party enough to take up the last remaining rooms. Maria had complained mightily about the poor quality of the inn, arguing that St. John had various lackeys scattered around the area who would take them in and provide them comfortable lodging. Simon's insistence that they remain near the road was unreasonable to her, and he appreciated the validity of the argument. However, he had no desire for Maria to realize that he had lied about the planned holiday, a ruse that would be revealed if he donned the same garments.

A soft sigh drew his attention back to Lysette. She was curled up in a wing chair, stripped to her chemise with her legs tucked up close and a blanket across her lap. Pale blonde curls were loosened from a previously stylish arrangement and left to lie carelessly against pale, creamy skin. She was reading, as she often did, devouring historical volumes of text with a voracity he found intriguing. Why such interest in the past? They had merely intended to make discreet inquiries, and she had brought a book along with her anyway.

Frowning, Simon moved to the bed and stripped down to his smalls. Then he crawled between the sheets. With lowered lids, he studied her, admiring her delicate golden beauty while considering why it was that he found her so unappealing. It was, to his knowledge, the only time in his life that he had found external attractiveness incapable of distracting from the internal flaws. Considering that Lysette rivaled Maria in loveliness, it was a startling realization to come to.

The women were similar in many ways, and that only emphasized their differences. Maria had a solid core within her, a spine of steel that was created by her unwavering determination. Lysette seemed sometimes as if she was uncertain of her life's path. He could not understand why she appeared to relish her role one moment, and then despise it the next.

His instincts were clamoring, and he had come to rely on them implicitly. Something told him that all was not right in Lysette's world. She was a hired killer, and her icy disposition supported her chosen profession. Yet her apathy for others was sometimes belied by brief flashes of confusion and remorse. He suspected she was a bit touched, and it was difficult to feel both sympathy and dislike toward the same woman.

"How did you come to work for Talleyrand?" he asked.

She jumped and glared at him. "I thought you were sleeping."

"Obviously not."

"I do not work for Talleyrand."

"Who then?"

"That is none of your business," she said smartly.

"Oh, I think it is," he drawled.

Her gaze narrowed as she looked at him. "Whom do you work for?" she countered.

"I work for no one. I am a mercenary."

"Hmm . . ."

"Are you?" he prodded, when she said no more than that.

Lysette shook her head, once again looking a bit lost. Her clothes were finely crafted and expensive, her manners and deportment faultless. She had begun life in far better circumstances than these. He knew why Maria had turned to a life of crime, but why had Lysette?

"Why don't you find a rich husband and enjoy yourself draining his coffers?" he asked.

Her nose wrinkled. "How boring."

"Well, that would depend on the husband, would it not?"

"Regardless, that does not sound appealing to me."

"Perhaps life as a mistress would suit you better?"

"I do not like men very much," she pronounced, startling him. "Why are you asking me such questions?"

Simon shrugged. "Why not? There is nothing else for me to do."

"Go to sleep."

"Do you prefer the company of women?"

She stared at him a moment. Then her eyes widened. "No! *Mon Dieu.* I prefer the company of books, but in lieu of that, men are my second choice. Most especially in the manner to which you are referring."

He smiled at her horror.

"Why don't you think about Cartland?" she suggested, "And leave me in peace."

His humor fled. "You think he will find Mitchell?"

"I think it would be impossible for him not to with this large a number of pursuers. He was given a sizeable contingent of men. I would be surprised if he was not watching all the major roads in and out of London." Her beautiful features lost all traces of humanity. "I would not have come with you if I thought of this as merely a family affair."

"Of course not," he murmured, the tiny flare of warmth he'd felt for her fading as rapidly as it had come. Such was the way of their relations—one minute he found her marginally attractive, the next he could not abide her. "And what of this man who rides with Cartland? Depardue? Do you think about him?"

"As little as possible."

There was something more there; he could tell by the edge that had entered her voice. "He is your rival, is he not?"

Her lips whitened, then, "No. He is not. If he succeeds, it does not reflect negatively on me."

"So why not allow him to proceed and spare yourself the blight on your soul?"

"I do what I must," she said with a trace of defensiveness. "You do not like that I can set aside my emotions to accomplish the tasks set before me, but the ability keeps me alive."

Heaving out his breath, Simon slid down to lie on his back. "Surviving in the manner that you and I do does not mean we have to be heartless. What would be the point of living if we have no heart?"

He heard the book slam shut. "Do not seek to lecture me!" she snapped. "You have no notion of what my life has been like."

"So tell me," he said easily.

"Why do you care?"

"I told you, there is nothing else to do."

"Do you want to have sex?"

His head shot up in surprise. She stared back with both brows raised.

"With you?" he asked, incredulous.

"Who else is here?" she retorted.

To his chagrin, Simon realized that as much as he enjoyed a quick, meaningless tumble, he had no real desire to tumble Lysette. However, damned if he wouldn't rise to the occasion. "I suppose we could . . ."

Her eyes widened at his obvious reluctance. Then she laughed, a sweet, lilting sound that he found enchanting. Who knew such a cold creature could have such a warm laugh? "You don't want to sleep with me?" she asked, grinning.

Simon scowled. "I can manage the task," he bit out.

Lysette looked pointedly at the general area of his cock. "It does not look that way to me."

"Never cast aspersions on a man's virility. You force him to prove it by fucking you raw."

A shadow passed over her features. She swallowed hard and looked away.

His irritation fled. Sitting up, he said, "I was jesting."

"Of course."

Scrubbing a hand over his jaw, Simon cursed inwardly. He did not understand the woman at all. She was too mutable. "Perhaps we should restrain our conversations to safer subjects?"

She looked at him. "Yes, I think you are right."

He waited for her to say something; then finally he took the lead. "I intend to capture Cartland and bring him together with Mitchell. Then you can see for yourself the differences between the two. If I know Cartland at all, he hopes to eliminate Mitchell before his secret is revealed."

"If there is such a secret to tell."

"Why do you not believe us?"

"Do not take offense," she said easily. "I do not believe Cartland either."

"Who do you believe, then?" he snapped.

"No one." Her chin lifted. "Tell me you would do differently in my place."

"You met Mitchell. He is an earnest young man with a good heart."

Her gaze hardened. "I am certain there are those who would laud Monsieur Cartland as well."

"Cartland is a lying murderer!"

"So you say. But did he not once work for you? Do you not have a grievance against him for revealing your traitorous activities in France? You have motive to want him dead, which leaves anything you say against him suspect."

Cursing under his breath, Simon plopped back onto the pillow and yanked up the counterpane.

"Are you going to sleep now?" she asked.

"Yes!"

"Bonne nuit."

His response was a frustrated growl.

Chapter 10

Amelia shivered as her bare back touched the cool counterpane and Montoya's warmth left her. If she kept her gaze trained downward, she could see a tiny sliver of the room and the glow of the fire in the grate. But she did not want to see, so she squeezed her lids shut.

In her mind's eye, she pictured Montoya as a rather exotic-looking man. Strong, handsome, and rather severe. The desire she felt to lighten his burdens and bring him some comfort was a goading force. She wanted to hear him laugh and press kisses to the dimples she saw far too rarely.

Suddenly, an image of Colin burst forth in all its glory, vivid and powerful. She stiffened in surprise.

"What is it?" Montoya murmured, the cessation of sound telling her that he had stopped undressing.

Inhaling sharply, Amelia brought her thoughts back to the present. Perhaps it was to be expected that she would think fondly of her first love at this moment, the one where she embarked on a similar journey with another. She lacked the experience to know.

"I am cold without you," she lied, holding her arms out to him.

"In a moment, you will be hot and damp," he purred, the bed dipping as he joined her atop it.

She felt the warmth of him along her side and then the gentle press of his firm lips to her shoulder. His hand drifted along the length of her, following the slight curves and valleys of her figure.

"I fear I am dreaming," he said softly. "I am afraid to blink in case I open my eyes and find you gone."

Amelia's hand came to rest on the flat plane of her belly just below her navel. "I feel flutters here," she confessed.

His hand covered hers and squeezed gently. "I will be there soon. Deep inside you." His fingertips tiptoed across her skin and touched the curls between her legs.

It tickled, making her laugh. When he pressed his lips to hers, she felt his returning smile. "I love you," he breathed before taking her mouth.

Her heart stopped, delaying her reaction to the deepening intrusion of his fingers. A callused fingertip parted her and her thighs squeezed together instinctively.

Gasping, Amelia turned her head away, the reaction to those whispered words hitting her with stunning force. She had never thought to hear those words again, not from the lips of a lover. Tears welled, burning her eyes.

"Open your legs," he urged, kissing her throat. "Allow me to pleasure you."

She began to quiver, the assault to both her senses and her heart rattling her to the core. "Reynaldo . . ."

"No." He came over her then, kissing her hard. "Call me anything but that. Lover or darling—"

". . . sweetheart . . ."

"Yes . . ." His tongue thrust deep, caressing hers, making her moan into his mouth. "Open," he said ardently. "Let me see you . . . touch you . . ."

Unable to deny him when he spoke with such passion, Amelia spread her legs and then arched upward as he stroked against the tender, throbbing point that begged for his attention.

"Oh!"

Montoya's kisses became more luxurious as he continued to fondle her with devastating skill. His callused fingertips rubbed her slick, aching sex in time to the rhythmic plunges of his tongue.

Awash in pleasure, yet struggling against the building tension that strained her body, she writhed and clutched at him. Beneath her grip his forearm muscles flexed with his movements, increasing her erotic awareness of how intimately he touched her.

Then one finger dipped lower, circling the clenching opening to her sex.

"How slick you are," he breathed reverently. "How greedily you suck at my fingertip." To prove his point, he pushed in the tiniest bit. Amelia cried out as her body spasmed around the gentle invasion.

"Dear God, you are so tight and hot," he praised gruffly. "You will kill me when I push inside you."

Amelia reached for his cock, wondering how she would accommodate him. He was so thick and hard. Her untried body was burning from the press of one finger.

Montoya groaned when she wrapped her hand around him. He was slick, too. With need and desire for her.

"You are ready to come," he said. "Feel how hard your clitoris is?" The pad of his thumb pressed lightly against the swollen protrusion and circled. In response, her body tightened around the single finger slowly easing into it.

She whimpered as he stepped up the pace, his finger thrusting in and out, deeper and deeper. His expert manipulation of her clitoris caused her skin to dampen with sweat and her breasts to ache. Desperate mewling poured from her throat, and she clung to him, trying to bring him closer.

"Tell me what you need," he whispered, his lips to her ear. "Tell me how to please you."

"My nipples . . ."

"They are beautiful. Puckered so wantonly. Eager to be sucked."

"Yes!" Amelia arched upward in blatant invitation.

"Say it, my love." His finger pushed deeper and touched her maidenhead. "Say what you want."

"I want . . ."

"Yes?" He continued to rub inside her.

"I want your mouth on my breasts."

"Umm . . . with pleasure," he purred.

She gasped when he obliged, the burning heat searing her tender flesh. Tension gripped her limbs, tightening with every tug of his lips, every thrust of his finger, every circle of his thumb.

The climax stole her breath when it hit. Her body

went rigid, her heart slammed against her ribs, her blood rushed through her ears.

And deep inside her, at the extremity of her orgasm, Montoya broke through the barrier between them. Amidst the onslaught of sensation, the loss of her virginity was barely noticed, and the tear that leaked from the corner of her eye was not from pain, but pleasure so intense she could hardly bear it.

As awareness returned after the rush, she heard his hoarsely voiced endearments and praise. Her first thought was of how grateful she was to share the sexual act with a man who felt such passion for her and inspired a returning desire for him. What might have been an act of duty was instead a joy.

There were a hundred emotions warring for dominance within her, all struggling to be freed through words. But her throat was too tight to release them.

Instead, she wrapped her arms around him and held him to her breast.

Colin listened to the sound of Amelia's heart slowing and knew he had never loved her more. She was a goddess in her passion, a creature of lust and longing, her beautiful body flushed and glistening. Earthy. Wild and hot, as she had longed to be. Built for sex.

With him.

No other man could unlock her. She said she felt nothing when he was gone. She felt alive when he was near. Warm and soft, wet and willing. Eager to be touched.

"That was"—she gave a soft, breathy sigh—"wonderful."

He rubbed his face against her breast and laughed, his heart filled with joy. He, too, felt reawakened after being dormant too long. She had pursued him, needing his desire to set free her own.

"Your whiskers burn," she complained, pushing at his head.

The image in his mind of such an obvious sexual mark on her made his cock throb in frustrated protest at its deprivation.

But the fantasy he had nurtured over the years was not of his own gratification. He wanted *hers*, needed it. Before the night was over he would bind her to him with pleasure, enslave her with desire, teach her all the many facets of sexual culmination. Her love was the ultimate prize, but her lust was vital, too.

"Can I burn you in other places?" he asked, lifting his head.

Her tongue darted out to wet her lower lip. Colin took over the task, licking across the plump curve with the very tip of his tongue. It was an enticement, an intimation, a hint.

From the way her breath caught, she comprehended his intent. "You jest."

"Never. I want to taste you, Amelia. On the outside and on the inside."

He could almost hear her brain working. Considering.

"I find it easier to conceive of my tasting you in that fashion," she said slowly, "more so than I can the reverse."

His arms shook at the thought, and he rolled to his back to avoid collapsing atop her.

"You would like that," she mused aloud, noting

his reaction. "Does a woman's mouth feel so different from her quim?"

"I love that you are inquisitive. I pray you will always be."

"One day I should like to teach you something."

"Siren. You already have me bewitched. Must you reduce me further?"

Her hand brushed lightly across the ridges of his abdomen and circled his upthrust cock. He exhaled harshly as she sat up and turned to face him. Reaching out, he caught her shoulder and stayed her. Despite her inability to see, she turned her head toward him. Her free hand reached for the fichu.

"Not yet," he said.

"I am ready now."

"I am not."

She seemed prepared to protest, then changed her mind. Instead, she stroked gently up the length of his shaft. He grit his teeth and fisted the counterpane.

"I want to do to you," she murmured, "what you did to me."

"You know men are less fastidious than women when we reach orgasm."

"But the sensation is the same, is it not?"

He smiled. "I would imagine so."

Amelia sat up and tucked her legs beneath her. With two hands, she fondled him, squeezing and caressing. The sensation originated at his cock, burned up his spine, and seared his heart. There was reverence in her touch. Awe.

The edge of a nail traced the line of a vein, and he groaned, a low, pained sound.

"Tell me what you like," she breathed. "Tell me how to please you best."

"You already please me best." Colin caressed the elegant curve of her spine.

"Then tell me how to please you better."

"If you did that, I would spend in your hands."

"Or my mouth?" Her head tilted to one side in question.

"Not tonight," he choked out. His bollocks drew up, and he pulled them down with a quick tug.

She felt blindly until she comprehended what he had done. "Why did you do that?" Her cool fingers touched his balls, rolling them gently, then tugging them.

Unlike when he had performed the task himself, Amelia's ministrations had the opposite result. Colin felt as if his testicles were attempting to crawl up inside his body. He pushed her hand away. "Bloody hell, do not do that!"

"That was amazing," she said, with that awed tone that drove him to madness.

Pushed to the edge of reason, Colin rolled over her and settled between her thighs. The makeshift blindfold twisted with his movements, but he caught it quickly and pulled it into place.

"You feel so good." Amelia's small hands moved across his shoulders. "You are so big and hard . . . everywhere."

He heard anxiety in her voice and sought to alleviate it. "I will please you," he promised, supporting his weight on one forearm and reaching low to massage the tender flesh of her cunt with the heel of his other palm. She moaned and rolled her hips into the pressure. "What you felt before is nothing to how it will feel when I am inside you."

Her slender arms wrapped around his neck and pulled him near. "I want that. I want that with you."

"Yes." He licked along the shell of her ear, making her shiver. "You are a sensual woman. It's there in the way you move, the way you look at me, the way you are built."

"I am too slender," she said in a quiet voice.

"You are perfect. Some women are fashioned to suit all men. You were crafted for me alone. My blood runs hot, my passions high; therefore you were made for endurance. Your limbs graceful, but lithe. Your curves lush, but not limiting."

He pushed a finger inside her, testing her soreness. Her answering moan of welcome was all the encouragement he needed. Fisting his straining cock, he positioned the thick head at the tiny slitted entrance to her body. Cum was dribbling from the tip, the shaft too eager and determined to lubricate his way. It wasn't necessary. Amelia was so wet and hot. With the veriest roll of his hips, the fat crown slipped inside her.

"Oh, God . . . !" she breathed, her mouth opening on gasping breaths.

Colin's entire body strained with the pleasure of her grip. The scalding heat inside her swept upward from his cock and over his skin. Sweat misted, then pooled in the small of his back as his back bowed with the effort he maintained to keep his entry slow. She would need time to adjust to his size and the novel intrusion of a man's body into hers.

Amelia's hands caught his hips, and her hips

began a tiny rolling motion that nearly unmanned him.

"Bloody hell!" he gasped, jolting as his seed spurted out in a desperate bid to relieve the torturous pressure in his bollocks.

"I need you deeper," she begged, and he was so grateful for her that he took her mouth in a lush, frantic kiss. Her lips closed around his tongue, sucking it with such fervor his cock swelled in jealousy.

Using his weight, Colin pinned her to the bed, sinking another inch inside her, his hands cupping her face and gentling her ardor.

"Amelia . . ." He groaned and nuzzled his sweat-slick cheek against hers. "You are making it impossible for me to initiate you as you deserve."

"I ache inside," she cried, holding him so tightly. "And you are not there yet."

"You are tiny and untried, and I am thick and hard. If I go too quickly, it will bring you pain now and soreness later."

"You are too big . . ."

"No, damn it all!" He did not want to be surly, but her hungry cunt was tugging on the head of his cock, goading his primitive instincts to take over and leave the gentlemanly ones behind.

"Then let me watch. Perhaps if I can see, I would be less anxious. This moment is too intense without my sight. Every noise, every touch is magnified."

Colin went rigid. Now was not the time, and yet he could not bear for any part of this night to distress her. He was in heaven. He wanted nothing more than for her to be also. "I am afraid of what will happen if you see me now. If you turned me away, I do not think I would survive it."

Her lower lip quivered. Then she asked, "Do you have one of your masks with you?"

"You ask me to withdraw?" He stared down at her with wide eyes. "Are you insane? I am *inside* you."

"Not all the way," she argued. "Not as I need you to be." Her voice took on the pleading, cajoling note that he had never been able to resist.

She would kill him, he realized with an odd mixture of pride and wryness. She would never be passive in the bedroom, just as she had never been passive out of it. He half feared the day when she'd be fully awakened sexually. How would he survive the full assault of her feminine wiles? He wasn't yet buried to the hilt and he felt like he was dying.

"It excites me," she whispered, releasing the stunning statement with panting breaths. "The sight of you in the mask." Her fingers came up and traced the shape of his lips. "You have such a wicked mouth. I have dreamt of it. Longed for it to move across my skin and whisper hot words of wanting."

Shuddering with desire, Colin pushed restlessly into her streaming cunt. She was melting around his cock. Her nipples were hard against his chest, her stomach was quivering against his.

"It would please me to watch you. Do not deny me." Her hands cupped his buttocks and tugged, pulling him fractionally deeper.

She became tighter the deeper he went, her virgin tissues resisting the remolding of her body to fit his.

"Please . . ." she breathed with such heartrending yearning. "Do not leave me in the darkness at this moment in my life."

Cursing, Colin wrenched himself free, his body shaking with its need. He rolled from the bed and stalked on nerveless legs to the armoire where his valise waited. Reaching inside it, he withdrew the mask, which he had kept as a tangible reminder of the stolen moments he had shared with Amelia.

He stared down at the gleaming white item in his hands with a building resentment for its purpose—that of keeping Colin Mitchell away from the woman he loved.

How he wished he would have seen where this deception would lead when he first purchased the mask! One look at Amelia—a sip of water for a man dying of thirst—was all he had expected the ruse to provide.

"Hurry," she urged in the throaty voice of a consummate seductress. The feminine allure so practiced and studied in other women was simply innate to her.

Colin lifted the half mask to his face and tied the black satin ribbons that would hold it in place, then retied the ribbon that restrained his queue. Turning his head, he looked at her and knew he would not leave this room as the same man who had entered it.

She reclined against the piled pillows, her legs and arms crossed modestly, the blindfold gone. In her verdant gaze he saw lust, longing, and appreciation of such magnitude that he could scarcely breathe.

Pivoting on his heel, he faced her directly, affording her a clear view of his raging cock and taut musculature. He watched her swallow hard and understood how intimidating the sight of him must be. She was a tall woman, but he was still much taller. He was more than twice her size, his body hardened by both his common lineage and frequent physical activity.

And he was in full rut. Thick veins pulsed with his raging blood, and he fisted the shaft to ease the pain of it.

"Does the sight of me this way arouse you," he asked, "or frighten you?"

Amelia licked her lips. "I am not frightened," she whispered. "I am nervous and perhaps apprehensive, but I do not fear you."

"You are a strong woman," he praised, striding swiftly toward her.

Without preliminaries, he kneeled on the bed and climbed over her, tugging her arm out of the way so he could claim a nipple with his mouth. He attended the stiff peak with hard, rhythmic suction, urging her silently to make some sound of her delight.

Her hands cupped the back of his head and held him to her breast. "Come inside me," she whispered. "I hate this feeling of uncertainty and ignorance."

Sitting back on his heels, Colin pulled her legs over either side of his own, spreading her thighs wide to expose her cunt to his gaze. With the angle of the pillows and her semireclined position, she had a clear view. Before she could register the size of her tiny pink slit compared to the girth and length of his cock, he was in her, pushing the thick head into the tender opening.

She whimpered and dug her nails into his thighs.

Holding her hips, he took her, rocking gently but relentlessly deeper and deeper. His gaze moved between the place of their joining and her beautiful face.

With his back shadowing her from the rapidly dwindling glow of the fading fire, he could not discern color, but he saw the telltale shimmer of sweat on her brow, and her eyes glistened with a sheen of tears.

"Am I hurting you?" he gasped, his fingers bruising her as she responded to his voice by rippling along the buried length of his cock. She was so damn tight and hot, it felt as if he were fucking into a tightly closed fist.

"No . . ." Her voice was thready and faraway sounding.

Colin lifted one of her hands from his skin and set it over her distended clitoris. "Stroke yourself," he instructed.

To his utter delight she obliged without embarrassment, her long, slender fingers circling the slick flesh with only slight hesitation.

Her lovely cunt responded as he had known it would, clenching and grasping at him with renewed fervor. With every suck, he pushed deeper, groaning with the ecstasy of it, gulping in desperate breaths of air filled with the scents of sex and honeysuckle.

She began to writhe and mewl in a show of such wanton craving, he would wonder later how he managed to work inside her completely without coming at the midway point. Finally, with a last desperate lunge, he hit the end of her, the sensation of being balls-deep inside her enough to make his eyes tear.

Amelia cried out as Montoya's hot, heavy length finally struck deep. A flare of torturous relief spread outward from the aching spot inside her that begged to be rubbed, and then coiled tight again.

When he held still, she struggled, circling her hips, grinding against the root of his shaft. The growl that left him was more animal than human, and her body shivered in response, spurred to greater lust by the sound.

He held her still with powerful hands, his gaze burning from within the eyeholes of the mask. His beautiful mouth was hard, his jaw taut.

"Why won't you move?" she cried.

"Because I am about to blow, and I refuse to go without you."

"I am ready!" Her voice was high with her distress, her womb clenching and tightening in a way that was nearly painful.

With effortless strength, he scooped her up and lifted to his knees, impaling her deeper on the rock-hard length of his cock. Amelia clung to his broad shoulders, her mouth suckling across the salty, whisker-roughened expanse of his throat. The room spun as he rearranged their positions, every movement sliding her over him until she bit him in retaliation for her sexual frustration.

Montoya cursed and pushed her away from him.

"Ride," he said roughly.

He sat on the edge of the bed, her legs astride his, his erection buried deep. So deep. Canting his arms back, he supported his torso and gave her full access to use him as she willed. The display he made was searingly erotic, his abdomen laced tight with muscle, his furred chest damp with sweat.

And the mask. Dear God, the mask added a dark, alluring mystery that urged her to recklessness.

"I—"

"Now!" he barked, making her jump.

Her shoulders went back and her chin lifted in answer to his challenge. She thought this must be difficult for him for reasons she had not considered before. He made love with the expertise of a man who had his choice of women, which suggested the marring of his face might have been a recent event. Perhaps she was the first woman to welcome him to her bed since the injury was inflicted. The thought added poignancy to an already remarkable event.

Amelia decided in that moment that she would love him well, with all that she had, better than any other woman ever could. She would reach for the turmoil she sensed inside him and soothe it with her passion, showing him with her body that it was his heart that lured her to him.

Setting her hands on his shoulders for balance, she pushed onto her knees and lifted, sliding her sex upward along the length of him. When she lowered, the feel of the broad head of his cock stroking over that quivering spot inside her made her gasp and shake violently.

"That's it," he praised in a dark whisper, watching her through thick black lashes. "See how well I fit you? I was made for your pleasure."

Biting her lower lip, she repeated the movement, venturing slowly as she found the way of it. Her thumb brushed across a scar that marred his shoulder, the wound so old, it had long since turned silver. She caressed it as she undulated, feeling the circular shape surrounded by ragged edges. In the back of her mind the injury bothered her, prodded at her . . .

Then he spoke, and everything else scattered from her mind.

"Sweet Amelia. You are mine."

Amelia rose and wrapped her arms around his torso, tilting her head to fit her mouth over his, lifting and falling, moaning at the feel of her swollen nipples brushing across the light dusting of coarse hair on his chest.

Claiming him as he claimed her.

Montoya thrust one hand into her tresses, holding her close as he murmured encouragement into her mouth, his hips circling beneath her in breathtaking thrusts, stealing her wits.

Stealing her heart.

As she gained confidence, she moved faster, breathing hard from her exertions, drops of sweat trickling down between her bouncing breasts.

"I want you this way daily." His words were heavy, slurred with pleasure. "I want you to feel empty when I am not inside you. Hungry. Starved for me."

Amelia knew it would be that way. She was mindless with lust, grinding, writhing, pumping onto his thick, straining erection as if she had done this before. As if she knew what she was doing.

His teeth nipped her throat and she cried out, everything clenching inside her until he cursed from the feel of it.

He was driving her to this madness—with his big body reclined, his eyes heavy-lidded behind the mask, his lips glistening from her mouth. He looked like a pagan sex god. Exotically beautiful. Endlessly controlled. Content to lie back and be pleasured by a wanton whose sole focus was the pursuit of orgasm.

With her lips against his cheek, she whispered, "Fuck me," surprising herself with how easily the crude word rolled off her tongue.

A brutal shudder wracked Montoya's frame in response.

"Make me *come*," she coaxed breathlessly, riding him still. "I want it . . . I want *you*. Wild. Deep. I need you with me—"

Before she could blink, he had twisted, pinning her to the bed. Feet on the floor and fists in the counterpane, he drove powerfully into her, every perfect downstroke wrenching a cry of rapture from her throat.

He loomed over her, watching her through the mask, his chest heaving, his abdomen lacing, his buttocks clenching beneath her calves as she lifted to meet his every plunge. His body was a study in sexual power. Built to fuck a woman into addiction.

The coiling tension in her womb tightened, forming a hard knot that made her head thrash against the brutal pleasure. And then it broke free in a riot of sensation, burning across her skin, seiz-

ing her lungs, spasming inside her in endless rapid
ripples that worshipped his straining cock.

The guttural roar that ripped from his throat
brought tears to her eyes and a name to her lips.
He paused in midstroke, rigid, and she mewled a
protest, undulating beneath him in delirious pleasure.

He resumed, increasing the strength and speed
of his thrusts until he swelled inside her, groaning
through gritted teeth. Embedded in her to the deepest point, his body jerked in time to the hot, thick
wash of his ejaculations inside her.

It was savage and primitive and beautiful. He
curled around her, his weight supported on his
forearms beneath her back, his skin sticking to
hers with their mingled sweat.

"I love you," he whispered ardently, his tongue
licking the trails of her tears. "I love you."

Amelia reached for the ribbons that secured the
mask.

Chapter 11

It was dark in the room, the banked fire incapable of casting a shadow more than a foot away from the grate. Sight was difficult, and yet Simon's instincts urged him to heed their warning.

Moving cautiously, he turned his head and found the space in the bed beside him to be empty. He exhaled carefully, maintaining the deep, even rhythm of sleep.

Something had woken him, and since he was sleeping with a woman who would kill him if necessary, he knew ignoring the disturbance would not be wise.

He looked toward the window and saw the gleam of silver moonlight on strands of golden hair. Lysette had the drapes parted a scant inch or two and was presently staring out the window.

"What are you doing?" he whispered, sitting up.

Her head might have turned toward him, but he could not be sure.

"I heard noises outside."

"What do you see?"

The curtain closed. "Three riders. One went inside briefly, I assume to wake the innkeeper. Then they continued on."

Shivering, Simon threw off the covers and moved to the grate. "I doubt anyone would go to such trouble for directions at this time of night."

"My thoughts exactly."

"Could you hear them? Were they French?"

There was a brief flare of light as she lit a match; then the wick of a single taper took over the illumination. "I think they were English."

He frowned into the flickering fire. "Perhaps I should wake Maria."

"No need. They rode forward, not backward. Whatever they are looking for, it has yet to be found."

As heat began to radiate outward from the grate, Simon stood and faced Lysette. She looked tired, and a crease marred the side of her lovely face. She wore her cloak over her chemise and clutched it to her chest with white-knuckled fingers.

He gestured toward the bed. "Fine. Let's go back to sleep. I am still sore from that blasted carriage and could use a bit more time on my back instead of my arse."

Lysette nodded wearily and sank into the chair she had been reading in earlier. *"Bonne nuit."*

"Bloody hell." Scowling, he asked, "Did you fall asleep there?"

She blinked up at him. *"Oui."*

"On purpose?"

"Oui."

Simon ran a hand through his hair and prayed

for patience. "I do not bite or snore or drool. I mean no offense when I say that I have no interest in tumbling you. The bed is perfectly safe."

"The bed may be," she said, watching him impassively, "but I have some doubts as to whether you are."

He opened his mouth to argue, then threw up his hands. "Bah! Rot in the chair, then."

Freezing, he hurried back to the bed and crawled between now-cooled linens. Curling into a ball, he prayed the warmth of the renewed fire would reach the bed soon.

"Curse you," he grumbled, glaring down the length of the bed at her. "It would be much warmer if there were two of us in here."

"You have more reason to want me dead than alive," she pointed out in a far too reasonable tone.

"At this moment, truer words were never spoken," he snapped. "The only reason I am not strangling you is because killing you would rob me of your body heat!"

Her pretty lips thinned primly.

"This is ridiculous, Lysette." He sat up, too frustrated to even attempt sleep. The impracticality of sleeping in the cramped wing chair after a long day of travel was so out of character for her. She was faultlessly practical, as was everyone who lived by their wits. "Why would I kill you now, when I have not before?"

She shrugged, but the way her gaze darted nervously belied the careless gesture.

Heaving out a long-suffering sigh, Simon once again tossed back the covers and stalked toward her. When she wielded a knife from between the edges of her cloak, he was not surprised.

"Put that away."

"Stay back."

"I am not attracted to you," he reiterated slowly. "And even if I was, I have no need to force myself on an unwilling woman."

Lysette frowned suspiciously. "I am fine in the chair."

"Liar. You look exhausted, and I cannot afford to drag you along while I attempt to clear Mitchell's name. You must carry your own weight."

She bristled at that. "I will not be a burden."

"Damned if you won't after a night spent sleepless and frozen. You will become ill and useless."

Pushing to her feet, she said, "I can take care of myself. Go back to bed and leave me in peace!"

Simon opened his mouth to argue further, then shook his head instead. He once again climbed between the sheets and turned his back toward the other side of the bed. A few moments later, the taper was extinguished. Shortly afterward he heard delicate snoring.

Faced with a deepening puzzle, Simon lay awake for some time.

Amelia studied the masked man in repose beside her and wondered how deeply he slept.

"We will wait until the sunrise to remove it," Montoya had said earlier.

"Why not now?" she countered, desperate to see beneath the now intrusive barrier. Her heart was smitten and her body no longer innocent. But what they shared could be no more than infatuation—it could not be love—if she did not see all sides of him.

"I want nothing to mar this evening," he had explained, withdrawing from her body and moving to the washstand behind the screen in the corner. He'd returned with a damp cloth and washed between her thighs, then cleansed himself before joining her in the bed. "In the morning, I will bare myself to you, strengthened by the memories of a blissful, perfect night in your arms."

In the end, she had reluctantly agreed, unwilling to be at odds with him over the matter of a few hours.

With his back to the headboard and her body curved to his side, he had asked her to share a beloved memory from her past. She had chosen a tale about Colin, relating how she had conquered her fear of heights by climbing a tree during a game of hide-and-seek.

"He passed below me several times," she said, her cheek resting over Montoya's heart. "I half hoped he would find me quickly, because it was frightening clinging to that limb, but the desire to surprise him was too great to give myself away."

His hand caressed up and down the length of her back. "You wanted to win," he corrected, laughing that low, deep laugh she had adored from the moment she heard it.

"That, too." She smiled. "When he finally forfeited, I was so pleased with myself. Colin spent his allowance on a new ribbon to mark the conquering of that fear."

Montoya sighed. "He must have loved you a great deal."

"I think he did, although he never told me. I would have given anything to hear those words from him." Her fingers sifted through the hair on his chest.

"Actions speak louder than words."

"I tell myself that. I still have that ribbon. It is one of my greatest treasures."

"What do you imagine your life would have been like now, if you two had never been parted?"

Lifting her head, she'd met his questioning gaze. "I have imagined it in hundreds of scenarios. The most likely one, I think, would be that St. John would have taken Colin under his wing."

"Would you be married?"

"I have always hoped so. But that would depend upon him."

"He would have asked you," Montoya said with conviction.

Amelia smiled. "What leads you to be so certain?"

"He loved you deeply. I have no doubt. You were simply too young for him at the time, and he was not in a position to offer for you." He brushed the backs of his fingers along her cheekbone. "Do you love him still?"

She hesitated, wondering at the wisdom of confessing a lingering affection for one man while warming the bed of another.

"Always tell me the truth," he urged softly, "and you will never be wrong."

"Part of me will love him forever. He helped to

mold me into the person I am today. He is weaved into the very fabric of my life."

Montoya had kissed her then, sweetly and with deep reverence. Breathless and enamored, she asked him to share a part of his past with her, expecting that he might speak of his lost love. He did not.

He chose to speak of his livelihood and the dangerous work he had done for the Crown of England. He shared how he'd traveled the length and breadth of the Continent, never having a true home or family, until the day he sought to resign and was instead embroiled in a life-threatening intrigue.

"That is why I attempted to maintain my distance from you," he said. "I did not want to taint your life with my mistakes."

"Is that how your face was scarred?" she asked, her fingertips lightly following the edge of the mask where it touched his skin.

He went rigid. "Beg your pardon?"

Instantly contrite for having distressed him, Amelia rushed to say, "I can understand your fear, but your disfigurement will not alter my affection for you."

"Amelia . . ." He seemed at a loss for words.

The conversation had died then, and they had simply clung to each other as Montoya fell asleep. She remained awake, her mind shifting through a multitude of thoughts. She planned what to say to Ware and Maria and mentally rehearsed how she would ask St. John for his assistance. She catalogued the various aches and pains that heralded her new awareness as a woman and speculated on how her relationship with Montoya would proceed once they were freed from all the unknowns that plagued them. She also wondered at her outrageous behavior of the last week and what it meant.

Only Maria truly understood what a monster Lord Welton was. That his blood ran through Amelia's veins made her ill at times. Externally, she was clearly his issue. Was she also like her father in ways she could not see? It was terrifying to realize that everything she had done these last few days had been selfishly motivated. She had disregarded the feelings and concerns of those who cared for her—Ware, Maria, and St. John—in favor of her desire to be with Montoya. Was she truly her father's daughter?

Amelia gazed into the licking flames and thought of the mask, ruminating about the man beneath it. The urge to peek beneath the guise was pressing. She tried to excuse the action with the reasoning that it was the mystery of his identity that had goaded her to act so rashly, not a defect in her character.

But what if Montoya was a light sleeper? What if he caught her and became angry? She dreaded the thought of exchanging furious words.

Perhaps she could test the depth of his slumber in some way . . . ?

Her hand lifted from the hard expanse of his abdomen, and her fingertips ran lightly along his thigh. The muscle twitched, but he made no other movement. Amelia tried again, caressing him with deeper pressure. This time, he moved not at all.

She became hopeful. He had loved her long and well, and extended journeys were known to make many a traveler weary.

Raising her head, her gaze roamed admiringly over the sculpted beauty of his chest. The scar on his shoulder was more visible now, the room lightened considerably by the fire Montoya had stoked into a hearty blaze to banish the pervasive chill. She studied the bullet hole with sympathy, guessing by the size and many radiating lines that it had been a nasty wound.

She kissed the evidence of injury, her lips brushing feather-light over the damaged flesh. The tempo of his breathing changed, and his nipples tightened while she watched in awe.

How fascinating the human body was. Tonight she had learned so much about her own. Amelia felt the sudden urge to know everything about his.

With the memories of his lovemaking still fresh and burning in her mind, she extended her tongue and licked across the tiny bead of darkened flesh. His skin was salty, the texture firmer than hers. She loved it, as she was beginning to love all of him.

Mimicking his earlier ministrations to her breasts, Amelia wrapped her lips around his nipple and sucked gently. He stirred, but not in the way she had anticipated.

Her thigh was draped over his, her knee bent and leg raised. As his cock swelled, she felt it, and she turned her head to see the thickening outline of his erection beneath the bedclothes. Her blood heated and began to move sluggishly. More surprising yet, her mouth watered.

She glanced at his face beneath lowered lashes. In the shadows of the eyeholes he appeared to be sleeping, with no telltale shimmer from liquid eyes to betray his cognizance.

Did she dare to explore further?

Her curiosity raging, she did not debate the question long. She slid downward, pulling the counterpane with her, eventually exposing his glorious cock to her avid gaze.

"You play with fire, love."

Montoya's voice startled her. She looked up at him and found him watching her with slumberous, burning eyes.

"How long have you been awake?" she asked.

"I've yet to fall asleep." His wicked mouth curved, revealing his dimple.

"Why did you keep your silence?"

"I wanted to see how far you would go." His hand lifted, his fingertips catching and caressing a stray curl of her hair. "Curious kitten," he murmured.

"Do you mind?"

"Never. Your touch is vital to me."

Considering that permission to proceed, she returned her attention to his erection. Amelia ran one fingertip from tip to root and smiled when it jerked at her touch.

"I find it astonishing that you fit in me," she confessed.

Remembering the rapturous feel of her cunt around his cock, Colin could not find the voice to reply. He was ferociously aroused and leashing himself by sheer will alone. When she'd begun to touch him, he had thought it by chance. Then she'd lifted her head and branded him forever with the feel of her lips upon the wound that had nearly killed him. It was the gunshot that had separated them so many years ago. The shot he'd taken while trying to save her.

Amelia slid lower still, stopping at eye level with his groin and leaving a trail of moisture along his leg. The evidence that the mere sight of his body was enough to arouse her to slickness made his bollocks tighten, forcing a perfect bead of semen to grace the tip of his cock.

His lungs seized as she eyed it hungrily. Would she be so bold?

A heartbeat later the question was answered as her tongue darted out and licked the droplet away.

Colin exhaled harshly at the whiplash of pleasure.

She studied him with narrowed eyes, a look he had come to know well over the years. It was a calculated glance, one she gave when considering how to tackle a challenge he presented. He smiled, understanding that she never sought to best him, only to equal him and be his match.

"You never answered me before," she said, circling the base of his cock with her thumb and forefinger. "Does a woman's mouth feel so different from her quim?"

"Yes."

"In what way?"

"In many ways. A cunt hugs every inch of a cock. It expands and contracts in ripples, and it is as soft as the finest silk. In contrast, a woman's mouth hugs through suction, not design. The pad of the tongue is textured and the muscle is agile. It can stroke like a finger, which stimulates the sensitive spot"—he pointed to the place on the underside of his cockhead—"here."

"Which do you prefer?" Her grip slid upward, then down again, making his teeth clench.

"Both have unique pleasures."

"That is not an answer," she murmured, caressing him again.

"It is difficult to think when you are fondling me," he managed.

She ceased and waited impatiently for him to gather his wits.

"My preference changes with my mood. There will be occasions when I will want to lose myself in you. I will want to hold you close and feel your body moving beneath mine. I will want to suck on your nipples and feast at your mouth. I will want to watch your face as you orgasm and hold you in the aftermath."

As he spoke he felt her grow wetter, hotter against the flesh of his leg. His voice deepened in response. "At other times, I will want to be serviced. I will want to lose myself to the pleasure in a way I cannot when I must see to your needs as well. The sight of your supplication will satisfy the primitive male in me, while my surrender to your care will be complete. I will be helpless and open, completely at your mercy."

The smile she gave him was impish. "I should like that."

"You might, or you might not. Many women do

not. They fail to see the power in the act. They feel demeaned and used. Others simply do not like the taste of a man's seed."

"Hmm . . ."

He knew that hum and its portent. She wanted to know which type of woman she would be. Sadly, they had run out of time.

"We must dress you and return you safely to your room before you are seen. When the hour is appropriate to protect your reputation, we will meet and I will bare myself to you—my face and my secrets."

"I am not finished with you," she complained with a seductive pout that hardened him to full, raging arousal.

"It will be with exquisite pleasure that I offer myself to your sexual experimentation, love," he said hoarsely. "But such play requires time free of interruptions. We do not have the luxury tonight."

"You speak of our future liaisons with such surety," Amelia said, staring at his cock and resuming her ministrations.

Colin set his hand over hers and stilled her movements. "I cannot think otherwise and advise you not to either."

"But you have not made your intentions known."

Fueled by heady lust and burning possessiveness, he promised, "My intention is to tear down everything that stands between us. Then I want to woo you properly, with great fanfare. I want to dazzle you with extravagance, and lay the world at your feet." His thumb caressed the back of her hand. "Then, when every recessed corner of your heart is filled with love for me, I will wed you."

He loved her. He could not imagine never having her, not after this night. Yet he could make her no promises with a price on his head.

Despite this, at the pinnacle of the orgasm of his life, he had pressed against her womb and emptied his seed inside her. He no longer had any time. The clock was ticking.

Colin watched her lovely face and could not guess her thoughts. "Amelia?"

She laid her cheek upon his thigh. "Do not wait until life meets some inner criteria to seize the day," she whispered. "I have learned that sometimes tomorrow never comes."

Her melancholy cut him, and he held his arms out to her, groaning his pleasure when she draped her nude body over his. Sexual desire simmered into the more complicated need to cling to something precious, yet unsecured.

Dawn approached, but neither was capable of releasing the other.

Chapter 12

It was a knock that woke her. At first groggy with the remnants of sleep, Maria took a moment to recognize her surroundings. Then the memories of the day before and the long, sleepless night rushed back in a deluge. She sat up abruptly, tossed back the covers, and rushed to the door.

"Christopher!" With joy, she flung herself into her husband's arms, and he crushed her to him, lifting her feet from the floor and stepping into the room.

"How did you find me so quickly?" she asked, as he kicked the portal closed behind him.

"It would have been quicker, damn you, if you had stayed in one of my inns and not this hovel! Why the devil are you here?"

"Simon insisted." She had tried to suggest they use one of the many homes Christopher owned across the entire length and breadth of the country. They were not grand. They were small cottages, inhabited by those who lived off pensions provided by St. John. The homes were safe, comfortable, and usually located in quiet corners where few questions were asked and fewer visitors came by. Nicknamed "inns" for both the accurate description of the service provided and also for the anonymity afforded by so generic a name, they were responsible for saving many lives.

"Damn him, too," Christopher said. Then he took her mouth, his head tilting to fit his lips to hers.

When she was limp and breathless, he muttered, "Vexing wench. Why must you torment me by being so troublesome?"

"This is not my doing!" she protested, tossing his hat aside.

"Damned if it isn't." He carried her to the bed and tossed her upon it, his gaze heating at the sight of her clad in only a chemise. Shrugging out of his fawn-colored coat, he said, "If you had not indulged Amelia in her fancy, we would not be taxed with chasing her, and I would not have spent the frigid night in a carriage."

"She would have gone alone, I know it." Maria crawled beneath the covers.

Christopher rebuilt the fire. Then he discarded his waistcoat, removed his boots, and climbed into bed with her, wearing his breeches and shirt-sleeves.

"Tell me how you found me with such haste," she said, curling into his side.

"When Sam returned with the news of where you had gone, he mentioned Quinn. I sent men to find his lodgings, and when they discovered where he was staying, they found his valet packing. I followed him and he led me here."

Frowning, Maria lifted her head. "How is that possible? We had no notion that we would be staying at this establishment until we chanced upon it."

"Quinn must have known. His valet and the abigail of his French companion came directly to this place. You did say he insisted."

"He insisted we stay near the road." But, now that she thought of it, she remembered that it was Simon who'd begged that they take shelter at the first inn they came to just before Reading. She had protested the sorry appearance of the lodging, but he had complained of a sore arse and growling stomach.

"I do not understand." She sat up and faced her reclining spouse. "Our meeting in the shop was unplanned, I am certain of it. Even if I were wrong about that, there was no way for Simon to know Amelia would run off as she did."

"But, if he knew who Amelia was chasing and where the man might be headed . . ." Christopher's words faded, leaving her to draw her own conclusions.

"He told me they were already intent on a holiday, yet you say his valet and belongings were not yet ready. Why the ruse? Why pretend to help me, when he had his own motives for following?"

"We will have to ask him those questions in a few hours, when we rise."

"A few hours?!"

He yawned and tugged her back into his arms. "His room is guarded, and the hour is still relatively early. I sent riders ahead to follow the trail. There is nothing pressing that cannot wait the duration of a much-needed nap. I require some sleep this morn or I will be useless the rest of the day. Besides—and you must forgive me for pointing this out—you do not look rested either."

Maria settled into her husband's embrace with lingering reluctance. She was a woman who acted swiftly. Doing so had kept her alive. "I cannot sleep well without you near," she confessed.

He hugged her tighter and pressed a kiss to her forehead. "It pleases me to hear that."

"I must have become accustomed to your snoring."

His head lifted. "I do not snore!"

"How would you know? You are asleep when you do it."

"Someone would have mentioned it to me before now," he argued.

"Perhaps you exhausted them so that they slept right through it."

Growling, he rolled and pinned her beneath him. She blinked up at him with mock innocence. No one dared to tease the fearsome pirate, except for her. Goading his ire was a delicious temptation she could not resist, because the more she agitated him, the more sexually focused he became.

"If you need exhausting, madam," he bit out, reaching between them to unfasten his breeches, "I am more than capable of managing that task."

"You said you were useless and required a nap."

He shoved up the hem of her chemise and cupped her sex in his hand. Instantly, she was wet for him. Hot and creamy with desire. She moaned as he stroked her, and he smiled arrogantly, pulling away to position his cock.

"Does this feel useless to you?" he purred, pushing the hard length into her.

"Oh, Christopher," she breathed, awash in heated delight. After nearly six years of marriage, her ardor for him had not lessened one bit. "I love you so. Please don't fall asleep before I come . . ."

"You will pay for that," he said in a voice slurred with pleasure.

He made certain she did. And it was wonderful.

Colin was rinsing off his razor when a stray noise caught his attention and arrested his movements. He listened carefully, his nerves already stretched by the upcoming confrontation.

Amelia had returned to her chamber some time ago, but he doubted she slept. She was too curious, too impatient by nature. Knowing her as well as he did, he imagined she paced her room and glanced repeatedly at the clock, counting down the minutes to the time when he would reveal his identity to her.

There. It came again. The perceptible sound of scratching at the door.

Setting his blade on the washstand, he grabbed a cloth and was drying his face when his valet opened the door. Jacques entered bearing a grim expression.

"Miss Benbridge has been found, *mon ami.*"

Colin stilled. "By whom?"

"Riders this morning. They spoke with the giant who came with her and then turned about."

Heaving out his breath, Colin nodded. "Did you arrange the private dining room as I requested?"

"*Mais oui.*"

"Thank you. I will be down in a moment."

The door shut with a quiet click, and Colin hastened his toilette. He had promised Amelia an explanation, and he intended to give it to her without interruption.

Nodding to his valet, he presented his back and shrugged into the coat he had selected that morning. It was a striking garment, reminiscent of a male peacock's beautiful plumage. The cost of the intricately embroidered ensemble, which included breeches and silver-threaded waistcoat, was obvious. The Colin Mitchell who Amelia remembered so fondly would never have been able to purchase clothing so expensive. He wore it now as an outward display of his rise in the world. His dream of becoming a man capable of affording her was now a reality, and he wanted her to see that straightaway.

Suitably attired and inwardly certain, Colin left his bedchamber and took the stairs to the main room. It took only a moment to find the large man who had accompanied Amelia. The giant sat with his back to the wall and his eyes trained on his surroundings. As Colin approached him, the man's gaze sharpened with examining intensity.

"Good morning," Colin greeted, coming to a halt directly before the table.

"Morning," came the deep, rumbling reply.

"I am Count Montoya."

"I gathered as much."

"There is much I need to explain to her. Will you give me the time and opportunity to do so?"

The man pursed his lips and leaned back his chair. "What do you 'ave in mind?"

"I have reserved the private dining room. I will

keep the door ajar, but I beg you to remain outside."

The man pushed to his feet, towering over Colin's not inconsiderable height. "That will suit both me and my blade."

Colin nodded and stepped aside, but as the giant moved to pass him, he said, "Please give her this."

He handed over the items in his hand. After a brief pause, they were taken from him. Colin waited until Amelia's guard had ascended the stairs; then he moved to the private dining room and mentally prepared for the most difficult conversation of his life.

The moment Maria entered the main room of the inn, Simon knew he was in trouble. She bore the glow of a woman well fucked, but if that had not given away the end of his gambit, her change of clothes would have. Confirmation came when Christopher St. John entered the space a few steps behind his wife.

"What a lovely way to begin the day," Lysette said with laughter in her voice. Much as he usually detested her enjoyment of drama, today it was a relief after her odd behavior the night before.

Simon heaved a resigned sigh and pushed to his feet.

"Good morning," he greeted, bowing to the striking couple. The combination of St. John's golden coloring and Maria's Spanish blood was an attractive one.

"Quinn," St. John said.

"Simon," Maria murmured. She lowered into

the chair her husband held out for her and linked her hands primly atop the table. "You know the identity of the man behind the mask. Who is he?"

Resuming his seat, Simon said, "He is Count Reynaldo Montoya. He was in my employ for several years."

"Was?" the pirate asked. "No longer?"

Simon related the events with Cartland.

"Dear God," Maria breathed, her dark eyes wide with horror. "When Amelia said the man was in danger, I never imagined it would be to this degree. Why did you not tell me? Why the lie?"

"It is complicated, Maria," he said, hating that he had betrayed the trust she bestowed so rarely. "I am not at liberty to divulge Montoya's secrets. He has saved my life many times over. I owe him at least my silence."

"What of my sister?" she cried. "You know how much she means to me. To know that she was at risk and not warn me . . ." Her voice broke. "I believed you and I were closer than that."

St. John reached over and clasped his wife's hand. The gesture of comfort pained Simon deeply. Out of all the women in the world, Maria was the dearest to him.

"I wanted to help you find her and then send her to safety with you," Simon said, "leaving Montoya and I to finish this business."

Maria's gaze narrowed in her fury. It radiated from her, belying the girlish image created by her delicate floral gown. "You should have told me, Simon. If I had known, I would have managed the situation far differently."

"Yes," he agreed. "You would have tasked dozens

of men with the search, which would have alerted Cartland and put her at greater risk."

"You do not know that!" she argued.

"I know *him*. He worked for me. I know all his strengths. Finding lost people and items is his forte. Lackeys scouring the countryside would attract the attention of a simpleton, and Cartland is far from that!"

It was the pirate's raspy drawl that cut through the building tension. "How do you signify, Mademoiselle Rousseau?"

Lysette waved one delicate hand carelessly. "I am the judge."

"And the executioner, if need be," Simon grumbled.

St. John's brows rose. "Fascinating."

Maria pushed back from the table and stood. Simon and St. John stood as well.

"I have wasted enough time here," she snapped. "I must find Amelia before anyone else does."

"Allow me to come with you," Simon asked. "I can help."

"You have helped quite enough, thank you!"

"Lysette witnessed three riders making inquiries in the dead of night." Simon's tone was grim. "You need all the assistance you can muster. Amelia's safety lies within your purview, but Cartland and Montoya lie within mine."

"And mine," Lysette interjected. "I do not understand why we do not contact the man you work for here in England. He would seem to be an untapped, valuable resource."

"St. John likely has a larger, more reliable web of

associates," Simon argued. "One more swiftly galvanized into action."

"Maria." St. John set his hand at the small of her back. "Quinn knows the appearances of both men. We do not. We would be blind without him."

She looked at Simon again. "Why does Montoya wear the mask?"

Careful to keep his face impassive, Simon used the excuse that Colin gave him. "He wore the mask for the masquerade. Later, he wore it to make it more difficult for Miss Benbridge to pursue him. He did not want to jeopardize her. He cares for her."

Maria lifted her hand to stem anything else he might say.

"We have an added complication," the pirate said. All eyes turned to him. "Lord Ware may follow."

"You jest!" Maria cried.

"Who is Lord Ware?" Lysette asked.

"Bloody hell," Simon muttered. "The last thing we require is the injury of a peer."

"He asked to accompany me," St. John said grimly. "But the departure of Quinn's valet made waiting impossible. Still, he asked for direction, and while I was deliberately vague in hopes that he would reconsider, he may prove more tenacious than other men of his station."

Maria exhaled sharply. "Even more reason to keep moving, then."

"I sent the town carriage back to London," the pirate said. "Pietro is loading the travel coach as we speak. We should make better time."

Simon, unfortunately, did not have a change of

equipage, but his bruised arse would have to make do.

With the sunrise lighting their way, they hastened toward Reading.

The moment the knock came to her bedroom door, Amelia ran to open it.

"Tim!" she cried, startled at the sight of her visitor and not very pleased. Perhaps he intended for them to leave now, which would necessitate her explaining about Montoya and her deception of the night before.

He took one look at her wild hair and disarrayed clothing and cursed with a viciousness that made her wince. "You lied to me last night!" he accused, pushing his way inside.

She blinked. How did he know?

Then she saw the items in his hand, and the answer to the question lost importance. "Let me see," she said, her heart racing at the possibilities. Tim had the mask. How? Why?

Tim stared at her for a long, taut moment, then offered her the mask and the missive with it.

My love,
    You have the mask. When next you see me, I will not be wearing it.
    Your servant,
    M

The sudden realization that Montoya could have fled after she departed made her feel ill.

"Dear God," she gasped, clutching the mask to her chest. "Is he gone?"

He shook his head. "'E waits for you downstairs."

"I must go to him."

Amelia hurried to the untouched bed where her corset and underskirts awaited donning. Montoya hadn't the time to dress her completely. His fear for her discovery in his room had driven him to haste. She had hoped to ask a chambermaid for help, but Tim would have to manage the task.

"I think you should wait until St. John comes," he said. "'E's on 'is way now."

"No," she breathed, pausing in midmovement. Her time with Montoya was too precious. The addition of her sister and brother-in-law would only add to the confusion she felt. "I must speak with him alone."

"You've already been alone with 'im," he barked, shooting a pointed glance at the untouched bed. "St. John will 'ave my 'ead for that. I don't need to give 'im any more to be angry o'er."

"You do not understand. I have yet to see Montoya's face. You cannot expect me to face such a revelation with witnesses who are in foul temper." She held a shaking hand out to him.

He stared at it for a long moment with his jaw clenched tight and his fists clenched tighter. "A moment ago, I admired 'im for seeking me out. Now I want to rip 'im to pieces. *'E should not have touched you.*"

"I wanted him," she said with tears in her eyes. "I pushed him. I was selfish and cared only about my own desires."

Just as her father would have done, curse him. And curse his blood which tainted her. Everything around her was in disarray because she could think only of herself.

"Don't cry!" Tim complained, looking miserable.

His discomfort was her fault. Somehow, she had to make everything right. The starting point was Montoya, as he was the pivotal figure who had begun this descent into madness.

"I have to go to him before they arrive." She shrugged out of her unfastened gown, wiggled into her corset, and presented her back. "I shall need your assistance to dress."

Tim muttered something as he stalked toward her, and by the glower he wore, she thought herself fortunate to have missed it.

"I think I'll wed Sarah after all," he growled, yanking on her stays so tightly, she lost her ability to breathe. "I'm too old fer this."

Gasping and lacking the air required to speak, she swatted at him to fix it. He scowled, then appeared to notice that she was about to faint, and why. He grumbled an apology and loosened the tapes.

"I 'ope yer 'appy," he snapped. "You've driven me to the altar!"

Amelia pulled on her underskirts. After Tim tied them to her, she caught up her dress from where it pooled on the floor and thrust her arms into the sleeves.

Tim's thick fingers fumbled with the tiny buttons that secured the gown.

"I love you." She looked over her shoulder. "I do

not know if I have ever told you that, but it's true. You are a good man."

The flush of his skin spoke volumes.

"'E'd best marry you, if that's what you want," he said gruffly, his gaze on his task. "Otherwise, I'll string 'im up and gut 'im like a fish."

It was some sort of peace offering, and she accepted it gratefully. "I would help you, if it came to that."

He snorted, but a quick glance over her shoulder revealed a wry curve to his lips. "'E doesn't know what trouble 'e's got 'imself into with you."

Amelia shifted impatiently. "I pray we can keep the man alive long enough to show him."

The moment Tim announced he was done, she pulled on stockings and shoes, and rushed toward the door. As she took the stairs with all the decorum she could muster, her breath shortened until she felt dizzy.

The next moments of her life would alter the future forever; she felt it in her bones. The feeling of portent was so strong, she was almost inclined to flee, but could not. She needed Montoya with a depth and strength she had thought she would never feel again. Part of her heart screamed silently at the betrayal of her first, dear love for Colin. The other half was older, wiser and understood that affection for one did not negate the affection she felt for the other.

Her hand shook as she reached for the doorknob of the private dining room. In the best of circumstances she would be nervous. She was about to face the man who had seen her and touched her in ways no one else ever had. The added tension brought on by the revealing of his face only deepened her disquiet and concern.

Taking a deep, shaky breath, Amelia knocked.

"Come in."

Before she lost her courage, she entered with as confident a stride as she could affect. She paused just inside, taking in the lay of the room with its cheerily blazing fire, large circular table draped in cloth, and walls covered in paintings of the countryside. He faced away from her before a window, his hands clasped at the small of his back, his broad shoulders covered in exquisite colorful silk, his silky black locks restrained in a queue that ended just between his shoulder blades.

The sight of his richly clad form in the simple country room was glaring. Then he turned, and her body froze in shock.

It cannot be him, she thought with something akin to panic. *It is impossible.*

Her heart ceased beating, her breath seized in her lungs, and her thoughts stuttered as if she had taken a blow to the brain.

Colin.

How was it possible . . . ?

As her knees gave way, she grappled blindly for a nearby chair but missed. She crumpled to the rug, a loud gasp filling the highly charged air as her instincts rushed to the fore and forced her to breathe.

"Amelia." He lunged toward her, but she held up a hand to stop him.

"Stay away!" she managed, through a throat clenched painfully tight.

The Colin Mitchell she knew and loved was dead.

Then, how is it, an insidious mental voice questioned, *that he is here with you?*

It can't be him . . . It can't be him . . .

She repeated that litany endlessly in her mind, unable to bear the thought of the years between them, the life he must have led, the days and nights, the smiles and laughter . . .

The betrayal was so complete, she could not credit that Colin was capable of it. Yet, as she stared at the dangerously handsome man who stood across from her, her heart whispered the agonizing truth.

I would know him anywhere, it said. *My love.*

How could she have missed the signs?

Because he was dead. Because I grieved long and deeply.

Freed from the confines of the mask, Colin's exotic Gypsy features left no doubt that it was he. He was older, the lines of his face more angular, but the traces of the boy she had loved were there. The eyes, however, were Montoya's—loving, hungry, knowing eyes.

The lover who'd shared her bed was Colin . . .

A wracking sob escaped her, and she covered her mouth with her hand.

"Amelia."

The aching tone in which her name was spoken made her cry harder. The foreign accent was gone, leaving behind the voice she heard in her dreams. It was deeper, more mature, but it was Colin's.

She looked away, unable to stand the sight of him.

"Have you nothing to say?" he asked quietly. "No questions to ask? No insults to hurl?"

A hundred words struggled to leave her mouth, and three very precious ones, but she leashed them tightly, unwilling to bare the depth of her pain. She stared at a small, square painting of a lake that adorned the wall. Her lower lip quivered, and she bit it to hide the telltale movement.

"My body has been inside yours," he said hoarsely. "My heart beats in your breast. Can you not at least look at me, if you will not speak to me?"

Her silent reply was the tears that flowed in a steady, endless stream.

He cursed and came toward her.

"No!" she cried, stilling him. "Do not come near me."

Colin's jaw clenched visibly, and she watched the muscle tic with an odd disconnection. How strange to see Montoya's maturity and polish within her childhood love. He looked the same and yet different. He was bigger, stronger, more vital. He was stunningly attractive, blessed with a novel masculine appeal few could rival. She used to dream of the day they would be wed and she could call him her own.

But that dream had died when he had.

"I still dream of that," he murmured, answering the words she had not realized she'd spoken aloud. "I still want that."

"You allowed me to believe you were dead," she whispered, unable to reconcile the Colin she remembered with the magnificently dressed man standing before her.

"I had no choice."

"You could have come to me at any time; instead you have been absent for years!"

"I returned as soon as I was able."

"As another man!" She shook her head violently, her mind filling with memories of the last weeks. "It was a cruel game you played with my affections, making me care for a man who does not exist."

"I exist!" He stood tall and proud, his shoulders back, his chin lifted. "I played no role with you. Every word that left Montoya's mouth, every touch, was from *my* heart. The same heart beats in both men. We are one and the same. Both madly in love with you."

She dismissed his claim with a wave of her hand. "You affected an accent and allowed me to believe you were disfigured."

"The accent was a façade, yes. A way to keep you from guessing the truth before I could tell you properly. The rest was a creation of *your* mind, not mine."

"Do not blame this farce on me!" Amelia struggled to her feet. "You allowed me to grieve for you. Have you any notion of what I have suffered these last years? How I have suffered these last weeks, feeling as if I was betraying Colin by falling in love with Montoya?"

Torment shadowed his features, and she hated the vicious satisfaction she felt at the sight of it. "Your heart was never fooled," he said roughly. "It always knew."

"No, you—"

"Yes!" His dark eyes burned with an inner fire. "Do you recall whose name you cried at the height of orgasm? When I was deep inside you, clasped in the very heart of your body, do you remember which lover's name came to your lips?"

Amelia swallowed hard, her mind shifting through the myriad of sensations that had assailed her untried body. She remembered the look of the bullet scar on his shoulder, the way the feel of it had plagued her in some fashion she could not pinpoint.

"You were driving me mad!" she accused.

"I wanted to tell you, Amelia. I tried."

"Later, you could have. I nearly begged you!"

"And have this discussion directly after we made love?" he scoffed. "Never! Last night was the culmination of my deepest, most cherished fantasies. Nothing could have induced me to ruin that."

"It is ruined!" she yelled, shaking. "I feel as if I have lost two loves, for the Colin I knew is dead, and Montoya was a lie."

"He is not a lie!"

Colin came toward her, and she hastily caught the back of a chair and pulled it between them. The sturdy wooden seat was no deterrent, however, and he shoved it aside.

She turned to flee, but he caught her, and the feel of his arms around her trembling body was too much.

Amelia hung in his embrace, devastated.

"I love you," he murmured, his lips to her temple. "I love you."

For so long she'd prayed to hear those words from his lips, but they were too little now and far too late.

Chapter 13

As her coach pulled into the courtyard of the inn specified by the outriders, Maria collected her hat and gloves in preparation for alighting.

"It is a rare sight to see you so anxious," Christopher murmured, his heavy-lidded gaze making him appear deceptively slumberous. She knew him too well to believe that.

"I am relieved we have found her and that she was of sound mind enough to drag Tim along with her, but there are still the matters of Montoya and Ware to address." Maria sighed. "As miserable as my youth was, I am grateful to have been too busy to indulge in reckless love such as this."

"You were waiting for me," Christopher purred, catching her hand before she gloved it and kissing the back.

She cupped his cheek and smiled. "You were worth the wait."

The coach rolled to a halt, and Christopher vaulted down. As she accepted his assistance, she said, "I am surprised that Tim is not out here to greet us."

"As am I," he agreed. He glanced up at the coachman. "Pietro, make arrangements for the horses, then unload Miss Benbridge's valise."

Pietro nodded and pulled away, taking the carriage to the stables several yards away.

"You think of everything," Maria praised, wrapping her arm around his.

"No, I think of you," he corrected, looking down at her with the melting intensity that had shattered her defenses so many years ago.

They waited for Simon and Mademoiselle Rousseau to join them. Then they all entered the quiet inn.

"I will inquire about Tim," Christopher said, striding to the counter. A moment later, he gestured for one of the lackeys at her side to join him. Together, the two men followed the innkeeper out of the room.

"What is going on?" Mademoiselle Rousseau wondered aloud.

"Let us order food," Simon said. "I am half-starved."

"You are always half-starved," she muttered.

"It requires a great deal of energy to tolerate you, mademoiselle," he retorted.

The bickering duo walked away, leaving Maria waiting with a lackey. She frowned as Christopher reappeared with Tim in tow.

Maria noted the grim look on Tim's face and moved forward to meet them. "Where is Amelia?"

"Apparently," Christopher drawled, "her phantom admirer has decided to step out from behind the mask."

"Oh." She glanced at Tim, who looked both pained and furious. "What is it?"

"They are speaking in the private dining room," Christopher explained, "with an open door for propriety's sake. From the sounds of it, it is not going well for the man."

"Why not?"

"When 'e approached me," Tim rumbled, "I thought 'e looked familiar, but I couldn't place 'is face. It came to me when I overheard them talking."

"What came to you?" she asked, looking between both men. "Who is he? Do we know him?"

"Remember the pictures I drew for you in Brighton?" Tim asked, harkening back to the days of her "courtship" with Christopher. After a failed attempt to retrieve Amelia, Tim had put both his excellent memory and talent for rendering to good use by drawing images of the servants who had spirited Amelia away.

Nodding, Maria recalled the stunningly beautiful drawings. "Yes, of course."

"The man she's speaking to is one of them."

Frowning, she tried to recall them all. There had been a drawing of Amelia and Pietro, as well as of a governess and a young groomsman . . .

"That is not possible," she said, shaking her head. "That young man was Colin, the boy who died trying to save Amelia."

"Pietro's nephew, was he not?" Christopher asked with one brow raised. "If there are any doubts about the man's identity, I am certain Pietro can help us to dispel them."

"Bloody hell," she breathed. Pivoting on her

heel, she looked for Simon and found him sinking into a chair. She marched toward him.

He glanced up and saw her coming, his blue eyes first sparkling with welcome, then narrowing warily. The smile that curved his sensual lips faded as resignation passed over his features. She knew then that it was true, and her heart ached for the torment her sister must be feeling.

"Out with it," she snapped, as he stood before her.

Simon nodded and pulled out the empty seat that waited between him and Mademoiselle Rousseau. "You might want to take a seat," he said wearily. "This might take some time."

"Release me, Colin."

Amelia held back a sob by dint of will alone. The feel of his big, powerful body pressed so passionately against her back was both a balm and a barb. Her nerves were raw; her emotions fluctuated between wild, heady joy and a feeling of abandonment too close to what she had felt in her father's negligent care.

"I cannot," he said hoarsely, his hot cheek pressed ardently to hers. "I am afraid if I let you go, you will leave me."

"I want to leave you," she whispered. "As you left me."

"It was the only choice that afforded me the opportunity to have you. Can you not see?" The tone of his voice was a rough plea. "If I had not left and made my fortune elsewhere, you would never be mine, and I could not bear it, Amelia. I would do anything to have you, even give you up for a time."

She tugged at his arms. Every breath she took was filled with the scent of him, a scent that awakened her body to memories of the passionate night behind them. It was an unbearable torment. "Release me."

"Promise to stay and hear me out."

Amelia nodded, knowing she had no choice. Knowing they had to find some closure to this so they could both move on with their lives.

Facing him with an uplifted chin, she tried to keep her face impassive despite the tears she could not stop. For his part, Colin made no effort to hide his torment. His handsome features were wracked with painful emotions.

"I might have felt differently," she said flatly, "if you had told me of your desire to build a different life for yourself, if you had made me a partner in your plans instead of cutting me out."

"Be honest, Amelia." He clasped his hands behind him as if to prevent reaching out for her. "You would never have allowed me to go, and if you had begged me to stay, I would not have had the strength to deny you."

"Why could you not stay?"

"How was I to afford you with a servant's meager pay? How was I to give you the world when I had nothing?"

"I could have borne any livelihood if only you were there to share it!"

"And what of the nights?" he challenged. "Would you feel the same while shivering because we must ration our meager stipend of coal? And what of the days? Where we must rise before the sun to work ourselves to exhaustion?"

"You could have kept me warm, as you did last night," she retorted. "A lifetime of such nights . . . I would damn the coal to hell if my bed was warmed by you. And the days. The passing of each hour would bring me closer to you. I could have tolerated anything if it led me back to you."

"You deserve better!"

Amelia stomped her foot. "It was not for you to decide that I was incapable of living such a life! It was not for you to decide that I was not strong enough!"

"I never doubted that you would make such an effort for me," he argued, his frame vibrating with an edgy intensity so reminiscent of the Colin of old. "What I doubted was *my* strength, *my* capability to live in that manner!"

"You did not even try!"

"I couldn't." Colin's voice grew more impassioned. "How could I bear looking at your cracked and reddened hands? How could I bear the tears that would come in the unguarded minutes when you longed for a moment's comfort?"

"Love requires sacrifice."

"Not when the entirety of the sacrifice is made by you. I could not live with myself knowing that my selfishness brought you to an unhappy end."

"You don't understand." Her hand lifted to cover her heart. "I would have been happy as long as I had you."

"And I would have hated myself."

"I see that now." Grieving anew, Amelia wondered how she could have been so wrong about their love for each other. "If we had never met, you would have been happy with the life you had, wouldn't you?"

"Amelia—"

"Your discontent stems from me and the expectations you imagined I had for you."

"No, that is not true."

"It is." The pain in her chest intensified until she could hardly breathe. "I'm so sorry," she whispered. "I wish we had never met. We might have been happy."

His eyes widened. "Dear God, do not say such a thing! Never. You are the only thing that has ever brought me happiness."

Suddenly, she felt so old and so tired. "Leaving your country and your family, traversing the Continent risking your life to gather information for the Crown . . . That is what you call happiness? You are deluded."

"Damn it," Colin growled, snatching her by the shoulders. "You are worth it, all of it. I would do it again a hundred times over to become worthy of you."

"I never thought you were unworthy, and you did not harbor these feelings of inferiority until you met me. That is not love, Colin. I do not know what that is, but I know what it is not."

Made anxious by Amelia's sudden composure, Colin considered ways to keep her connected to him. Last night they had been as close as two lovers could ever hope to be, and now they were as distant as strangers. "Whatever doubts my revelation may inspire, do not belittle my feelings for you. I love you. From the moment I first saw you, I loved you, and I have never stopped. Not for a moment."

"Oh?" Amelia wiped at her tears with hands so steady, he felt a prickling disquiet. "What of the times when you gained the expertise at lovemaking you displayed so beautifully last night? Were you in love with me then?"

"Yes, damn you." He pulled her closer, pressing the full length of his heated body to hers. "Even then. Sex is sex to a man, nothing more. We require the spending of our seed to be healthy. It has nothing to do with elevated feelings."

"Simply slaking your needs as you did behind the store when we were younger?" She shook her head. "Last night, with every touch ... every caress ... I wondered how many women you must have entertained in order to acquire such skill."

"Jealous?" he lashed, bleeding inside and frightened by her rapid retreat. She spoke with no inflection, no feeling, as if she cared not at all. "Do you wish it had been you who served my baser needs with no emotion or caring? No affection or concern?"

"I am jealous, yes, but also sad." Her beautiful eyes were empty. "You lived a full life without me, Colin. At times, you were likely content with your lot. You should not have come back. Those women did not make you wish to be someone you are not, as I do."

"I never think of them," he vowed, cupping her beloved face in his hands. "Never. All the while I thought of you and how deeply I wanted you. I wished they were you. It was an ache that never faded. I learned, yes. I became skilled, yes. For *you!* So that I could be everything to you, so that I could satisfy *you* in every way. I wanted to be all you needed, all you wanted."

"How miserable," she said. "It breaks my heart to know that I have prevented you from being happy."

Furious at his helplessness and confused by the turns the conversation was taking, Colin held her still and took her mouth, thrusting strong and sure into the hot, moist depths.

He tasted her pain and sorrow, her bitterness and anger. He drank it all, stroking across her tongue with his, before sucking fiercely.

Clutching his forearms with both hands, she moaned and trembled in his arms. Her body could not resist his, even now. It was a weakness he hated to exploit, but he would if necessary.

"My mouth is yours," he said hoarsely, brushing his wet lips back and forth across hers. "I have shared kisses with no one but you. Never."

He caught her hand and held it over his heart. "See how strongly it beats? How desperately? Because of you. Everything, *everything* I have ever done has been with you in mind."

"Stop . . ." she panted, her breasts thrusting against his arm with her labored breathing.

"And my dreams." He pressed his temple to hers. "My dreams have always been yours. I aspire to be a better man to be worthy of you."

"And when will that day come, Colin?"

He pulled back, frowning.

"All these years, and yet you still found reasons to put me aside until last night when I forced your hand." Amelia sighed, and he heard a note of finality in the forlorn sound. "I think we saw in each other only what we wanted to see, but in the end the gulf between us is too wide to cross with mere illusions."

Colin's blood froze, a not inconsiderable feat with her body pressed so tightly to his. "What are you saying?"

"I am saying that I am tired of being left behind and forgotten until some preordained time arrives. I have lived the whole of my life under such a cloud and refuse to do so any longer."

"Amelia—"

"I am saying that when we leave this room, Colin, it will be farewell between us."

The slight scratching on the open door drew Simon's attention from the maps spread out across his desk. He looked up at the butler with both brows raised. "Yes?"

"There is a young man at the door asking for Lady Winter, sir. I did tell him that neither she nor you were at home, but he refuses to leave."

Simon straightened. "Oh? Who is it?"

The servant cleared his throat. "He appears to be a Gypsy."

Surprise held his tongue for the length of a heartbeat. Then Simon said, "Show him in."

He took a moment to clear away the sensitive documents on his desk. Then he sat and waited for the dark-haired youth who entered his study a moment later.

"Where is Lady Winter?" the boy asked, the set of his shoulders and jaw betraying his mulish determination to get whatever it was he came for.

Simon leaned back in his chair. *"She is traveling the Continent, last I heard."*

The boy frowned. *"Is Miss Benbridge with her? How can I find them? Do you have their direction?"*

"Tell me your name."

"Colin Mitchell."

"Well, Mr. Mitchell, would you care for a drink?" Simon stood and moved to the row of decanters that lined the table in front of the window.

"No."

Hiding a smile, Simon poured two fingers of brandy into a glass and then turned around, leaning his hip against the console with one heel crossed over the other. Mitchell stood in the same spot, his gaze searching the room, pausing occasionally on various objects with narrowed eyes. Hunting for clues to the answers he sought. He was a finely built young man, and attractive in an exotic way that Simon imagined the ladies found most appealing.

"What will you do if you find the fair Amelia?" Simon asked. *"Work in the stables? Care for her horses?"*

Mitchell's eyes widened.

"Yes, I know who you are, though I was told you were dead." Simon lifted his glass and tossed back the contents. His belly warmed, making him smile. *"So do you intend to work as her underling, pining for her from afar? Or perhaps you hope to tumble her in the hay as often as possible until she either marries or grows fat with your child."*

Simon straightened and set down his glass, bracing himself for the expected—yet, surprisingly impressive—

tackle that knocked him to the floor. He and the boy rolled, locked in combat, knocking over a small table and shattering the porcelain figurines that had graced its top.

It took only a few moments for Simon to claim the upper hand. The time would have been shorter had he not been so concerned about hurting the lad.

"Cease," he ordered, "and listen to me." He no longer drawled; his tone was now deadly earnest.

Mitchell stilled, but his features remained stamped with fury. "Don't ever speak of Amelia in that way!"

Pushing to his feet, Simon extended his hand to assist the young man up. "I am only pointing out the obvious. You have nothing. Nothing to offer, nothing with which to support her, no title to give her prestige."

The clenching of the young man's jaw and fists betrayed his hatred for the truth. "I know all of that."

"Good. Now"—Simon righted his clothing and resumed his seat behind the desk—"what if I offered to help you acquire what you need to make you worthy—coin, a fitting home, perhaps even a title from some distant land that would suit the physical features provided by your heritage?"

Mitchell stilled, his gaze narrowing with avid interest. "How?"

"I am engaged in certain . . . activities that could be facilitated by a youth with your potential. I heard of your dashing near rescue of Miss Benbridge. With the right molding, you could be quite an asset to me." Simon smiled. "I would not make this offer to anyone else. So consider yourself fortunate."

"Why me?" Mitchell asked suspiciously, and not without a little scorn. He was slightly cynical, which Simon thought was excellent. A purely green boy would be of no use at all. "You don't know me, or what I'm capable of."

Simon held his gaze steadily. "I understand well the lengths a man will go to for a woman he cares for."

"I love her."

"Yes. To the point where you would seek her out at great cost to yourself. I need dedication such as that. In return, I will ensure that you become a man of some means."

"That would take years." Mitchell ran a hand through his hair. "I don't know that I can bear it."

"Give yourselves time to mature. Allow her to see what she has missed all of these years. Then, if she will have you anyway, you will know that she is making the decision with a woman's heart, and not a child's."

For a long moment, the young man remained motionless, the weight of his indecision a tangible thing.

"Try it," Simon urged. "What harm can come from the effort?"

Finally, Mitchell heaved out his breath and sank into the seat opposite the desk. "I'm listening."

"Excellent!" Simon leaned back in his chair. "Now here are my thoughts . . ."

"Why did you say nothing to me?" Maria asked when the tale was finished, staring at Simon as if he were a stranger. She felt as if he were.

"If I had told you, *mhuirnín*," Simon said softly, "would you have withheld the information from your sibling? Of course not, and the secret was not mine to share."

"What of Amelia's pain and suffering?"

"Unfortunate, but not something I could alleviate."

"You could have told me he was alive!" she argued.

"Mitchell had every right to make himself worthy of Amelia's esteem. Do not fault him for pursuing the woman he loves in the only manner available to him. Of all men, I understand his motivations very well." He paused a moment, then spoke in a calmer voice. "Besides, what he did with his life was no concern of yours."

"It is a concern of *mine,*" drawled a voice from behind them, "now that it affects Miss Benbridge."

Maria turned in her chair and faced the man who approached. "Lord Ware," she greeted, her heart sinking.

The earl was dressed as casually as she had ever seen him, but there was a tension to his tall frame and a tautness to his jaw that told her leisure was far from his mind. His dark hair was unadorned but for a ribbon at his nape, and he wore boots instead of heels.

"This is the fiancé?" Mademoiselle Rousseau asked.

"My lord," Christopher greeted. "I am impressed by your dedication."

"Until she tells me otherwise," the earl said grimly, "I consider Miss Benbridge's welfare one of my responsibilities."

"I have not had this much fun in ages," the Frenchwoman said, smiling wide.

Maria closed her eyes and rubbed the space between her brows. Christopher, who stood at her back, set his hand on her shoulder and gave a commiserating squeeze.

"Would someone care to fill me in?" Ware asked.

She looked at Simon. He raised both brows. "How delicately should I phrase this?"

"No delicacy required," Ware said. "I am neither ignorant nor cursed with a weak constitution."

"He does intend to marry into our family," Christopher pointed out.

"True," Simon said, though his gaze narrowed. He relayed the events leading up to the present moment, carefully leaving out names like Eddington's, which could not be shared.

"So this man in the mask is Colin Mitchell?" Ware asked, scowling. "The boy Miss Benbridge fancied in her youth? And she does not know it is him?"

"She knows it now," Tim muttered.

"Mitchell is telling her as we speak," Christopher explained.

There was a thud behind them, and they all turned to find Pietro, who stood gaping with a dropped valise at his feet. "That isn't possible!" the coachman said heatedly. "Colin is gone."

Maria glanced at Simon, who winced.

"This grows more fascinating by the moment," Mademoiselle Rousseau said.

"You are a vile creature," Simon snapped.

Looking up at Christopher, Maria signaled her intent to stand, and he stepped back. "I should go see how things are progressing."

"No need," he murmured, his gaze trained beyond her.

All heads turned toward the hallway that led to the private dining room. Amelia appeared with reddened eyes and nose and disheveled hair, the picture of tormented heartbroken loveliness.

Mitchell came into view directly behind her, and the sight of him took Maria aback, as it did everyone who saw him. Elegantly attired and proud of bearing, he left no traces of servitude clinging to his tall frame. He was an arrestingly beautiful man, with dark, sensual eyes framed by long, thick lashes and a voluptuary's mouth framed by a firm, determined jaw. He, too, looked devastated and gravely wounded, and Maria's heart went out to both of them.

"Amelia . . ." Ware's cultured drawl was rough with concern.

Her verdant gaze met his and filled with tears.

A low growl rumbled from the earl's chest.

"Colin." Pietro's agonized tone deepened the trauma of the day's revelations.

Distracted by the many unfolding events, Maria did not foresee Ware's intent until he stalked up to Mitchell and asked, "Do you consider yourself a gentleman?"

Mitchell's jaw tightened. "I do."

Ware threw a glove down at Mitchell's feet. "Then I demand satisfaction."

"I will give it to you."

"Dear God," Maria breathed, her hand at her throat.

Christopher left her side. He drew to a halt beside the earl and said, "I would be honored to serve as your second, my lord."

"Thank you," Ware replied.

"I will serve as Mitchell's," Simon said, joining them.

"No!" Amelia cried, her horrified gaze darting between the grim masculine faces. "This is absurd."

Maria pulled her away. "You cannot intercede."

"Why?" Amelia asked. "This is not necessary."

"It is."

"I have a home in Bristol," Ware said. "I suggest we retire there. Our audience will then be made up of those we trust."

Mitchell nodded. "That was my destination, so the location is convenient for me as well."

"I caused this." Amelia looked pleadingly at Maria. "My selfishness has led to this end. How do I stop this?"

"What is done, is done," Maria said, rubbing her hand soothingly down Amelia's spine.

"I want to go with them."

"That would not be wise."

Christopher turned to her, and she saw in his face that he disagreed. She did not understand why he would wish them to go, but she could learn his motives later. As it was, she trusted him implicitly and knew that his first concern was always for her health and happiness.

"I want to go," Amelia said again, with more strength.

"Shh," Maria soothed. "We can discuss this over a hot bath and a change of clothes."

Her sibling nodded, and they moved away to order heated water and a tub. With everyone distracted with their own thoughts, no one noted the man who occupied a shadowed seat in the far corner. He attracted even less attention when he left.

Stepping outside, Jacques tugged the brim of his hat down and sauntered across the drive toward the carriage that waited a short ways down the lane.

He opened the door and looked inside. "Mitchell was just challenged to a duel."

Cartland smiled. "Come in and tell me everything."

Chapter 14

It never ceased to amaze Amelia how a man as vibrant and impossible to ignore as Christopher St. John could fade into oblivion when he chose to. As it was, she hardly noticed that he shared the same squab with Maria as they traveled to Bristol. He held his tongue as she poured out her heart, and she was grateful to him for his silence. Few would believe that the notorious criminal could tolerate hours upon hours of a weeping woman's lamentations over love, but he did and he did it well.

"You told him you would not see him again?" Maria asked gently.

"Until Ware challenged him, that had been my intent," Amelia said from behind the handkerchief she held to her nose. She had refused to talk about anything yesterday on the ride to Swindon. Only today did she feel capable of discussing Colin without crying too copiously to speak. "We will be happier apart."

"You do not look happier."

"I will be, over the duration of my life, as will Colin." She sighed. "No one can be happy pretending day after day to be someone they are not."

"Perhaps he is not pretending," Maria suggested softly.

"Regardless, the new Colin harbors the same doubts as the old. Despite all that he has accomplished, he still believed Ware was the better choice until just days ago. He continues to make decisions regarding my welfare without consulting me. I had enough of such treatment in my childhood."

"You are allowing your past to cloud your present."

"You champion his actions?" Amelia asked with wide eyes. "How can you? I can find nothing good in what he has done. He is wealthy, yes—that is obvious in the quality of everything he owns—but accepting that end as being worthy of my grief and heartache puts a price on my love, and I cannot abide that."

"I do not champion his actions," Maria murmured, "but I do believe he loves you and that he thought he was acting in your best interests. I also believe that you love him. Surely, there is something good in that?"

Amelia ran a hand over her skirts and gazed out the window. Behind them, Colin rode in his carriage with Jacques, Mr. Quinn, and Mademoiselle Rousseau. Ware led their procession in his coach. She was trapped between the two, both figuratively and literally.

"I have come to the realization that passion is not as the poets would have us believe," she said.

There was a suspicious choking sound from the

opposite squab, but when she shot a narrowed glance at St. John, his face was studiously impassive.

"I am quite serious," she argued. "Prior to these last weeks, my life was orderly and comfortable. My equanimity was intact. Ware was content, as were both of you. Colin, too, had an existence that was progressing in its own fashion. Now all of our lives are in disarray. You've no notion of how it pains me to realize that my resemblance to Lord Welton is more than skin deep."

"Amelia. That is absolute nonsense." Maria's voice was stern.

"Is it? Have I not done exactly as he would do? Cared only for my own pleasure?" She shook her head. "I would rather be a woman who lives for duty than one who lives for her own indulgences. At least I would have honor then."

Concern filled Maria's dark eyes. "You are overwrought. It has been a long journey and the inn in Swindon had little to recommend it, but we are almost to Bristol, and then you must rest for a day or two."

"Before or after the duel?" Amelia asked testily.

"Poppet—"

There was a distant shout heard outside, and then the carriage turned. Leaning forward, she looked out the window and watched a long, manicured lane empty into a circular drive graced by a sizeable center fountain. The lavish manse beyond that was breathtaking with its graceful columns and massive portico flanked by abundant, cheery flowerbeds.

The line of carriages rolled to a halt before the

steps, and the front door opened, allowing a veritable swarm of gray- and black-liveried servants to flow out. St. John exited first. He then assisted Maria and Amelia down to the graveled drive.

"Welcome," Ware said, as he joined them. His mouth curved in a rakish half smile as he lifted Amelia's gloved hand to his lips. He looked dashing in his garb of pale blue breeches and coat the exact color of his eyes, and the strained smile she returned had true appreciation for his charm behind it.

"Your home is lovely, my lord," Maria murmured.

"Thank you. I hope you will find it even lovelier once you are inside."

In unison, they turned to look toward Colin's coach. Amelia steeled herself inwardly for his appearance, expecting that he would look at her as he had done all of yesterday—with entreaty in his dark eyes.

Sadly, no preparation on her part could mitigate the effect he had on her as he vaulted down from his carriage and approached with an elegant stride that was entirely sensual. Damn the man. He had always moved with an animal grace that made her tingle all over. Now that she knew how well that latent sexuality translated to bedplay, the response was worse.

She looked away in an effort to hide the irresistible attraction she felt.

"My lord," Colin said, his smooth voice roughened by obvious dislike. "If someone could kindly provide direction to the nearest inn, I will be on my way. Mr. Quinn will return later to make the necessary arrangements."

"I would like you to stay here," Ware said, startling everyone.

Amelia looked at him with mouth agape.

"That is impossible," Colin protested.

"Why?" Ware challenged with both brows raised.

Colin's jaw tightened. "I have my reasons."

"What is it?" St. John asked, a note in his voice alerting Amelia. Apparently he saw something in the exchange that she did not. "Allow me to help you."

"That will not be necessary," Colin said stiffly. "Keep Miss Benbridge safe. That is all the assistance I require."

"If you are in danger," Maria said, "I would prefer to keep you close. Perhaps we should stay at the inn as well."

"Please," Ware said in his customary drawl, as composed as ever. "Everyone will be safer here than in a public venue with frequent traffic."

"St. John," Colin said. "If I could have a moment of your time."

St. John nodded and excused himself. The two men moved a short distance away and spoke in tones too low to overhear. They became more animated, the conversation more heated.

"What is going on?" Amelia asked Maria.

"I wish I knew," Maria replied.

"Allow Mrs. Barney to show you to your rooms," Ware said, gesturing to the housekeeper who waited on the lower step with a soft smile.

"I want to know what is happening," Amelia said.

"I know you do," Ware murmured, setting his hand at her lower back and leading her toward the manse. "And I promise to tell you everything as soon as I know it."

"Truly?" She looked up at him from beneath the brim of her hat.

"Of course. When have I ever lied to you?"

She understood the message. *I am not Mitchell*, it said. *I have always been true to you.* Grateful for him, Amelia offered a thankful, shaky smile. Maria joined her, and together they followed Mrs. Barney into the house.

Colin watched Lord Ware lead Amelia toward the manse and fought the urge to wrench her away. It was unbearable to see her with another man. It ate at him as acid would, burning and stinging and leaving a gaping hole behind.

"I think you should stay," St. John said, drawing Colin's attention away from Amelia's departing back.

"You do not understand," Colin argued. "We have been followed ever since we left Reading. If I keep my distance from Miss Benbridge, I will draw the danger away from her."

St. John looked grim. "Unless she has a mind to follow you again," he pointed out. "Then she will be far more vulnerable than if she were to remain here."

"Bloody hell. I did not think of that." Lifting a hand to the back of his neck, Colin rubbed at the tense muscle that pained him. "In her present mood, I do not think she will go to the trouble."

"But you cannot be certain, and neither can I. Therefore, I think it best to err on the side of caution."

"Can you not deter her in some way?" Colin asked. "Cartland cannot be allowed anywhere near her. If he suspects how much she means to me, he will exploit her."

"Have *you* been able to deter her? Do not expect miracles from me." St. John smiled. "My wife is considered the Deadliest Woman in England, and she taught her sibling everything she knows. Amelia can cross swords with the best of men, and she can throw a knife better than anyone, even me. If she decides to follow you, she will find a way."

Colin blinked, then gave a resigned exhalation. "Oddly enough, I am not as surprised by that revelation as I should be."

"I would have liked to have met their mother. She must have been extraordinary."

"I do not have the time to socialize," Colin growled. "I must be either the hunter or the prey, and the latter role does not suit me."

St. John nodded. "I understand."

"I wish Mademoiselle Rousseau would believe Jacques's witness of the events of that night, but she refuses. I cannot collect why. Why dismiss him so completely? How can she trust Cartland's word over anyone else's?"

"I do not know what it is she seeks, but I will lend you whatever support you need. There is little that requires your attention tonight. Allow my men to begin the search in town. You can pick it up tomorrow. I think one night of domesticity will soothe Amelia enough to keep her from haring after you."

The thought of spending an intimate evening in the company of Amelia and Lord Ware was a torment unparalleled.

"Will you stay?" the earl asked, joining them. "Rooms are being prepared for you and your acquaintances as we speak."

"Thank you." It was all Colin could manage. "I will tell the others." He turned on his heel and walked away.

St. John watched him go, noting the stiffness of his posture and the anger evident in his stride. "He loves her."

"I see that."

Turning his head, St. John found the earl watching Mitchell with a narrowed glance. "I know why I think he should remain. I cannot collect why you do."

"Our differences will be more obvious in direct contrast." Ware met his gaze. "I am the best choice for her. If I doubted that for a moment, I would step aside. I want her happiness above all else. I do not think he is capable of giving it to her."

"He is a formidable opponent in the challenge ahead. Mitchell has lived by his wits and his sword for several years."

"I am not without skill of my own," the earl said easily, "regardless of the civilized manner in which I acquired it."

St. John nodded and followed Ware's urging to move into the house. Tim was overseeing the removal of both trunks and servants from the trailing coach. Mitchell was scowling at Quinn, who was assisting a grinning Mademoiselle Rousseau down from their carriage.

For his part, St. John wondered if other men went through such difficulties when attempting to marry off a younger sibling. Shaking his head, he climbed the stairs and moved directly to the suite assigned to him where he knew he would find his wife. Together, they would strategize the events of the coming few days.

The thought made him smile.

Bathed, dressed, yet inwardly shaky, Amelia slipped out of her bedchamber and hurried down the long gallery. Maria had told her to nap in preparation for afternoon tea, but Amelia could not sleep. What she felt was the urge to roam, to stretch her legs, to breathe fresh air and clear her head. As a child, she had learned that a brisk walk was capable of alleviating many ills, and she felt in strong need of that now.

"Amelia."

She paused at the sound of her name. Turning, she found Lord Ware exiting a room a few doors behind her. She curtsied. "My lord."

He shot a pointed glance at her walking boots. "May I join you?"

She briefly considered voicing a kind objection, then thought better of it. As much as she wished to be alone with her thoughts, Ware deserved an explanation and the opportunity to chastise her, if he so wished. "I would be honored."

He smiled his charming, dashing smile and came toward her. He was dressed as a country gentleman, and the more leisurely appearance suited him well. It reminded her of their meeting in Lincolnshire, and the smile she returned to him was genuine.

"How lovely you are," he murmured, "when your smiles reach your eyes."

"It is because you look so handsome," she returned.

Ware lifted Amelia's hand to his lips and his gaze beyond her shoulder, where he saw Mitchell at the end of the hall, watching them both with daggers in his eyes. Tucking Amelia's hand around his arm, he led her away toward the stairs, which would take them to the lower floor and the rear garden.

He felt his rival's stare burning a hole in his back for the entire way.

Colin watched Lord Ware's proprietary handling of Amelia with something so akin to blood rage, it frightened him.

He could not bear it.

"You must find something to occupy yourself with, *mon ami,*" Jacques said, startling Colin with his sudden, silent appearance. "You will act regrettably if you think endlessly of her."

"I have always thought endlessly of her," he bit out. "I know of no other way to live."

"She requires time. I admire your fortitude in giving it to her."

Colin's fists clenched. "It is not fortitude. I simply do not wish to kill a man in front of her."

"*Alors* . . . you must leave. Distract yourself with a task."

Inhaling sharply, Colin nodded. He had been set upon that end when he chanced upon Amelia with Ware. He forced himself to look away from where the couple had stood mere moments ago. "That was my intent. I was seeking you out."

"What do you want me to do?" the Frenchman asked, looking grim as always.

"I cannot go into town. There is some concern that Miss Benbridge will follow, and while I find that highly unlikely, the request is valid, so I must stay for now."

"I understand."

"St. John is sending a man to rally those who work for him in Bristol. Go and direct the search. Tell them what to look for, what to expect. If you find anything of import, send for me."

Jacques nodded and set off immediately. The Frenchman took the main staircase; Colin took the servants'. It emptied by the kitchen, and he ignored the startled glances sent his way as he exited out the delivery door and headed toward the stables.

Every step he took grew heavier, his heart weighed upon by the upcoming confrontation that would cut him nigh as deeply as the one with Amelia had.

He entered silently and inhaled deeply, finding the smells of hay and horses both familiar and soothing. The many beasts inside snorted and shifted restlessly as his scent filled the air and disturbed their equanimity. Glancing about, he looked for the groomsmen's quarters. His stride faltered when he found the doorway. A man leaned against the jamb, watching him with wounded, angry eyes.

The years had been kind to Pietro. Aside from a

slight pouch at the belly, the rest of his body was still fit and strong. Strands of silver accented his temples and beard, but his skin was smooth and free of wrinkles.

"Uncle," Colin greeted, his throat tight with sorrow and affection.

"My only nephew is dead," Pietro said coldly.

Colin flinched at the repudiation. "I have missed you."

"You lie! You let me think you were dead!"

"I was offered the chance at a different life." Colin held out his hands in a silent plea for understanding. "I had one chance to accept and no time to second-guess."

"And what of me?" Pietro demanded, straightening. "What of my grief? Was that nothing to you?"

"You think I was not grieving?" Colin bit out, stung by the condemnation of yet another person he loved. "I might as well have been dead."

"Then why did you do it?" Pietro came forward. "I have tried to see what would make you do such a thing, but I don't understand."

"I had nothing to offer anyone before. No way to create a life of comfort for those I loved."

"Comfort from what? The only discomfort in my life has been my mourning for you!"

"What of freedom from work?" Colin challenged. "What of a life of travel and discovery? I can offer you those things now, when I could not before."

Pain wracked Pietro's handsome features. "I am a simple man, Colin. A roof over my head . . . food . . . family. Those are all I need to be happy."

"I wish my needs were as simple." Colin moved to the nearest stall and set his crossed arms along the top of it. "I need Amelia to be happy, and this was the only way I could conceive of to have her."

"Colin . . ." He heard his uncle sigh. "You love her still."

"I have no notion how *not* to love her. It is ingrained in me, as much a part of me as my hair and skin color."

Pietro joined him at the stall door. "I should have raised you in the camp. Then you wouldn't want things that are beyond your reach."

Colin smiled and looked aside at him. "Amelia and I would have met at some point, at some time."

"That is your Romany blood talking."

"Yes, it is."

There was a long silence, as each attempted to find the right thing to say. "How long have you been in England?" Pietro asked finally.

"A few weeks."

"A few weeks and you didn't come to me?" Pietro shook his head. "I don't feel that I know you at all. The boy I raised had more care for the feelings of others."

Aching from the pain he had inflicted, Colin reached out and set his hand atop Pietro's shoulder. "If my love is in err, it is not due to lack of it for you but to a surfeit for her. I would have done anything, gone anywhere, to become worthy of Amelia."

"You seem to have accomplished what you set out to do," Pietro said quietly. "Your clothes and carriage are fine indeed."

"It seems a waste now. She is as angry as you are.

I do not know if she will forgive me, and if she does not, all is lost."

"Not all. You'll always have me."

Tears came to Colin's eyes, and he brushed them away with jerking movements. His uncle looked at him a moment, then heaved out his breath and embraced him.

"There is still some of the Colin of old in you," he said gruffly.

"I am sorry for the pain I caused," Colin whispered, his throat too tight to speak any louder. "I saw only the end, not the interim. I wanted everything, and now I have nothing."

Pietro shook his head and stepped back. "Don't give up yet. You've worked too hard."

"Can *you* forgive me?" If he could manage to win back the love of one, perhaps there was a possibility that he could win back the other.

"Maybe." A grin split the depths of his uncle's beard. "I have six horses to groom."

Colin's mouth curved wryly. "I am at your service."

"Come on." Pietro put his arm around Colin's shoulders and urged him toward the groomsmen's quarters. "You'll need to change your clothes."

"I can buy more if these are ruined."

"Hmm . . ." His uncle looked at him consideringly. "How wealthy are you?"

"Obscenely."

Pietro whistled. "Tell me how you did it."

"Of course." Colin smiled. "We have time."

* * *

It was late afternoon. The sun was dipping to the west and supper was being prepared. Ware's guests would eat earlier tonight than they would in Town, then spend the evening in the parlor, attempting to ignore the tension simmering between all parties. It would no doubt be unpleasant, but Ware understood the emotional undercurrents that were affecting everyone but him. He cared for Amelia and thought her the most suitable bride for his needs. That was his only tie to all of the rest.

"Mitchell stayed," he said to Amelia, as they strolled through the rear garden.

"Oh."

She stared straight ahead. With a sigh, he drew to a halt, which forced her to do the same.

"Talk to me, Amelia. That has always been the core strength of our friendship."

With a shaky smile, she canted her body to face his. "I am so sorry to have done this to you," she said remorsefully. "If I could go back and alter the events of this last week, I would. I would go back years and have married you long ago."

"Would you?" He tugged her closer, and set his hands lightly on her hips. Behind her, a profusion of climbing roses hugged an archway that led to a pond. Dandelion seeds drifted in the breeze, creating an enchanting backdrop for an enchanting woman.

"Yes. All these years I mourned him and he was thriving." Something deliciously like a growl escaped her. "He finds it far too easy to leave me behind. I am sick of being left behind. First my father, now Colin."

Amelia wrenched away and began to pace, her long legs moving with a lithe, determined elegance.

"I have never left you," he said, pointing out what he knew to be his greatest strength. "I enjoy your company far too much. There are precious few people in this world about whom I feel similarly."

"I know. Bless you. I love you for that." She managed a brief smile. "That is what has decided my mind. You will be steadfast and supportive. You do not seek to be someone you are not. You inspire me to be decorous and deport myself in a manner befitting a lady. We rub along well together."

Ware frowned, considering. "Amelia. I should like to discuss your thoughts on decorum and deportment in greater detail. Forgive me, but I find it rather odd to mention those traits as being most attractive. I would think our friendship and ease of association would lure you most."

She halted, her pale green skirts settling gently around her feet. "I have come to realize something these past days, Ware. I have reckless tendencies, just as Welton did. I require a certain environment in order to restrain those selfish impulses."

"And I provide this environment."

Amelia beamed at him. "Yes. Yes, you do."

"Hmm . . ." He rubbed his jaw. "And Mitchell inspires your reckless nature?"

"'Goads' would be a more apt word choice, but yes, he does."

"I see." Ware smiled wryly. "His role sounds more fun than mine."

"Ware!" She looked affronted, which made him laugh.

"Sorry, love. I must be honest. In one breath,

you point out that I do not seek to be someone I am not—in opposition, I presume, to Mr. Mitchell. Then in the next breath, you say that I inhibit a part of your nature that you are not proud of. Is that not seeking to be someone you are not . . . in a fashion?"

Her lower lip quivered in that way it had when she was upset. She set her hands on her hips and demanded, "Do you *want* me to be with him?" she cried. "Is that what you are saying?"

"No." All traces of amusement left him, and he bared the emotions he kept hidden below the surface. "I do not think he is the man for you. I do not think he deserves you. I do not believe he can provide a life that would content you. But that does not mean I want to live with only half of you."

Amelia blinked. "You are angry."

"Not at you," he said gruffly, reaching for her again. He gripped her by the elbows and pulled her close. "But I may eventually become so and I do not want that. I resent that I can have only the one side of you. If you choose me, Amelia, I can make you happy. The question left is whether you can make me happy, and I wonder if that is possible if I am forever waiting for the return of that precocious girl who asked me to kiss her."

"Ware . . ."

She cupped his cheek with her hand, and he nuzzled into it, inhaling the sweet scent of honeysuckle that clung to her.

"I do not deserve you," she whispered.

"Is that not what Mitchell said to you?" he asked, altering his hold to embrace her fully. Resting his cheek against her temple, he said, "I will leave you now. I have arrangements to make, and you require time to think."

"I do not want you to fight him."

"It is too late to change that end, Amelia. But I demand first blood, nothing more."

He felt relief relax the tautness of her spine. "Thank you," she said.

Ware brushed away the lone tear that stained her cheek, and stepped back.

"I am available to you at all times. Do not hesitate to seek me out if you have a need."

Amelia nodded, and watched Ware turn about and head toward the manse. When he disappeared from her view, she glanced around her, feeling lost and alone. No one knew how she felt, how deeply wounded she was by Colin's reappearance after all these years.

She stilled, her heartbeat stumbling for a moment over a sudden realization.

There was one person who loved Colin as she had. One person who would be equally devastated by his betrayal.

Knowing Pietro would need comfort as she did, Amelia lifted her skirts and hurried toward the stables.

Chapter 15

Francois Depardue assumed a vaguely bored expression as he entered the inn in Bristol. He took the stairs to the guest rooms above and knocked on the appropriate door. A shout of permission for entry was heard from the interior, and he answered it by stepping inside.

"Well?" Cartland asked impatiently, glancing up from the maps he had spread across the small, round table.

It was with great effort that Francois bit back an angry retort. With every day that passed, he disliked the brash, arrogant Englishman more and more. He'd argued with and then begged his superiors to have Cartland held in custody until he could ascertain who was truly guilty of Leroux's murder, but to no avail.

If he is lying, they said, *he will be close at hand for you to eliminate.*

They had insisted that Cartland join the search, and the Englishman had immediately assumed that he was in charge. He was an excellent tracker and even better killer, but those skills were tempered by his mistaken belief in his own superiority.

"It appears that Mitchell will be staying with Lord Ware. The manse is heavily guarded for some distance around. I would guess that is due to the presence of Christopher St. John."

Cartland smiled. "The earl is likely concerned that Mitchell will flee like the coward he is before the challenge can be met."

"So you say," Francois said.

The Englishman's features darkened. "I think the presence of Mademoiselle Rousseau has spoiled your temper."

Lysette. Francois smiled at the thought of her. Once, she had been harmless, but he and his men had ensured that she would never be harmless, or innocent, again. Aside from his sincere desire to see justice brought to Leroux's killer, his one pleasure in this miserable assignment was the thought of crossing paths with Lysette again.

His blood heated in anticipation. She would fight him, she always did, and she improved with every encounter. The harder she resisted him, the more he enjoyed it. Now that the *Illuminés,* on whose behalf she worked, had tasked her with ensuring either Cartland or Mitchell paid for Leroux's death, he imagined his inevitable domination of her body would be that much sweeter.

Perhaps the *Illuminés* thought he would welcome their assistance, but he did not like being second-guessed, which was how he viewed their interference.

"Do you have any suggestions for how we should proceed?" Francois asked.

"We could possibly lure the bulk of the guards away, using me as bait. Then we can attack the manse at night and kill him."

"But that will not tell me who is guilty, will it?"

Pushing to his feet, Cartland snapped, "I am obviously innocent, or they would not have sent me to find Mitchell!"

"Why, then, is Mademoiselle Rousseau here?" Francois smiled. "You think she is merely present to observe and support my efforts? Surely you are not so stupid. It was well planned to send you with me and Quinn with her. Nothing has been left to chance. You think your spy"—he gestured to the stocky man in the corner with a jerk of his chin—"gives you an advantage, but you are wrong."

"What do you suggest we do?" Cartland's face flushed.

Francois debated a moment, then shrugged. "Mitchell is dueling over a woman. Perhaps she is the key to his confession."

The Englishman paled. "You think to take St. John's sister-in-law? Are you insane?"

"Surely he cannot be as fearsome as is rumored," Francois scoffed.

"You've no notion," Cartland muttered. Then his features took on a mien of wily determination. "Then again . . . perhaps you are right." He smiled smugly. "I will think of a way. Give me time."

Francois shrugged, but inwardly he was making his own plans. "Fine. I will go eat downstairs. Either of you care to join me?"

"No. We both have work to do."

"As you wish."

Cartland watched Depardue leave with a narrowed glance.

"He is becoming more trouble than he is worth," he muttered. "Since killing him myself is out of the question, we must find another way to hasten the man to his reward."

"Send him to capture the girl, then," Jacques replied easily. "Since it was his idea, he should not object."

Grinning, Cartland considered the beauty of the plan. If Mitchell or St. John took care of Depardue for him, it would only strengthen his own protestations of innocence.

"Can you arrange for him to gain entry?"

"*Mais oui.*"

"Excellent. See to it."

Amelia found Pietro leading a bridled horse from the nearby corral to the stable yard. For a long moment, she was struck dumb by the resemblance he bore to Colin. With her memories of her childhood love arrested in the past, she had not noticed before. Now that she had seen him as a man, the similarities were unavoidable and agonizing. Tears welled, and though she tried to blink them back, they were plentiful and blurred her vision. She wiped them angrily away.

"Miss Benbridge." Pietro looked at her with commiseration in his dark eyes. "It hurts. I know."

She nodded. "How are you faring?"

"I'm angry," he admitted, "but grateful to have him back. If you still love the boy he was, perhaps you feel the same?"

"I am glad he is alive," she managed. "Is there anything you need?"

A smile lifted the corner of his mouth. "It is sweet of you to think of me during this time. I can see why he adores you as he does."

Her face heated at the gentle praise.

"He has loved you a long time, Miss Benbridge." Pietro's deep, slightly accented voice soothed her, though his words did not. "From the beginning, I tried to discourage him, but he wouldn't listen. I think it says a great deal that you both care so deeply for each other after all these years apart."

"That does not change the fact that he feels inferior to me"—she released a shaky breath—"or that I do not like the person I become trying to convince him of his worth."

He watched her for a long moment, then nodded. "Will you help me?"

"Of course." Amelia stepped closer. "What do you need?"

"Can you lead this horse into the stable for me? I have a few more to round up before the sun sets."

She accepted the proffered reins. The smile he gave her was strange, but presently everything in her life felt odd.

"Thank you," he murmured, then walked away.

Amelia turned and moved through the open stable door. The moment she stepped inside, she realized Pietro's intent. She paused, her breath caught in a mixture of surprise and volatile lust.

Colin worked with his back to her, but his identity was never in question. His torso was bare, his legs clad in worn coarse breeches, his calves hugged lovingly by polished Hessians. Powerful muscles bunched and flexed beneath sweat-sheened skin as he stroked a brush rapidly over a horse's flanks.

The sudden assailment of memories from their youth almost brought her to her knees. The sight of scratches left by her nails in the golden flesh added a carnal claim to his beautiful body that she longed to enforce.

As she watched, he stilled. Her exhale was a pant, and his head swiveled to face her in a lightning quick movement.

"Amelia."

He straightened and pivoted, baring the chest she had worshipped with both mouth and hands.

Dear God, he was divine. So handsome and virile, he made her heart ache.

"Are you alone?" he asked.

"Utterly."

Colin flinched and stepped toward her.

"Please do not come closer," she said.

His jaw tightened and he halted. "Stay. Talk to me."

"What is there to say? I heard your reasons. I understand why you acted as you did."

"Is there hope for us? Any at all?"

She shook her head.

Agony transformed his features. "Look at me," he said in a broken voice. "Look at where we are. This is where I would be if I had not left—tending St. John's horses while you lived your life in a manse I am not allowed to enter. How could we have been together? Tell me that."

Amelia covered her mouth to stifle a sob.

"What if I gave it all away?" His words were laced with a desperation that broke her heart into even smaller pieces. "What if I resumed my place as a servant in your household? Would you have me then?"

"Damn you," she cried, her shoulders straightening in self-defense. "Why must you change yourself to suit me? Why can you not simply be who you are?"

"This *is* who I am!" He spread his arms wide. "This is the man I have become, but he is still not what you want."

"Who cares what I want?" She stalked toward him. "What about what you want?"

"I want *you!*"

"Then why are you so quick to leave my side?" she snapped. "If you want me, fight for me. Do it for you, not for me."

Amelia thrust the reins at him.

He caught her hand and held it. "I love you."

"Not enough," she whispered, yanking free. Then she turned and ran from the stable in a flurry of skirts and lace.

Colin stared after her for long moments, attempting to reason what more he could do, what more he could say to win her love back. He had done everything, lost everything . . .

A dark shape filled the doorway, and he pushed his roiling emotions aside. "St. John."

The pirate stared at him with knowing eyes. "There was a lone rider spotted on a hill nearby. He is being followed back to town."

Colin nodded. "Thank you."

"Supper will be served shortly."

"I do not think I can bear it." The thought of the façade he would have to wear while Ware publicly laid claim to Amelia was too much.

"I will make your excuses, then."

"I owe you a great deal."

St. John hesitated a moment, then stepped farther inside. "Did you ever have the misfortune to meet Lord Welton?"

"Once. Briefly."

"What do you recall about him? Any impressions that lingered?"

Frowning, Colin thought back to the long-ago day. "I remember thinking he had no warmth in his eyes."

"Nothing like Miss Benbridge."

"Bloody hell. Nothing like her at all."

"Yet she seems to think they are similar creatures," St. John murmured. "Or at least that she is capable of becoming more similar. Any action she takes that is prompted by her desires rather than her reason is a suspected weakness."

Colin digested the information carefully. With him, Amelia was a creature of passion. She always had been. But they had been separated at the same time she'd learned of her father's treacherous nature. Certainly the revelation of Welton's true evil would have changed her, altered her in some way. In his heart he was attempting to woo the girl of old, but she was not that same girl any longer. He had to take that into consideration.

"Ware is the reasonable choice," Colin said, but he no longer thought the earl was the best choice. Amelia's vitality came from the passionate fire within her. It needed to be celebrated, as it would be with Colin. Not extinguished by the decorum Society would demand from Ware's wife.

"Yes," St. John agreed. "He is."

The pirate made his egress as silently as he'd arrived, leaving Colin with a great deal to consider.

Amelia sat stiffly during dinner, highly conscious of the fact that Colin took his meal in his room. The discussion she'd had with him in the stables prodded at her and gave her no rest. She was poor company, speaking little and casting a dark cloud over everyone's already somber mood. Despite her best efforts, she could not forget the sight of Colin working in the stable, a station he might still occupy if he had stayed in her employ. It was a shocking revelation to her, and she did not know what to think of it.

She retired early and hoped exhaustion would claim her, but fate was not so merciful. Unable to sleep, Amelia spent long hours tossing about in her bed. She finally abandoned the effort and left the confines of her disheveled linens. Donning her robe over her night rail, she slipped downstairs to the library.

The hour was late, all parties abed, leaving her the massive manse to herself. There were many times she roamed the St. John house at night, finding comfort in the silence and feeling of aloneness so reminiscent of her youth. Her imagination wandered, creating stories and tales in her mind, her memories picking up various passages from favorite books until she found herself at the library.

The door was slightly ajar, the flickering light of a blazing fire betraying the presence of someone inside. A shiver of awareness coursed over her skin in a wave of gooseflesh, urging her to forsake thoughts of reading and return to the safety of her bed. She debated a moment, internally examining why she would proceed when she valued stability so highly.

Ever since Colin had returned to her life, she had been acting with reckless disregard for anything but her own wants and needs. The correlation to her pater could not be ignored, and her jaw clenched with determination. It was most likely Ware in the library, and his presence would ground her and mitigate the riot of emotions she did not know how to deal with.

She pushed open the door.

Entering on silent feet, she noted the shirt-sleeve-clad arm hanging over the side of a wing chair and the large hand holding a crystal goblet at a careless angle. From the darkened color of the skin, she knew she had incorrectly guessed the occupant's identity, but she did not retreat. Something about the way the glass was held alarmed her. The amber liquid inside was tilted perilously close to the rim, threatening to spill onto the English rug.

The room was warm and comfortable, the walls lined floor-to-ceiling with bookcases displaying a mixture of worn volumes and priceless artifacts. Overstuffed furniture was scattered around the space, as were many side tables. It was a library that was actually used, rather than serving as merely an ostentatious display of wealth. Despite the inevitable upcoming confrontation with the man in the chair, she was soothed by the smells of parchment and leather, and took comfort in the silence inherent in a place of learning and discovery.

Amelia rounded the wingback and found Colin sprawled within its cradle, his long legs stretched out to rest his booted feet atop a footstool, his torso sans a coat and waistcoat, his throat bared by a missing cravat. He looked at her with heavy-lidded, emotionless eyes and lifted the goblet to sculpted lips. There was a scratch near his brow and a trail of dried blood below it.

"What's wrong?" she asked softly. "How were you hurt?"

"Stay away," he said in low, rough tone. "I am in a dark place, Amelia, and I have consumed more liquor than is wise. I cannot say what I will do if you come too close."

Draped on the carved wooden arm of a nearby chair were his waistcoat, coat, and weapons—a small sword and dagger.

"Where did you go?"

"I have yet to leave." He turned his head to look into the fire.

She heard the sadness and despair beneath the words, and her heart hurt for him. For her. "I am glad you did not go out."

"Are you?" Colin's head turned. In the light of the flickering fire, his beautiful face was hard, his dark eyes cold. "I am not."

"What could you have done in this condition?"

"There is no reason for me to evade Cartland. I should turn myself over to him and spare everyone the jeopardy my presence creates."

"Your life is the reason!" she protested. "If you concede, you will die."

A wry smile tugged at the corner of his lips. "Without any hope of having you, perhaps such a fate would be merciful."

"Colin! How can you say such a thing?" She covered her mouth and fought the tears that welled.

He cursed softly. "Go away. I am not fit company, as I warned you."

"I am afraid to leave you." She feared that he would do as he threatened and surrender.

"No, you are not. You already left me, remember?"

Amelia almost said more, but his dangerous mood stilled her tongue. She had seen St. John in similar moods at times and had always wondered at Maria's fortitude in seeking him out when he was so afflicted.

He needs me, Maria would say in explanation.

It was obvious that Colin needed comfort, too. And Amelia had distanced herself from him, which left him only the bottle to turn to for solace.

She approached him with shoulders squared, lifting the hem of her robe to her lips where she wet it. Reaching him, Amelia raised his chin with one hand and used the other to smooth away the blood. He was still, his eyes watchful, the tension that gripped him reaching out and surrounding her as well, making every nerve ending tingle and every breath a pant.

With an edgy snarl, Colin turned his head and pressed his lips to the sensitive skin of her wrist. She froze, unable to move as his tongue stroked over her now madly fluttering vein.

His glass hit the rug with a soft thud and a splash, and then he was on her, wrapping his big body around her and pulling her to the floor.

"I want you." His hot open mouth moved ravenously over the tender flesh of her throat. "So badly, it's eating me alive."

"Colin . . ." The feel of him, over six feet of potently aroused male, ignited her simmering passion to a raging fire. "We shouldn't . . ."

"Nothing can stop it," he said, his hand pushing open the halves of her robe and cupping her breast. "You belong to me."

Her gaze turned to the door she had left open when she entered. "The door—"

His lips surrounded her nipple through her night rail. Amelia gasped and clutched his hair.

"Remember that night," he whispered against her breast. "Remember how I felt inside you. Remember how deep . . . how I filled you . . ."

She quivered in longing, her blood hot, her breasts heavy and aching. His callused fingertips rolled and tugged at her nipple, sending waves of pleasure along the length of her body.

"Colin—"

He came over her and took her mouth, inundating her senses with the taste of brandy and the exotic spice that was uniquely his. She moaned in delight, sucking at his thrusting tongue in a desperate effort to drink in more of him.

Distantly, she felt his hands on her thighs. The chill of the evening air over feverish skin betrayed the lifting of her gown. As everything tightened and coiled in anticipation of his touch, Amelia whimpered into his mouth. His knee intruded between hers, urging her legs apart. Shameless, she complied, spreading her thighs to give him access to the throbbing flesh at the apex.

Colin lifted his head and watched her as he cupped her sex in his hand. "You melt for me," he breathed, his chest lifting and falling rapidly. He pushed two fingers inside her, and she arched in helpless pleasure. "You were made for me."

The feel of him there, where she ached, was too much. Wrapping her arms around his shoulders, she breathed, "Come in me. Fill me."

His gaze darkened, the irises swallowed by dilated pupils. "There is so much I can do to your body, Amelia. So many ways to impart pleasure. Shall I show you what you will miss when we part?"

"You left me first."

"I came back." His seductive tone was in sharp contrast to the pain she saw on his features. "Will *you* come back? If I love you well enough . . . if I addict your body to mine . . . will you come back to me?"

Her lower lip quivered and he licked across it, his breath hot and scented of liquor. His fingers advanced and retreated, plunging shallowly into her clenching sex, building her ardor with tender skill. It was searingly intimate, but in a different way than before. The emotions they bared were not hope and pleasure but despair and pain.

"It would be worth everything," he said in a serrated whisper, "if there was any chance that you might love me again."

"I never stopped." She cried softly, tears trailing down her temples to wet her hair. "Lack of love for you is not the problem."

Colin pressed his cheek to hers. "My greatest regret is that I could not be enough for you, despite my best efforts."

Amelia turned her head and pressed her lips to his, unwilling to argue again about their differences when he was already hurting. He took her kiss with tangible desperation, his heart beating so violently, she could hear it over her own racing pulse. All the while his shoulders flexed beneath her touch, the muscles working to propel his fingers into her drenched, aching sex. She cried out softly, a thready sound of female surrender and lust.

The sound changed him; she felt it. The wounded boy from her past gave way to the determined man of her present. Desperation altered to dominance; despair altered to desire. When his head lifted and he met her gaze again, he had the devil in his eyes.

"If only you could see what I see," he murmured, gentling his fingers, pulling free of her to slide across her clitoris with a slick, expert touch.

She gasped, her hips lifting involuntarily in an effort to increase the pressure of his teasing rubbing.

"Always hungry," he whispered, "always passionate. You burn for me, Amelia, as if you had Gypsy blood in your veins."

Colin nipped at her chin, then slid lower, licking along her throat until he reached the obtrusive ruffled neckline of her night rail. He moved, taking a kneeling position, hovering over her in a way that made her feel ravished. She was splayed beneath him, her clothes in disarray, his fingers touching her as only a husband should. The wantonness of her pose only increased her ardor, made her hotter and more desperate.

He pushed up her gown, higher and higher, until her stiffened nipples were kissed by the air and then by his mouth. His tongue was an instrument of pleasure and agony. The gentle licking over the tight peak made her clutch at his hair and pull him closer. As he suckled her, his cheeks hollowed, goading the sensations bombarding her until there was no way to register them all.

Colin. Her beautiful, exotic Colin was making love to her as she had never dreamed he would, and she could not resist him. His need and longing tapped into her own, freeing her of her inhibitions, making her a willing supplicant to his demands.

"Such beautiful breasts," he praised, kissing across the valley between them to pay a like service to her neglected, jealous nipple. Colin cupped the swollen flesh with his hand, plumping it with gentle kneading, rolling the beaded point between thumb and forefinger. "You are so sweet and soft. I could lose myself in you for days . . . weeks . . ."

The thought of being the recipient of the full force of his desires was as arousing as his touch, and Amelia rode his hand, the need to orgasm becoming a driving urge. "Please . . ."

His teeth bit into her nipple, eliciting a gasp of surprise. Then he traveled lower to circle her navel with the point of his tongue. "Not yet."

"Now," she begged, her need so intense, she could hear how wet she was. "Please . . . now."

Colin reared up to a kneeling position, leaving her bereft of his warmth and touch. He smiled as she protested, revealing the rakish dimples she had always loved. His shirtsleeves were tugged from the confinement of his breeches and pulled over his head, baring a sculpted chest and abdomen that made her mouth water. His skin was dark and stretched tightly over a highly defined musculature. She loved his body, always had. She adored the way hard labor made him powerful and strong.

"The way you look at me will keep us up all night," he said with darkly sensual promise.

He reached for the placket of his breeches and freed the straining length of his erection. Whatever arguments of reason she might have uttered died a fiery end, her entire focus narrowing to encompass only the man before her. He was a sensual fantasy come to life with his glistening torso bared to the waist and his thick, hungry cock curving upward in proud enticement.

Licking her lips, she sat up and reached for him.

"Amelia . . ." His tone was a warning, but he made no move to deter her as she angled him down to meet her waiting mouth.

"Just a taste," she whispered, licking her lips. "One taste . . ."

Her tongue swept across the tiny hole at the tip.

Colin's breath hissed out between his teeth.

The skin was softer than anything she had ever touched before, and the taste of him, salty and primitively male, was an aphrodisiac. With a moan, Amelia circled the wide, flared head with her lips and gave a tentative suck.

"Dear God," he groaned, shuddering. His hands came up to cup the back of her head.

Emboldened by his response and a wild desire to have him at her mercy, Amelia tilted her head and licked the pulsing length from top to bottom. The point of her tongue followed the path of a pulsing vein to the thick crest. She licked around and around, tasting the thick essence of his seed.

Colin was certain he would die of the pleasure Amelia bestowed with such enthusiasm. She seemed lost in the act, less focused on him and more on her own enjoyment. Her beautiful face was flushed, her green eyes glassy with arousal, her lips red and swollen and stretched tightly around his girth.

"Yes," he whispered, as she moaned and sucked harder. "Your mouth is heaven . . . take me deeper . . . yes . . ."

His body ached with the force under which he leashed it. He was trembling, burning, gasping for air. The sight of his cock sliding in and out of the ring of her lips was killing him. An hour ago, he had thought he would never touch her again, never hold her or feel her hot and wet around his cock as she climaxed beneath him. The pain of that loss was nearly too much to survive. To lose all hope and be left with nothing, only to see this— his breeches barely parted, his cock engorged and throbbing with need, and Amelia . . . the love of his life . . . servicing his lust with such passionate fervor. It made the ecstasy of her luscious mouth agonizingly intense.

"My love . . . I won't last . . ." His voice was so guttural, he barely understood himself, but she knew. She collected his meaning. He felt it in the way she touched him, saw it in the way she looked at him.

"Do it," she breathed, her words warm against his wet skin. Her hand fisted around him and pumped, drawing up his bollocks and making his thighs quake with the intensity of his rising climax. She cupped him there, her fingers sliding through the rough hair and fondling his sack.

He cursed, the tension in his spine painfully acute. "I will flood you—damn it . . ."

Her eager mouth flowed over the aching head of his cock in a burning caress of drenching heat and hungry suction. His lungs seized, his vision darkened, his fingers tightened on her scalp.

He was moving on instinct alone; his hips bucked and thrust, running his cock over her flickering tongue and against the back of her throat. Her clenched hand prevented him from moving too deep, kept him from taking too much. Amelia moaned in sensual supplication, the vibration tingling up the length of his erection and freeing his coiling orgasm.

Colin growled as he erupted, his cock jerking with every wrenching pulse of semen, his fingers tangling in her hair. Over the mad beating of his heart and harsh, panting breaths, he heard her seductive mewls and desperate swallows as he came such as he'd never come before, pumping hard and fast into the milking depths of her mouth until he was completely and utterly spent.

She released him with a last, lingering suck, her lips shiny with his seed and curved in a purely woman's smile. Colin stared down at her in a daze, his thoughts lost in an alcohol-soaked, orgasm-induced fog. His heart, however, was as alive as it had ever been.

Had he truly thought sex would temper his love for her and make it more manageable? He loved her more now than ever, with a reckless, saturating abandon.

Lose her? *Never.*

Pushing her back, he slid down. He parted her thighs with his palms and buried his face in the slick, humid paradise of her glistening sex. Colin licked her, parting the pouty lips to stroke across her clitoris.

"Colin!" she cried out, her voice filled with startled, embarrassed pleasure.

He smiled against her, then kissed her deeply, turning his head to push his tongue inside the tiny, clenching slit that was made to hold his cock. The taste of her intoxicated him, addicted him.

"No . . . *Please.*"

There was something in her voice, a note of panic that urged him to lift his head. He stared at her, saw the wild light in her eyes and asked, "What is it?"

"Please. Stop."

He frowned, noting the high flush on her cheeks and the trembling of her thighs beneath his hands. She was hopelessly aroused, yet she stayed him.

"Why?"

"I cannot think . . ."

Reason. Conscious thought. She wanted it. Servicing him gave her power. Being serviced by him took it all away.

"You think too much," he said hoarsely. "Give in. Free the woman who took me to her bed without care for anything or anyone."

She struggled beneath him. "You want t-too much . . ."

"Yes," he growled. "All of you. Every piece . . ."

He was in her then, giving her pleasure with avid lips and tongue, eating at her, drinking her in, inhaling the primal scent of her deep into his lungs. The innate hunger he felt for her stirred in response, rousing and climbing, swelling his cock as if she had not just drained him.

Amelia twisted beneath Colin, clawing at his shoulders, begging for mercy in a voice roughened by pure female lust. She was on the edge of a steep cliff that terrified her, and he was pushing her, giving her no quarter, allowing her no space to retreat.

His tongue was an instrument of torturous pleasure, lashing and flickering, driving her higher and harder. His lips circled her clitoris, sucking and pulling. And the noises he made. The wet smacking, the rumbling purrs, the groans of need that made her slicker and hotter.

Thick skeins of dark hair tickled her inner thighs, moving as he did, narrowing her focus until all she knew was the tightening of her womb and the helpless rolling of her hips.

He demanded her response, forced it from her, turned her into a mindless creature of desire and need and desperate wanting.

"No . . . no . . . no . . ." she gasped, fighting him even as her fingers tangled in his locks and pulled him closer.

So that he could not leave her again.

Colin cupped her buttocks and lifted her, altering the angle, urging her thighs to widen so that he could take everything. He thrust his tongue hard and fast into the spasming opening, and she climaxed violently, her arms falling heavily to the floor, her nails clawing at the rug.

"Colin!"

She was devastated, destroyed. But he was not done with her. Before she could catch her breath, he was over her, inside her, pushing deep into the heart of her with the thick, hot length of his cock.

"Yes." He groaned, sliding his arms beneath her shoulders, holding her in place as he lunged with sensual grace and seated himself to the hilt. "Jesus . . . you feel so good."

He ground his hips against her, rubbing deep inside her, making her feel every throbbing inch of him.

Gasping, writhing, Amelia accepted his possession with ravenous greed, her swollen tissues parting for his relentless drives with a quivering welcome. He gripped her throat with one hand, her hip with the other, pinning her down. Dominating her. Possessing her. Branding her as his.

"Mine," he growled, sliding in and out of her, the movements of his hips leisurely, though nothing else about him was.

There was a look on his flushed and sweat-dampened face. Part agony, part pleasure. So austere and focused. So intent. His eyes blazing with heat. His handsome features stretched tautly with strain. It was searingly erotic. Intimate.

Colin was making love to her. He was alive and in her arms, in her body. Whispering words of love and desire, making dreams come true that she had thought were forever dead to her.

Again the tension built and coiled, causing her to tighten around his straining cock and ripple along its length, making him curse and growl. She felt the chafing rubbing of his waistband between her thighs, heard the sound of his boots digging into the weave of the rug, realized he was still partly dressed just as she was.

The image in her mind of how they must look— she with parted robe and lifted night rail, he with boots and breeches lowered just enough to free his beautiful cock, both locked on the floor in carnal congress—took her to orgasm.

"There," he purred, watching her with a feral smile of possession, thrusting strong and sure, extending her pleasure until she thought it might kill her. The surge of sensation was unbearable, tingling across her skin until it was too tight and sensitive.

When she was limp and whimpering, he sought his own pleasure, his dark head thrown back, his neck corded tightly, his cock so thick and hard.

Amelia watched him as he had watched her, her legs wrapped around his working hips, her hands at his waist. Pulling him into her.

His pace picked up, his grip tightened. She felt the climax coming, felt it grip him in a fist, felt it tighten his lungs. It burst from him in shocking spurts of molten liquid inside her, again and again, the breaking dam heralded by his ragged, extended groan and jerking, wrenching shudders.

"Dear God," he gasped, quaking, rubbing his

pelvic bone against her swollen, oversensitive clitoris and making her come again. Suffusing her body with delight that seeped into her bones and heart and soul. Making them one.

"My love," he breathed, rubbing his big body against hers, drenching her in the scent of his skin. "I won't release you. You're mine—"

She stemmed further words with a desperate kiss.

Chapter 16

*A*melia woke to a hand held over her mouth. Scared beyond measure, she struggled against her assailant, her nails clawing at his wrist.

"Stop it!"

She stilled at the command, her eyes opening wide, her heart racing madly as her sleep-fuzzy brain came to an awareness of Colin looming over her in the darkness.

"Listen to me," he hissed, his gaze darting to the windows. "There are men outside. A dozen at least. I don't know who they are, but they are not your father's men."

She yanked her head to the side to free her mouth. "What?"

"The horses woke me as the men walked by the stable." Colin stepped back and yanked off her counterpane. "I snuck out the back and came round to fetch you."

Embarrassed to be seen in only her night rail, Amelia yanked the covers back over her.

He yanked them off again. "Come on!" he said urgently.

"What are you talking about?" she asked in a furious whisper.

"Do you trust me?" Colin's dark eyes glittered in the darkness.

"Of course."

"Then do as I say, and ask questions later."

She had no notion of what was happening, but she knew he wasn't jesting. Sucking in a deep breath, she nodded and slipped from the bed. The room was lit only by the moonlight that entered through the window glass. The heavy length of her hair hung down her back in a thick, swinging braid, and Colin caught it, rubbing it between his fingers.

"Put something on," he said. *"Quickly."*

Amelia hurried behind the screen in the corner and disrobed, then slipped the chemise and gown she had worn earlier over her head.

"Hurry!"

"I cannot close the back. I need my abigail."

Colin's hand thrust behind the screen and caught her elbow, tugging her from behind it so that he could drag her to the door.

"My feet are bare!"

"No time," he muttered. Opening her bedroom door, he peered out to the hallway.

It was so dark, Amelia could barely see anything. But she heard male voices. *"What is going—"*

Moving with lightning speed, Colin spun and covered her mouth again, his head shaking violently.

Startled, it took her a moment to understand. Then she nodded her agreement to say nothing.

He stepped out to the hallway with silent steps, her hand in his. Somehow, despite her shoeless state, the floorboard beneath her squeaked, when it hadn't under Colin's boots. He froze, as did she. Below them, the voices *she had heard were also silent. It felt as if the house were holding its breath. Waiting.*

Colin placed his finger to his lips. Then he picked her up and hefted her over his shoulder. What followed was a blur. Suspended upside down, she was disoriented and unable to discern how he managed to carry her from her second-floor bedroom to the lower floor. Then a shout was heard upstairs as she was discovered missing, and pounding feet thundered above them. Colin cursed and ran, jostling her so that her teeth ached and her braid whipped his legs so hard, she feared hurting him. Her arms wrapped around his lean hips, and his pace picked up. They burst out the front door and down the steps.

More shouting. More running. Swords clashed and Miss Pool's screams pierced the night.

"There she is!" someone shouted.

The ground rushed by beneath her.

"Over here!"

Benny's voice was music to her ears. Colin altered direction. Lifting her head, she caught a glimpse of pursuers, and then more men intercepted them, some she recognized, others she didn't. The new additions to the fray bought them precious time, and soon she could not see anyone on their heels.

A moment later she was set on her feet. Wild-eyed, she glanced around to catch her bearings, and found Benny on horseback and Colin mounting the back of another beast.

"Amelia!" He held out one hand to her, the other expertly holding the reins. She set her hand in his, and he dragged her up and over, belly down across his lap. His powerful thighs bunched beneath her as he spurred the horse, and then they were off, galloping through the night.

She hung on for dear life, her stomach heaving with the jolting impacts. But it did not last long. Just as they reached the open road, a shot rang out, echoing through the darkness. Colin jerked and cried out. She screamed as her entire world shifted.

Sliding, falling . . .

Amelia awoke to a hand held over her mouth and a whisper in her ear.

"Shh . . . Someone is in the house."

Colin's voice anchored her in the semidarkness. For the space of several heartbeats, the horror and fear from the vivid dream lingered. Then the feel of Colin's body pressed to her back and his strong arms around her provided much needed comfort.

Awareness seeped in slowly. She noted the elaborate moldings on the ceiling and felt velvet beneath her calf.

They were on the settee in the library. From the look of the fire in the grate—now reduced to mere embers—she had been asleep for at least a couple of hours.

Turning in Colin's embrace, she faced him and pressed her mouth to his ear. "Who is it?" she whispered.

Colin shook his head, his dark eyes glittering.

Amelia held still, absorbing the tension that gripped his frame. Then she heard it. The sound of a booted foot falling on the parquet floor.

Boots. At this hour.

Her heartbeat leaped from the steady rhythm of slumber to a racing tempo. Unlike her dream, this time it was Colin who was endangered.

He pressed his lips to hers in a quick, hard kiss. Then he slid silently off the edge of the couch. On his knees, he fastened his breeches. He drew his discarded shirtsleeves over his head, then reached for his small sword.

She, too, slid to the floor and belted her robe.

"Secure the door when I leave," he whispered, pulling his blade free of its scabbard with torturous slowness to avoid making any sound.

Denying him with a shake of her head, Amelia crawled over to where a faint glimmer betrayed the jeweled hilt of his dagger lying atop his waistcoat and coat. The moment her hand wrapped around it, he was behind her.

"No."

"Trust me." She turned her head to press her cheek to his.

His jaw clenched. "My sanity hinges on your safety."

"You think I feel differently about you?" She touched his cheek with a shaking hand, tracing the faint line that marked the spot where a dashing dimple appeared when he was happy. "Rest easy. My sister is the Wintry Widow."

There was a long pause, his throat working as he considered what she was saying.

"Let me help," she breathed. "How will we ever move forward together if you always leave me behind?"

She knew how the thought of her in danger tormented him, because she felt likewise about him.

Finally, Colin managed a jerky nod. With a swift kiss to his parted lips, she pulled the dagger free of its sheath.

I love you. The words were spoken soundlessly, his lips against hers.

Amelia lifted his hand and kissed the back.

Colin wrenched away from her and moved to the door. At some point while she was sleeping, he had closed it. Now, he turned the knob and cracked it just wide enough to see. The well-oiled hinges made no sound.

In the blink of an eye, he was gone. She counted to ten, then slipped out after him.

Bolstered by the feel of the dagger hilt, Amelia crawled along the runner toward the stairs, her senses acute. The sound of the wind blowing and the nocturnal call of a preying owl grounded her to the moment. She breathed shallowly, her emotions suppressed by the instinct to survive and the need to protect Colin. There was a sudden silence, as if the house held its breath, and then she heard the barest hint of sound—a stealthy footfall straight ahead.

She paused. Pushing to her knees, she huddled in the darkness.

A clear shot, just one.

To her right, a movement caught her eye. Holding the blade and aiming the hilt, Amelia prepared to throw. Her arm was steady, her nerves taut but manageable. She had never killed before, but if it became necessary, she would act first and face the consequences later.

Her arm went back, her focus narrowed on a slim shaft of moonlight lying directly across the bottom step.

Although there was no discernable sound of

progress, Amelia sensed the intruder moving closer to that tiny beam of light.

Closer . . . closer . . .

Suddenly, Colin lunged. She knew it was him by the white of his shirt, as he arced through the moonlight. He crashed into a body so well concealed by shadows that Amelia had been unable to see the outline of it at her present angle. A loud crash heralded the colliding of the two figures into a breakable object.

She leaped to her feet. Crossing the hallway, she reached the opposite wall, improving the chances of a successful strike.

It was too dark to identify one form or the other. With both figures tangled in a writhing mass of limbs, she could do nothing but pray.

Mercifully, a door opened on the upper floor. She bit back a sob of relief. The light cast by an approaching lantern bearer was sufficient illumination to catch an uplifted blade too short to be Colin's small sword. Amelia pulled back her arm and threw, putting weight behind the volley with an oft-practiced lunge.

It spun hilt-over-blade in a lightning quick roll. A pained grunt rent the air. The knife that had been aimed at Colin clattered noisily, yet harmlessly, to the parquet.

St. John rushed down the staircase with a pistol held in one hand and a lantern held aloft in the other. Maria was directly behind him with a foil at the ready.

Light spilled across the foyer, revealing Amelia's target. Clutching his chest, the intruder sank to his

knees. The hilt of the dagger protruded from between his clutching hands. He swayed morbidly
for a long moment, then fell forward.

"Bloody hell," Colin breathed, rushing to her
side. "Beautifully done."

"That was excellent, Amelia," St. John said with
much pride, his gaze on the body lying slumped at
his feet.

"What in hell is transpiring out here?" Ware demanded, descending the staircase. Mr. Quinn and
Mademoiselle Rousseau joined the gathering in
short order.

"Depardue," the Frenchwoman said. She lowered
to a crouch and set her hand on his shoulder, pushing him gently to his back. *"Comment te sens-tu?"*

The Frenchman groaned softly and opened his
eyes. "Lysette . . ."

She reached for the dagger and withdrew it.
Then stabbed him again, this time through the
heart.

The sound of the blade scraping across a rib
bone and a sharp abbreviated cry from Depardue
made Amelia shudder violently. "Good God!" she
cried, feeling ill.

The Frenchwoman's arm lifted and fell again.
Mr. Quinn lunged and yanked her back, the dagger pulling free with her retreat and hitting the
floor. "Enough! You killed him."

Mademoiselle Rousseau fought her confinement,
hurling expletives in French with such venom,
Amelia took an involuntary step backward. Then the
woman spat on the corpse.

The display left everyone in stunned silence for
a long moment. Then St. John cleared his throat.

"Well . . . that one is no longer a threat. However, there must be more of them. I doubt the man would come alone."

"I will search the downstairs." Colin looked at Amelia. "Go to your room. Lock the door."

She nodded. The sight of the dead man and the rapidly spreading pool of blood at her feet made her stomach churn. Now that help was at hand, the full effect of her actions began to seep into her consciousness.

I found something.

All eyes turned toward the direction of the foyer, where Tim appeared, carrying Jacques by the scruff of his neck.

"'E was sneaking about outside," the giant rumbled.

No one could fail to note the Frenchman's fully dressed state.

"I was not 'sneaking' about!" Jacques protested.

"I think 'e let that one"—Tim jerked his chin toward Depardue—"in."

"Do we have a traitor in our midst?" St. John asked ominously.

A cold chill swept across Amelia's skin.

"*Ça alors!*" Mademoiselle Rousseau threw up her hands, one of which was covered in blood. "Should we be wasting time on him when there could be others outside?"

Tim looked at St. John. "We caught three more, not including these two."

Colin's face hardened. "We will question all of them, then. Someone will tell us something of import."

Mademoiselle Rousseau snorted. "*Absurde.*"

"What do you suggest we do?" Simon asked with exaggerated politeness. "Torture him slowly over many days? Would that better slake your blood lust?"

She waved her hand carelessly. "Why exert yourself? Kill him."

"Salope!" Jacques yelled. "You would eat your own young."

St. John's brows rose.

"She works with me," the Frenchman cried, struggling in Tim's grip. "I, at least, can bear witness to Mitchell's innocence in the matter of Leroux's murder. She has nothing of value."

"I beg your pardon?" Colin said, his frame stiffening. "Did you say you both work together?"

Amelia wrapped her arms around her waist, shivering.

"Ta gueule!" Mademoiselle Rousseau hissed.

Jacques's smile was maliciously triumphant.

"I think we should separate them," Colin suggested.

St. John nodded.

"I will take Lysette," Simon said with a hard edge to his voice.

When the Frenchwoman shivered with apparent apprehension, Amelia looked away and fought a flare of sympathy for the woman.

"Come along, poppet," Maria murmured, linking arms with her. "Let us gather tea and spirits for the men. We have a long night ahead of us."

Colin stared at the man he'd thought was a friend and attempted to comprehend the fullness of the plot being explained to him. "You have been work-ing with Mademoiselle Rousseau from the begin-ning? Before you met at the inn a few days ago?"

Jacques nodded. He was bound to a damask and gilded chair in Ware's study, his calves tied to the legs, his hands restrained behind the back. "We did not meet at the inn. I have known her for some time now."

"But you both acted as if you had just become acquainted," Simon argued. When Mademoiselle Rousseau had proven to be more stubborn in hold-ing her silence, he had left her bound and guarded in a guest room and joined the rest of the party in questioning her coconspirator.

"Because we had to make you believe that this matter was about Cartland and his murder of Ler-oux," Jacques explained.

"Is that not what this has all been about?" St. John asked, frowning.

"No. The *Illuminés* sought to end your inquiries and activities in France, which have become in-creasingly troublesome. I was sent to discover the identity of your superior."

Colin froze. "The *Illuminés?*" He had heard whispers of a secret society of "enlightened" mem-bers who sought power through hidden channels, but the rumors were unsubstantiated. Until now. "What do they have to do with Leroux?"

"None of this had anything to do with Leroux," the Frenchman snapped. "In fact, Cartland's mur-der of Leroux has been a complication."

"How so?" Simon asked from his position on the settee. Dressed in his evening robe and holding a cheroot in one hand, he looked the part of a man at leisure, which was definitely not the case.

"The *Illuminés* learned that Mitchell was returning to England," Jacques said. "I secured a cabin aboard the same ship with the intent to befriend him on the journey. It was hoped that our association would eventually lead to a disclosure of the identity of the man you work for here in England. I followed Mitchell the night we were to set sail, and I took advantage of the opportunity presented to me. I used the situation to build a friendship with Mitchell."

"Fascinating," St. John murmured.

"And what of Lysette?" Simon asked.

"Mitchell was my target," the Frenchman said. "You were hers. The *Illuminés* do not like to leave anything to chance."

"Bloody hell." Colin growled his frustration. "And what of tonight? What role did Depardue play?"

"He was responsible for discovering the truth regarding Leroux's death, which is a personal matter to the agent-general."

"So I am still wanted in France," Colin said, "and someone must pay for Leroux's death. My predicament has not changed, merely your and Mademoiselle Rousseau's role in it."

Jacques smiled grimly. "Yes."

"And now Depardue is dead."

"Do not regret that outcome, *mon ami*. As Mademoiselle Rousseau can attest, he was a far from honorable man. I would never allow you to suffer for his crimes. I assured you of that from the beginning."

"But you allowed Depardue into my house," Ware pointed out. "Why?"

"Cartland sent him to find Miss Benbridge," Jacques explained. "I agreed to assist him, but my intent was not to let him succeed. I had hoped to be the one to 'discover' him and kill him, thereby deepening your trust in me."

"I do not understand." St. John stepped closer. "Why does Cartland trust you?"

"Because of Depardue. When Mitchell and I were still in London, I searched for Cartland. I found Depardue and told him I was working with Lysette to apprehend Leroux's killer. Lysette's involvement made Depardue wary. This created an opening with Cartland, who needed alternate French support because Depardue did not believe him."

"Where is Cartland now?" Colin asked.

"At the inn, waiting for word."

Colin looked at Quinn, who stood.

"I will change swiftly," Quinn said.

St. John rose. "I shall come along, as well."

"I will stay here with the women," Ware offered. Then he smiled. "Though I doubt they need my protection."

Colin left the room and moved toward the library with a rapid, eager stride. Quinn fell into step beside him.

"It appears that your vindication is at hand," the Irishman said.

"Yes. Finally." Anticipation thrummed through Colin's veins and made his heart race. The divide separating him from Amelia still existed, but the scent of their lovemaking clung to his skin and gave him hope. She loved him. The rest would come in time.

He and Quinn parted ways by the staircase, and Colin returned to the library to collect his coats. His fist curled around the empty sheath that normally held his dagger, and his mind returned to the moment when Amelia had come to his aid, defending him to the death. Earlier today he had thought it impossible to love her more than he did. Now he realized he was falling in love with her all over again. With the woman Amelia had grown into.

For the first time, Colin was absolutely certain there was no other man in the world better for Amelia. And even if that were not the case, damn them all regardless. She belonged to him. With perseverance he might convince her to believe that, too.

Resolute and determined, he shrugged into his garments and left the room. Ware was standing at the foot of the staircase, staring down at the location where Depardue's body had lain not long ago. The scene was tidied now, but Colin suspected the memory would haunt the earl for years to come.

At the sound of footfalls, Ware turned his head, and his gaze narrowed upon seeing Colin.

"If you capture Cartland," Ware said, "you will have no further business here." His jaw tightened. "Except for one."

"Shall we meet at dawn?" Colin suggested. The duel was one more impediment to his future with Amelia. He wanted it dispatched immediately. "We will both have been awake through the night. No advantage for either of us."

"Perhaps you will fight at length or return wounded," the earl said grimly. "However, if neither of those conditions applies, dawn will suit me well."

Colin bowed and hastened toward the stables, spurred by the thought that the sun could rise upon an entirely new life for him. He found St. John waiting with a dozen men. Quinn appeared shortly after.

Within a half hour, a troop of over a dozen riders was on its way into town.

Chapter 17

Cartland heard the sounds of many booted feet approaching his room and reached for the gun resting on the table before him. Sending Depardue along with four others had been a gamble he would have preferred to avoid, but sometimes such risks reaped the greatest rewards.

Holding a pistol lightly in one hand, he waited for the knock and then called out for entry. The door opened, and one of his men entered in a rush.

"I cannot be certain," the man said; "perhaps I am overcautious, but a group of three heavily armed gentlemen entered the tavern below."

Cartland tucked his weapon into his waistband and reached for his coat. "Better to be cautious than foolhardy." He caught up his small sword and moved swiftly toward the door. "Are the others below?"

"Yes, and two in the stables."

"Excellent, come with me."

Moving with long, rapid strides, Cartland made

his egress by way of the servants' staircase. Straight ahead was the rear exit, but he turned left instead and went through the kitchen to the delivery door. It always paid to be careful.

The door was ajar, allowing the cool night breeze into the hot kitchen. Cartland saw nothing but darkness beyond the small pool of spilling light, but he rushed outside to the alley in a near run to give himself a better chance of escape if a trap was set.

Once he was shrouded by the enveloping moonlit night, he felt safer.

Until he heard the pained grunt of the lackey who ran just behind him.

Startled, Cartland stumbled over a loose bit of gravel. He spun, pulling his gun free as he did so, his gaze wild and seeking.

"So good to see you again," Mitchell called out.

The light of the moon illuminated the narrow alley and the prone body on the ground with the knife hilt protruding from its back. The lackey groaned and writhed and was absolutely useless to Cartland.

"You!" he sputtered, unable to see the man who hunted him.

"Me," Mitchell agreed from the shadows.

The echo created by the surrounding buildings made it difficult to determine where Mitchell was.

Meanwhile, Cartland was out in the open.

Brandishing his firearm, Cartland said, "The French won't believe that I am at fault. They trust me."

"Allow me to worry about that."

There was a thud to the left, and Cartland fired in that general direction. When a large, round rock rolled down the shallow incline to rest against

his booted foot, he knew he'd been tricked. Had
he not been so panicked, he would have known
better. His heart sank into his gut, frozen by terror.

Mitchell's laughter filled the night. Then the
Gypsy appeared in a flurry of a swirling cape like
some phantom apparition. In each hand was a
weapon. One was a pistol, which left Cartland with
no options beyond death or surrender. His useless,
smoking gun fell from his nerveless fingers and
clattered to the alley floor.

"I can help you," he offered urgently. "I can
speak on your behalf and clear your name."

Mitchell's teeth flashed white in the darkness.
"Yes, you will—by returning to France and paying
for your crimes."

Amelia jolted awake just before dawn. Her heart
was racing as if she'd run a great distance, but she
could not discern why.

She lay abed for a long moment, blinking up at
the canopy above her. Her bleary gaze lingered
upon the gold tassels that framed the edges, and
she attempted to regulate her panting by concen-
trating on every breath.

Then she heard an unmistakable noise that filled
her with dread—the sound of swords clashing outside.

For a moment, she feared the men had not suc-
ceeded with their early morning capture of Cartland,
but the lack of shouting and mayhem dispelled that
thought.

The duel!

She called out for her abigail as she leaped up from the bed. "Anne!"

Hurrying to the window, she threw the drapes wide, cursing under her breath to see the pale gray-and-pink sky.

Amelia rushed to her armoire and pulled out a shawl. "Anne!"

The door opened, and she turned in an agitated flurry. "Why did you not wake me before—Maria!"

"Amelia."

The note of sympathy in Maria's voice caused gooseflesh to flare across Amelia's arms. "No!" she breathed, rushing past her sister to the gallery.

"Poppet! Wait!"

But she did not. She ran with all the strength she had, nearly crashing into an industrious chambermaid before skittering around the corner and stumbling down the stairs. As she approached the lower floor, the unmistakable ring of clashing foils iced her blood. Amelia was nearly to the French doors that led to the rear terrace and the lawn beyond that when she was caught in a crushing embrace and restrained. She attempted a scream, but was gagged by a massive hand over her mouth.

"Sorry," Tim muttered. "I can't let you distract 'em while they're fighting. That's 'ow men are killed."

She shuddered violently at the thought of either man being injured. Struggling like a madwoman, Amelia fought for freedom, but even grown men could not best Tim. As the sounds of fighting continued, tears welled and coursed freely. Every clang of steel clashing against steel struck her like a blow, causing her to jerk repeatedly in Tim's arms. He cursed and pressed his cheek to hers, murmuring things meant to soothe, but nothing could alleviate her distress.

Then . . . silence.

Amelia froze, afraid to breathe in case the sound would overpower the heralds of whatever was transpiring outside.

Tim carried her to a nearby window and pushed up the sash a bare inch. A damp, chilly breeze blew through the tiny gap, making her shiver.

"You are the better man."

Colin's voice drifted to her ears, and her lips quivered against Tim's palm.

"You are the reasonable choice," he continued in a grim tone. "You have been steadfast and true to her. Unlike my estate, your wealth and title are long-standing. You can give her things that I cannot."

Amelia hung limply in Tim's arms, sobbing silently.

"Most importantly, her affection for me is not something she welcomes, while she gratefully embraces her future with you."

Her head turned to the side, her tear-stained cheek pressing against Tim's thundering heart.

Colin was leaving her, as he had so many times before.

Tim's hand fell away from her mouth.

"Release me," she whispered, her spirit broken. "I will not go outside."

He set her down and she turned away.

"Poppet." Maria waited at the bottom of the stairs with her arms wide open. Amelia walked gratefully into them, her knees weakening, forcing them both to sit on the bottom step.

"I had hope," Amelia whispered, her chest crushed by grief such as she had not felt since she first believed Colin had died. "I hate myself for having hope. Why can I not learn from the past? Those I love do not stay in my life. They all leave. Every one of them. Except for you . . . only you stay . . ."

"Hush. You are overwrought."

Strong arms curved beneath her as Tim lifted her up. She curled against his chest as he carried her back to her bedchamber with Maria in tow.

Colin straightened from his low bow, his eyes meeting Ware's as the earl mimicked his movements. He felt the hot trickle of blood weeping from the shallow wound caused by Ware's blade, but he did not care. Ware had satisfaction, but that was all he would have. It would have to be enough for the earl, for Colin intended to take the spoils.

"But regardless of everything that recommends you, my lord," Colin continued, "I concede only this duel. Not Miss Benbridge. Her deeper affection is for me, as always. And I believe my feelings for her are quite obvious to one and all."

"Which is why you abandoned her for several years?" the earl scoffed.

"I cannot alter the past. However, I can assure you that from the present moment onward, nothing on Earth can take her from me."

Ware's blue eyes narrowed, and thick tension filled the air between them. Then the corner of the earl's mouth lifted. "Perhaps you are not the man I thought you were."

"Perhaps not."

They bowed again, then quit the lawn, both men heading in the separate directions their lives would now take them.

The next half hour of Amelia's life—or was it an hour?—passed in a daze. Maria forced tea upon her, as well as a hefty dose of laudanum.

"It will calm you," her sister murmured.

"Go away," she muttered, slapping at the many hands that sought to soothe her brow.

"I will read quietly," Maria said, "and send your abigail away."

"No. You go, too."

Eventually they gave up and went away, leaving Amelia to curl into herself and fall back into a dreamless, drug-induced sleep.

Sadly, the respite did not last long. Far too soon another hand brushed the curls back from her face.

"I suppose I have only myself to blame for your lack of faith."

Colin's voice brushed across her skin like a tangible caress. She rolled into him, grasping with her hands. He caught them with his own and squeezed.

"You were supposed to sleep straight through this morning," he murmured, pulling the blankets back from her. "I wanted to spare you any possibility of distress."

She was lifted and cradled to a warm, hard

chest. The scent of his skin, so alluringly masculine and uniquely Colin, urged her to bury her tear-streaked face in his cravat.

She was distantly aware of being carried. It felt as if they descended a staircase, and then fresh air was drifting over her skin, making her shiver.

"There's a blanket in my carriage," he murmured. "A minute more and then you will be comfortable again."

A moment later she was jostled into a carriage, and it set off with a lurch, the wheels crunching across gravel. She was held securely in Colin's lap and covered warmly. Tears leaked out between her closed eyelids, and she prayed that she would never wake from such a wonderful dream.

His firm lips pressed tightly against her forehead. "Sleep."

Drugged by the laudanum, she did.

It was the sudden cessation of motion that woke Amelia. Blinking, she fought off the remnants of sleep.

"The horses are fatigued and I am near starved." Colin's deep voice pulled her from half awareness to full cognizance in an instant.

The duel . . .

Bolting upright, the top of her head made sharp contact with his chin, causing them both to cry out.

"Ow, damn it," he muttered, rearranging her atop his lap as if she weighed nothing at all.

Wild-eyed, Amelia took in the luxurious appointments of Colin's travel coach and then leaned out the window. They were in the courtyard of what appeared to be an inn.

She glanced at him and found him rubbing his chin. "Where are we?"

"On our way."

"To where?"

"To be wed."

Amelia blinked. "What?"

His smile revealed his dimples and reminded her of the boy she had fallen so deeply in love with. "You said that we had no hope of moving forward together if I was forever leaving you behind. Since I had no further reason to enjoy Lord Ware's hospitality, it was time for us to go."

She stared at him for a long moment, trying to collect what it was that he was saying. "I do not understand. Did you not duel this morning?"

"Yes, we did."

"Did he not win? Did you not say he was the better man? Dear God, am I losing my mind?"

"Yes, yes, and no." Colin tightened the arm banded around her waist and pulled her closer. "I allowed him first blood," he explained. "He had a right to it. When I took you, you were still his."

Amelia opened her mouth to protest, and he covered her lips with his fingertips. "Allow me to finish."

She stared at him for a long moment, absorbing the sudden gravity reflected on his countenance. Then she nodded and slipped free of his embrace, moving to the opposite squab so that she could think properly.

It was then she noted that she was dressed in her night rail. For his part, Colin was beautifully attired in a velvet ensemble of dark green. She still encountered difficulty correlating the Colin before her with the Colin of old, but she had no difficulty loving him, regardless. The sight of him filled her with pleasure, just as it always had.

"There is no point in denying that Ware can offer you things that I cannot," Colin said, his dark eyes watching her with a mixture of love and determination. "That is what you overheard this morning. However, I have come to realize that I don't care."

"You don't?" Amelia's hand went to her fluttering stomach.

"No, I don't." He crossed his arms, revealing the powerful muscles she found endlessly arousing. "I love you. I want you. I intend to have you. Every other consideration be damned."

"Colin—"

"I've stolen you, Amelia. Run away with you, just as I have always wanted to do." He smiled again. "Within a fortnight, you and I will be husband and wife."

"Do I have no say in the matter?"

"You can say 'yes' if you like. Otherwise, you have no say."

Amelia laughed even as tears fell.

Colin leaned forward and set his elbows on his knees. "Tell me those are happy tears."

"Colin . . ." She gave a shaky sigh. "How can I say yes? Discarding Ware so callously for my own pleasure is exactly the sort of behavior my father excelled at. I could not live with myself if I acted so selfishly. Perhaps I would even grow to resent you for tempting me into such reckless deportment."

"Amelia." He straightened. "If I tell you that Ware would want nothing more than your happiness, it might alleviate your concern and goad your agreement, but that is not what I want."

She frowned.

"Yes, we are acting impetuously," he continued. "Yes, we are seizing the day and our love without a care for the world. That is who we are. That is our affinity. You and I are not ones to restrain our joys."

"People cannot live in that manner."

"Yes, they can. As long as doing so brings no pain to others." His voice grew more impassioned, arresting her. "Ware does not love you, not as I do. And you do not love him. I also suspect that you do not love yourself, not as you should. You accused me of molding myself into someone I am not, yet you are guilty of the same offense. You seek to mold yourself into a woman of decorum and duty, but that is not who you are! Do not be ashamed of the facets of you that I love so much."

"Welton was an awful man," she cried. "I cannot be like him."

"You never could be." Colin caught up her hands. "You are filled with love for life and family. Your father was filled with love only for himself. Two very different things."

"Ware . . ."

"Ware knows what I am doing. He could stop us if he wishes, but he won't. Regardless, I am altering myself to have you. I am taking this day and you, and forsaking all of the rest. It is frightening, yes. We will both have to leave the cages we created for ourselves and venture into the unknown. But we will have each other."

Cages. She had been caged for so long, one part of her hating the restrictions, the other part grateful that they restrained her from being too much like Welton. "You know me so well," she whispered.

"Yes, I know you better than anyone. You told me to believe that I was worthy of you. Now it is your turn to believe that you are worthy of me. Trust that you are free from whatever defect of character your father suffered. Trust that I am smart enough to love a wonderful woman."

He pressed his lips to her knuckles. "Make the leap with me, Amelia. I am holding on to our love with both hands, despite all the reasons why I shouldn't. Do the same. Embrace your wild nature and run with me. Be free with me. We shall all be happier for it."

She gazed at him for a long moment, her vision blurring with tears. Then she threw herself into his arms.

"Yes," she whispered with her cheek pressed to his. "Let's be free."

Christopher, Simon, and Ware were engrossed in a discussion when Maria burst into the room with her skirts held in one hand and a missive in the other.

All three men rose immediately. Christopher and Simon both stepped toward her with frowns marring their handsome features. Ware merely raised his brows.

"I found this atop Amelia's pillow! Mitchell has absconded with her."

Simon blinked. "Beg your pardon?"

"Truly?" Christopher smiled.

"He says he intends to marry her." She glanced down at the note to read it again. "They are already headed north."

"We must hurry or we will miss the nuptials," Ware said.

"You knew?" Maria stared at him with wide eyes.

"I hoped," he corrected. "I am pleased to see the man has come to his senses."

Maria opened her mouth, then shut it again.

"Well, let's not dally," Christopher said, catching her elbow and spinning her back around toward the door. "We have packing to see to. Tim can guard Mademoiselle Rousseau and Jacques while we are absent."

"North," Simon muttered. "May I ride in your carriage, my lord?"

"Certainly."

Still finding it difficult to believe, Maria glanced over her shoulder at Ware.

"This is a happy occasion, Mrs. St. John," he drawled, following directly behind them. "You should be smiling as I am."

"Yes, my lord."

She looked at Christopher, who nodded. With that, she shrugged and laughed aloud. Then she lifted her skirts and raced her husband up the stairs.

Epilogue

"We set sail in a few hours," Quinn said, fingering a coined tassel on a multicolored pillow. "My trunks and valet are aboard, and Lysette is safely restrained in my cabin."

They sat in the family parlor of Colin's new town house in London. It was a large room, beautifully decorated in shades of soft blue and gold. Around the room, Amelia had added colorful touches of his heritage—pillows encased in glorious scarves, small carved figurines, and bowls of Romany trinkets given to them by Pietro as wedding gifts. The style was unfashionable and would be considered horrifyingly gauche by many, but they both loved the space and spent a great deal of time curled up together there.

Embrace who you are, she had said, with a new confidence that aroused him unbearably. She, too, was embracing the reckless side of herself that she had fought to contain for so long. Fears of becoming too much like her father were banished, just as

Colin's fear of being unworthy of her no longer had power to dictate his actions.

Colin leaned back in his chair and asked Quinn, "Did the French agree to release your men in a trade for the return of Mademoiselle Rousseau and Cartland?"

"And Jacques. They want him, too. But I am only taking Lysette with me for now. They can have the other two back after I am certain they will honor their end of the agreement."

"I do not envy you that trip," Colin said, wincing. "I cannot imagine Mademoiselle Rousseau makes a very good prisoner."

"She is miserable, but I am enjoying the whole thing immensely."

Colin laughed. "Because you're a cad. When will you return?"

"I am not certain." Shrugging, Quinn said, "Perhaps after I ensure that the others are released. Or perhaps not even then. Maybe I will travel some."

"You are good to your men, Quinn. It is a trait I have always admired in you."

"They are not my men any longer. I have resigned." He nodded at Colin's raised brows. "Yes, it's true. My work for Eddington was diverting for a time, but now I must find new ways to amuse myself."

"Such as?"

"Some sort of trouble will come up." Quinn grinned. "Seeing you in your evening finery reminds me that a life of social indulgence is not for me. It would bore me to tears."

"Not with the right woman."

Quinn threw his dark head back and laughed, a rich, full sound that brought a smile to Colin's lips.

"Even when I was maudlin with love for Maria," Quinn said, pushing to his feet, "I thankfully never spouted such nonsense."

Colin rose with him, flushing sheepishly. "One day, I hope to remind you of your protestations and watch you eat your words."

"Ha! That day will be a long time coming, my friend. Likely, neither of us will live long enough to see it."

As Quinn turned to leave the room, Colin felt more than a small measure of sadness at their parting. Quinn was a wanderer by nature; therefore, they would see each other far less often. After all they had endured and experienced together, he thought of Quinn as a brother and would miss him accordingly.

"Farewell, my friend." Quinn clapped him on the back when they reached the foyer. "I wish you much joy and many children in your marriage."

"I wish you happy, as well."

Quinn touched his brow in a smart salute, and then he was gone. Off to find his next adventure.

Colin stared at the closed front door for a long moment.

"Darling."

Amelia's throaty purr sent a wave of heat across his skin.

He turned to face her with a smile and found her paused at the top of the stairs, dressed in only her robe. Her hair was beautifully, intricately arranged with twinkling diamonds weaved among the powdered strands.

"You have yet to dress?" he asked.

"I was nearly finished."

"It does not appear that way to me."

"I had to stop when Anne brought me the finishing touches to my ensemble . . . and the final piece of yours."

"Oh?" His smile widened. He knew well that look of seductive mischief in her eyes.

Her left arm lifted gracefully, the emerald of her wedding ring glinting in the candlelight from the foyer chandelier, her delicate fingers wrapped with lustrous black satin and dangling a familiar white mask.

Every muscle in his body hardened.

"If you like," she murmured, "we can go to the masquerade as planned. I know it took you some time to dress."

He strode toward the stairs. "It would take me considerably less time to undress," he purred.

"I should like you to wear this."

"I set it out for a reason."

"Wicked man."

Colin took the steps two at a time and caught her up, relishing the feel of her soft, unfettered body pressed to his. *"I'm* wicked? It is you, Countess Montoya, who lures me away from a staid social outing in favor of a night of licentious revelry."

"I cannot resist." She lifted the mask to his face and secured the ribbons. "I have a passion for you."

"Indulge it," he growled, his lips to her throat. "I beg of you."

Her laughter was filled with joy and love. It filled his heart then, and over the course of many hours afterward. Along with other, equally wondrous sounds.

Don't miss *Ask for It*, the first book in Sylvia Day's Georgian series.

London, April 1770

"Are you worried I'll ravish the woman, Eldridge? I admit to a preference for widows in my bed. They are much more agreeable and decidedly less complicated than virgins or other men's wives."

Sharp gray eyes lifted from the mass of papers on the enormous mahogany desk. "*Ravish*, Westfield?" The deep voice was rife with exasperation. "Be serious, man. This assignment is very important to me."

Marcus Ashford, seventh Earl of Westfield, lost the wicked smile that hid the soberness of his thoughts and released a deep breath. "And you must be aware that it is equally important to me."

Nicholas, Lord Eldridge, sat back in his chair, placed his elbows on the armrests, and steepled his long, thin fingers. He was a tall and sinewy man with a weathered face that had seen too many hours on the deck of a ship. Everything about him was practical, nothing superfluous, from his manner of speaking to his physical build. He presented an intimidating presence with a bustling London thoroughfare as a backdrop. The result was deliberate and highly effective.

"As a matter of fact, until this moment, I was not aware. I wanted to exploit your cryptography skills. I never considered you would volunteer to manage the case."

Marcus met the piercing gray stare with grim determination. Eldridge was head of the elite band of agents whose sole purpose was to investigate and hunt down known pirates and smugglers. Working under the auspices of His Majesty's Royal Navy, Eldridge wielded an inordinate amount of power. If Eldridge refused him the assignment, Marcus would have little say.

But he would not be refused. Not in this.

He tightened his jaw. "I will not allow you to assign someone else. If Lady Hawthorne is in danger, I will be the one to ensure her safety."

Eldridge raked him with an all-too-perceptive gaze. "Why such passionate interest? After what transpired between you, I'm surprised you would wish to be in close contact with her. Your motive eludes me."

"I have no ulterior motive." At least not one he would share. "Despite our past, I've no desire to see her harmed."

"Her actions dragged you into a scandal that lasted for months and is still discussed today. You put on a good show, my friend, but you bear scars. And some festering wounds, perhaps?"

Remaining still as a statue, Marcus kept his face impassive and struggled against his gnawing resentment. His pain was his own and deeply personal. He disliked being asked about it. "Do you think me incapable of separating my personal life from my professional one?"

Eldridge sighed and shook his head. "Very well. I won't pry."

"And you won't refuse me?"

"You are the best man I have. It was only your history that gave me pause, but if you are comfortable with it, I have no objections. However, I will grant her request for reassignment, if it comes to that."

Nodding, Marcus hid his relief. Elizabeth would never ask for another agent; her pride wouldn't permit it.

Eldridge began to tap his fingertips together. "The journal Lady Hawthorne received was addressed to her late husband and is written in code. If the book was involved in his death . . ." He paused. "Viscount Hawthorne was investigating Christopher St. John when he met his reward."

Marcus stilled at the name of the popular pirate. There was no criminal he longed to apprehend more than St. John, and his enmity was personal. St. John's attacks against Ashford Shipping were the impetus to his joining the agency. "If Lord Hawthorne kept a journal of his assignments and St. John were to acquire the information—bloody hell!" His gut tightened at the thought of the pirate anywhere near Elizabeth.

"Exactly," Eldridge agreed. "In fact, Lady Hawthorne has already been contacted about the book since it was brought to my attention just a sennight ago. For her safety and ours, it should be removed from her care immediately, but that's impossible at the moment. She was instructed to personally deliver the journal, hence the need for our protection."

"Of course."

Eldridge slid a folder across the desk. "Here is the information I've gathered so far. Lady Hawthorne will apprise you of the rest during the Moreland ball."

Collecting the particulars of the assignment, Marcus stood and took his leave. Once in the hallway, he allowed a grim smile of satisfaction to curve his lips.

He'd been only days away from seeking Elizabeth out. The end of her mourning meant his interminable waiting was over. Although the matter of the journal was disturbing, it worked to his advantage, making it impossible for her to avoid him. After the scandalous way she'd jilted him four years ago she would not be pleased with his new appearance in her life. But she wouldn't turn to Eldridge either, of that he was certain.

Soon, very soon, all that she had once promised and then denied him would finally be his.

Sylvia Day's Georgian series continues with *Passion for the Game.*

"If all angels of death were as lovely as you, men would line up to die."

Maria, Lady Winter, shut the lid of her enameled patch box with a decisive snap. Her revulsion for the mirrored reflection of the man who sat behind her made her stomach roil. Taking a deep breath, she kept her gaze trained on the stage below, but her attention was riveted by the incomparably handsome man who sat in the shadows of her theater box.

"Your turn will come," she murmured, maintaining her regal façade for the benefit of the many lorgnettes pointed in her direction. She had worn crimson silk tonight, accented by delicate black lace frothing from elbow-length sleeves. It was her most-worn color. Not because it suited her Spanish heritage coloring so well—dark hair, dark eyes, olive skin—but because it was a silent warning. *Bloodshed. Stay away.*

The Wintry Widow, the voyeurs whispered. *Two husbands dead . . . and counting.*

Angel of death. How true that was. Everyone

around her died, except for the man she cursed to Hades.

The low chuckle at her shoulder made her skin crawl. "It will take more than you, my dearest daughter, to see me to my reward."

"Your reward will be my blade in your heart," she hissed.

"Ah, but then you will never be reunited with your sister, and she almost of age."

"Do not think to threaten me, Welton. Once Amelia is wed, I will know her location and will have no further need for your life. Consider that before you think to do to her what you have done to me."

"I could sell her into the slave trade," he drawled.

"You assume, incorrectly, that I did not anticipate your threat." Fluffing the lace at her elbow, she managed a slight curve to her lips to hide her terror. "I will know. And then you will die."

She felt him stiffen and her smile turned genuine. Ten and six was her age when Welton had ended her life. Anticipation for the day when she would pay him in kind was all that moved her when despair for her sister threatened paralysis.

"St. John."

The name hung suspended in the air between them.

Maria's breath caught. "Christopher St. John?"

It was rare that anything surprised her anymore. At the age of six and twenty, she believed she had seen and done nearly everything. "He has coin aplenty, but marriage to him will ruin me, making me less effective for your aims."

"Marriage is not necessary this time. I've not yet

depleted Lord Winter's settlement. This is simply a search for information. I believe they are engaging St. John in some business. I want you to discover what it is they want with him, and most importantly, who arranged his release from prison."

Maria smoothed the bloodred material that pooled around her legs. Her two unfortunate husbands had been agents of the Crown whose jobs made them highly useful to her stepfather. They had also been peers of great wealth, much of which they left to her for Welton's disposal upon their untimely demise.

Lifting her head, she looked around the theater, absently noting the curling smoke of candles and gilded scrollwork that shone in firelight. The soprano on the stage struggled for attention, for no one was here to see her. The peerage was here to see each other and be seen, nothing more.

"Interesting," Maria murmured, recalling a sketch of the popular pirate. Uncommon handsome he was, and as deadly as she. His exploits were widely bandied, some tales so outrageous she knew they could not possibly be true. St. John was discussed with intemperate eagerness, and there were wagers aplenty on how long he could escape the noose.

"They must be desperate indeed to spare him. All these years they have searched for the irrefutable proof of his villainy, and now that they have it, they bring him into the fold. I daresay neither side is pleased."

"I do not care how they feel," Welton dismissed curtly. "I simply wish to know who I can extort to keep quiet about it."

"Such faith in my charms," she drawled, hiding how her mouth filled with bile. To think of the deeds she had been forced into to protect and serve a man she detested . . . Her chin lifted. It was not her stepfather she protected and served. She merely needed him alive, for if he were killed, she would never find Amelia.

Welton ignored her jibe. "Have you any notion what that information would be worth?"

She gave a nearly imperceptible nod, aware of the avid scrutiny that followed her every movement. Society knew her husbands had not died natural deaths. But they lacked proof. Despite this morbid certainty of her guilt, she was welcomed into the finest homes eagerly. She was infamous. And nothing livened up a gathering like a touch of infamy.

"How do I find him?"

"You have your ways."

Enjoy more of Sylvia Day's Georgian series with *Don't Tempt Me.*

Paris, France—1757

With her fingers curled desperately around the edge of the table before her, Marguerite Piccard writhed in the grip of unalloyed arousal. Gooseflesh spread up her arms and she bit her lower lip to stem the moan of pleasure that longed to escape.

"Do not restrain your cries," her lover urged hoarsely. "It makes me wild to hear them."

Her blue eyes, heavy-lidded with passion, lifted within the mirrored reflection before her and met the gaze of the man who moved at her back. The vanity in her boudoir rocked with the thrusts of his hips, his breathing rough as he made love to her where they stood.

The Marquis de Saint-Martin's infamously sensual lips curved with masculine satisfaction at the sight of her flushed dishevelment. His hands cupped her swaying breasts, urging her body to move in tandem with his.

They strained together, their skin coated with sweat, their chests heaving from their exertions.

Her blood thrummed in her veins, the experience of her lover's passion such that she had forsaken everything—family, friends, and esteemed future—to be with him. She knew he loved her similarly. He proved it with every touch, every glance.

"How beautiful you are," he gasped, watching her through the mirror.

When she had suggested the location of their tryst with timid eagerness, he'd laughed with delight.

"I am at your service," he purred, shrugging out of his garments as he stalked her into the boudoir. There was a sultriness to his stride and a predatory gleam in his dark eyes that caused her to shiver in heated awareness. Sex was innate to him. He exuded it from every pore, enunciated it with every syllable, displayed it with every movement. And he excelled at it.

From the moment she first saw him at the Fontinescu ball nearly a year ago, she had been smitten with his golden handsomeness. His attire of ruby red silk had attracted every eye without effort, but Marguerite had attended the event with the express aim of seeing him in the flesh. Her older sisters had whispered scandalous tales of his liaisons, occasions when he had been caught in flagrant displays of seduction. He was wed; yet discarded lovers pined for him openly, weeping outside his home for a brief moment of his attention. Her curiosity about what sort of shell would encase such wickedness was too powerful to be denied.

Saint-Martin did not disappoint her. In the simplest of terms, she did not expect him to be so . . . *male.* Those who were given to the pursuit of vice and excess were rarely virile, as he most definitely was.

Never had she met a man more devastating to a woman's equanimity. The marquis was magnificent, his physical form impressive and his aloofness an irresistible lure. Golden-haired and skinned, as she was, he was desired by every woman in France for good reason. There was an air about him that promised pleasure unparalleled. The decadence and forbidden delights intimated within his slumberous gaze lured one to forget themselves. The marquis had lived twice Marguerite's eight and ten years, and he possessed a wife as lovely as he was comely. Neither fact mitigated Marguerite's immediate, intense attraction to him. Or his returning attraction to her.

"Your beauty has enslaved me," he whispered that first night. He stood near to where she waited on the edge of the dance floor, his lanky frame propped against the opposite side of a large column. "I must follow you or ache from the distance between us."

Marguerite kept her gaze straight ahead, but every nerve ending tingled from his boldness. Her breath was short, her skin hot. Although she could not see him, she felt the weight of his regard and it affected her to an alarming degree. "You know of women more beautiful than I," she retorted.

"No." His husky, lowered voice stilled her heartbeat. Then, made it race. "I do not."